There Are Doors

is the story of a man who falls in love with a goddess from an alternate universe. She flees him, but he pursues her through doorways to the other place, determined to sacrifice his life if necessary for her love. For to love her . . . is to die.

GENE WOLFE
THERE ARE DOORS

A TOM DOHERTY ASSOCIATES BOOK
NEW YORK

THERE ARE DOORS

Copyright © 1988 by Gene Wolfe

A TOR Book
Published by Tom Doherty Associates, Inc.
49 West 24 Street
New York, NY 10010

Cover art by Richard Bober

ISBN: 0-812-50301-5   Can. ISBN: 0-812-50302-3

Library of Congress Catalog Card Number: 88-19717

First edition: November 1988
First mass market edition: September 1989

Printed in the United States of America

0 9 8 7 6 5 4 3 2 1

NOTE

Indoor moopsball, as played by the patients and staff of United General Psychiatric Hospital, is taken from "Rules of Moopsball," by Gary Cohn, and used with his permission. "Rules of Moopsball" originally appeared in *Orbit 18*, edited by Damon Knight.

· I ·

Lara

"Do you believe in love?" he asked her.

"Yes," Lara replied. "And I hate it."

He did not know what to say. It all stuck in his throat, everything he had planned that afternoon walking home from the store.

"We use it, you see," she told him. "My women and I. We must."

He nodded. "Women do use love, of course. But so do men, and men usually use it worse. Don't you think that only proves it's real? If it wasn't, nobody could use it." The brandy had gone to his head; by the time he had finished speaking, he was no longer quite sure what they had been talking about.

"It's real, all right," Lara told him. "But I am not a woman."

"A girl—" He was groping.

So was she, a hand in his pajamas.

"A lady." His glass was at his lips. He took it from her hand and drank.

". . . and then the men die. Always. She holds his sperm, saves it, and bears his children, one after another for the rest of her life. Perhaps three children. Perhaps three dozen."

"I love you," he said thickly. "I'd die for you, Lara."

"But this is better—your way is so much better. Now I'll go back. Listen. There are doors—"

She did not go back at once. They embraced again, on the floor in front of the gas log. For the second time that evening he poured himself into her.

And afterward he held her to him, tightly, oh, so tightly, feeling as though the two of them were in a boat upon the sea, a little boat that rocked and spun with every billow; that only his body against hers, her body against his could save them both from freezing in the freezing spume.

"You must be careful," she said when he was almost asleep. "Because we've been so close."

He woke up with a throbbing headache. Sunlight was pouring through the window; from its angle he knew that he had missed work that day. He got up and made himself drink three glasses of water.

Lara was gone, but that was to be expected; it was nearly eleven. She had probably gone out to look for a job, or to get some clothes, maybe even to get some lunch.

He called the store. "Flu—came on last night. Sorry, so sorry I didn't call in sooner." I sound like a Jap, he thought. Too long selling Sonys.

Ella in Personnel said, "I'll mark you down. Don't feel bad—it's your first sick day this year."

2

Aspirin, he thought. You're supposed to take aspirin. He swallowed three.

There was a note on the coffee table, a note in Lara's angular writing.

> Darling,
>   I tried to say good-bye last night, but you wouldn't listen. I'm not a coward, really I'm not.
>   If it weren't for the doors I wouldn't tell you a thing— that would be the best way. You may see one, perhaps more than one, at least for a little while. It will be closed all around. (They must be closed on all sides.) It may be a real door, or just something like a guy-wire supporting a phone pole, or an arch in a garden. Whatever it is, it will look *significant.*
>   Please read carefully. Please remember everything I'm saying. *You must not go through.*
>   If you go through before you realize it, don't turn around. *If you do it will be gone. Walk backward at once.*
> Lara
> PS: You always put these on, don't you? At the end. At the end, I loved you. I really did. (Do.)

He read it three times and put it down, feeling that it was wrong, that something important had been left out, that his eyes had followed four smokestacks down to three chimneys. Was that underlined word really *significant,* and if so, just what did it signify? It might be *signature.*

He stuck his head under the shower and let the icy water beat his hair and the back of his neck full force. When he had stood there (bent, a hand braced against the tile) for so long that the slow drain had allowed the tub to fill, he washed his face seven times, shaved, and felt better.

If he went out, there was a chance that somebody from the store would see him; but it was a chance he would have to take.

Knotting his brown tie, he studied the door of the apartment. It did not look significant, though perhaps it was.

Capini's was only a block and a half. He had a glass of red wine with his linguine, and either the wine or the linguine made him feel almost normal.

But Mama Capini was gone or back in the kitchen, and it was Mama Capini he would have to talk to. There were three or four sons—he had never learned their names—but they were not likely to tell him anything. Mama Capini might, and he decided to come back for dinner. Meanwhile, the police, the morgue . . .

"I'm looking for a woman," he told the gray-haired, buck-toothed woman at the Downtown Mental Health Center who saw him at last. And then, because that sounded so dirty, he added, "A particular woman."

"And you think we might know where she is?"

He nodded.

"What was her name?"

"Lara Morgan." He spelled it. "I don't know if that was her real name or not. I never saw any identification."

"Then we'll hold off running it through the computer for a moment. Can you describe her?"

"About five foot nine. Red hair to her shoulder blades. Dark red. Auburn, is that what you call it?"

The buck-toothed woman nodded.

"Very pretty—beautiful, in fact. Viridian eyes. A lot of little freckles. A buttermilk complexion, you know what I mean? I doubt if I'm much good at estimating women's weight, but maybe a hundred and twenty pounds."

"Viridian, Mr. . . . ?"

"Green—viridian's a bluish green. You'll have to excuse it. I

4

sell tape decks and so on now, but I used to be in small appliances. Viridian has more blue than avocado."

"I see. And how was this woman dressed the last time you saw her?"

He bit back the impulse to say she wasn't. "A green dress. Silk I guess, or maybe it was nylon. High-heeled boots, I think lizard, though they might have been snake. A gold necklace and a couple of gold bracelets—she wore a lot of gold jewelry. A black fur coat with a hood. Maybe it was fake, but it looked and felt real to me."

The buck-toothed woman said, "We haven't seen her, Mr. Green. If someone who looked and dressed like that had come here, I'd know about her. If she's seeing someone, which I doubt, it's a private psychiatrist. What makes you think she may be disturbed?"

"The way she acted. Things she said."

"And how did she act, Mr. Green?"

He considered. "Like, she didn't know about ice-makers. She went to the refrigerator one time to get ice—she was going to make lemonade—and she came back and said there wasn't any. So I went and showed her how it worked, and she said, 'How nice, all these little blocks.'"

The buck-toothed woman frowned, putting her hands together fingertip to fingertip like a man. "Surely there must have been something more than that."

"Well, she was afraid that somebody was going to take her back. That's what she told me."

The buck-toothed woman's expression said now we're getting someplace. She leaned toward him as she spoke. "Take her back where, Mr. Green?"

He started to ask how she knew his name (he had refused to

give it to the temporary receptionist) but he thought better of it. "She didn't say, Doctor. Through the doors, I guess."

"The doors?"

"She talked about doors. This was just before she left—the doors, or one door anyway, that was how she got here. If they came to take her back, they'd pull her through a door, so she was going to go on her own first." When the buck-toothed woman offered no comment, he added, "At least, that was the way it seemed to me."

"These doors would appear to indicate an institution of some kind, then," the buck-toothed woman said.

"That's how they sounded to me."

"Has it struck you that the institution might be a prison, Mr. Green?"

He shook his head. "She didn't seem that way. She seemed, well, smart. But a little disconnected."

"Intelligent people who've been institutionalized often do. I take it she was about your own age?"

He nodded.

"And you are . . . ?"

"Thirty."

"Then let us say this beautiful woman who calls herself Lara Morgan is thirty also. If she had committed a serious offense in her teens—a murder, perhaps, or if she'd had some complicity in a murder—she would have been sent to a girls' correctional center until she was of age, and then transferred to a women's prison to complete her sentence. Thus she might easily have spent the last ten or twelve years in one or the other, Mr. Green."

He began, "I don't think—"

"You see, Mr. Green, escapees from our mental hospitals are not punished. They are ill, and one does not punish illness. But prisoners—criminals—who escape *are* punished. I'm glad that you've come back to us, Mr. Green. I was getting rather worried about you."

He was shaking when he left the Center; he had not really known he cared about Lara so much.

The Downtown Mental Health Center stood on one corner of a five-way intersection. The five streets were all congested, and when he looked down each they seemed to spin around him like the spokes of a wheel, each thronged, each noisy, each straight and running to infinity, thronged, noisy, and congested. None was like the rest; nor were any—when he looked again—exactly the way they had been when he had come in. Hadn't that theater been a bowling alley? And weren't fire trucks supposed to be red, buses yellow, or maybe orange?

Were the doors here? "It may be something like a guy-wire supporting a telephone pole." That was what Lara had written. Looking up, he saw that he stood under a maze of wires. There were wires to hold traffic signals, thin black wires going from building to building, wires for the clanging trolleys. There were buildings on the sides, streets and sidewalks below, the wires above. A dozen—no, two dozen at least—two dozen doors, and all of them looked significant. Had there been a hospital for dolls there before? Had there ever been such a shop in the world? Feeling rather like a broken doll himself, he started toward it.

·2·

Hell or Paradise, Who Say?

The room was lined with shelves eight or nine inches apart, and upon all these shelves stood little beds, dolls' beds. In each bed lay a doll.

"Yes, sir. Have you come for a doll?"

He ducked the question. "What an interesting place you've got here. I don't think I've ever seen a shop quite like this." Lara would like it, he thought; aloud he added, "Are all these broken?"

"Why, no," the shopkeeper said. He was about his own age, a stooped man who did not seem to know that the long hair that spilled to his thin shoulders was retreating.

"Then why—"

"All of them were broken when they came," the shopkeeper explained. He pulled down the blanket and sheet of the nearest doll. "They're fine *now*."

8

"I see."

"You've got a doll to be fixed? We need a deposit. It'll be refunded when you come back for your doll."

"You're holding deposits on all these?"

The shopkeeper spread his lean hands. "We've got to make money someway. We've got to keep the place going. We used to charge for the repairs, but hardly anyone came back when their doll was fixed. So now we take a pretty big deposit and charge nothing for the treatment. If the owner does come back for his doll—or like it is usually, the owner's mother—we gain shelf space, and he gets his deposit back in full. If he doesn't . . ." The shopkeeper shrugged.

"Don't you ever sell the dolls?"

The shopkeeper nodded. "When the owner's dead."

"Then you must keep some of them for a long time."

The shopkeeper nodded again. "There's a few we've had ever since we opened. But see, sometimes when a boy gets older, he remembers about his doll. Sometimes he finds the receipt in his mother's old papers. But we get the name of each owner when we accept his doll, and we watch the obituaries." The shopkeeper reached up to the highest shelf behind him and took down a small bed. "Here's one that's for sale now. If there's somebody you know . . ."

It was Lara.

Lara in miniature, ten inches high. But unmistakably Lara— her darkly red hair, her freckles, her eyes and nose and mouth and chin.

He managed to say, "Yes," and reached for his wallet.

"It *is* a pretty expensive doll, sir," the shopkeeper said. "Not just walk and talk—all the functions."

"No kidding?" He tried to cock an eyebrow.

"Yes, sir. It's the kind you wet with a salt solution. That's

9

what provides the electrolyte. It'll be pretty well dried out now, I'm afraid. It's been here a long time."

"I see." He examined the doll more closely. A name, *Tina*, was embroidered on the tiny blouse.

"It's still the goddess, naturally, sir," the shopkeeper said. "The goddess at sixteen. The boy who owned her's been dead now for about eight years. Malicapata. Pretty sad, sir, isn't it? Only now she'll bring years of pleasure to another child. Life goes on."

"Sometimes," he said.

"Sir?"

"And where could I find the goddess herself?"

"In Overwood, I suppose, sir. I'm afraid I've got to ask a hundred and fifty for that, sir, if you really want it."

"I'll have to write a check."

The shopkeeper hesitated, then said, "Okay."

The doll fit nicely into the breast pocket of his topcoat, its slender form well suited to the pocket's narrow shape.

Standing on the sidewalk once more, he looked around to get his bearings. Buildings rose from the five corners—a health-food store, a real-estate agency, a bookshop, a law office, a liquor store, a boutique advertising "Genuine Silk Artificial Flowers," and an antique shop. The streets that stabbed the aching distance seemed utterly unfamiliar. A brick-red trolley rattled by, and he recalled that trolleys had not run even when he was a child.

As if his mind had room for no more than a single puzzle, the answer to the first occurred to him: he had turned wrong on leaving the doll hospital; this was a different intersection. He reversed his steps, waving to the shopkeeper as he went past and noting with some amusement that there was already a new doll in the tiny bed that had been Tina's.

"Didn't even change the sheets," he muttered.

"They never do," the red-faced man walking beside him said.

The red-faced man gestured toward a shop, and he saw that the sheet music in its window was yellowed and dusty. "Find Your True Love" was printed at the top in the florid lettering favored at the turn of the century. A dead fly lay upon its back at the bottom.

"Looks quaint," he said. It was what they said at the store when they wanted to insult a rival operation.

"Get you anything you want," the red-faced man said, and laughed.

The social ice had been broken, and he was eager to ask someone. "Could you direct me to Overwood?"

The red-faced man halted and turned to face him. "Why, no," he said. "No, I can't."

"All right."

"However," the red-faced man raised a finger. "I can tell you how to get close, if you want to. Once you're close, maybe you can get more specific directions."

"Great!" he said. (But where was Overwood, and why had the shopkeeper called Lara "the goddess"?)

". . . to the station. Marea's right there at the foot of the mountains, and from there somebody may be able to direct you."

"Fine."

The red-faced man pointed. "Also, if you'll look right across the street, you'll see a little cartography store. You can probably get a map from them."

Though the store was small, it had a high ceiling. The owner had taken advantage of it to display several very large maps. One was a city map, and as he had expected, there were several five-way intersections; he crossed the store to study it, hoping to trace his route from the apartment to Capini's, and from there to the Downtown Mental Health Center.

But he could not locate his own neighborhood, or even find the address of the department store in which he worked. Though the store had only display windows, he felt certain it was near the river. Several rivers snaked across the map, and at one point two appeared to cross. None seemed quite as large as the river he recalled, or as straight.

A clerk said, "Can I help you?" and he turned to face her. She was a short, cheerful-looking girl with chestnut hair.

"A map to Overwood," he said.

She smiled. "Not many people want to go there."

There was something questionable in her look, he decided. It was the look of a clerk who remains perfectly pleasant while signaling frantically for the department manager. "I didn't say I wanted to go there," he told her. "But I'd like a map showing the location."

"They're pretty expensive, you know, and we don't guarantee them."

"That's all right," he said.

She nodded. "As long as you understand. Step this way, please."

A manic gaiety seized him. "Madame, if I could step that way I wouldn't need the lotion." It was the ancient wheeze at which he himself had dutifully snickered a hundred times.

She ignored it, or more probably did not hear it. "Here we are, sir. Slumberland, Disneyland, Cleveland, and Heaven, Hell, and Limbo—all three on this one map." She shot him a quizzical glance. "Quite a saving."

"No," he said. "Overwood."

"Overwood." She had to stand on tiptoe to pull it out of the highest pigeonhole in the rack. "Last one, too. They're on backorder, I think. That will be twenty-nine ninety-eight, plus tax."

"I want to make sure it's what I'm looking for first." He unfolded part of the map, which was thick and folded with great complexity.

"There's the Overwood area." She pointed. "Crystal Gorge, the Metal Forest, and so forth."

He nodded, bending over the map.

"That's twenty-nine ninety-eight, plus tax."

There were no paths, no roads, no buildings that showed on the map. He got out his wallet, a twenty, a ten, and a five.

The clerk glanced at them and shook her head. "That isn't real money. Not here, anyway. Where are you from?"

He said, "What do you mean? I just bought a doll down the street." Then he recalled that he had written a check for the doll.

The clerk walked hurriedly to her cash register and pressed a button. "Mrs. Peters, I think you'd better get in here."

He began to refold the map. In a moment he would have lost it forever.

"Wait a minute!" the clerk shrieked at him. *"Hey!"*

He was out the door and sprinting down the street. He had not thought she would chase him, but she did, knees pumping, one black high-heeled shoe in each hand, flying along with her skirt at her thighs. *"Stop him!"*

A woman tried to trip him with her umbrella; he staggered but ran on. A big, rough-looking man shouted, "Go it, Neddy!" Horns blew as a mounted policeman spurred his skittish horse through traffic.

An alley gapped ahead; on TV, fleeing criminals always ran

down alleys; he was well down this one before it occurred to him that they were probably pretty familiar already with the alleys they chose to run down.

This one became narrower and stranger with each stride he took, turning and turning again, as though it would never reach another street.

The clatter of hooves behind him sounded like a cavalry charge in a movie. He heard their rhythm break as the horse jumped the same overturned garbage can he himself had leaped only a moment before, then the animal's awful scream, and a sickening thud as its steel shoes slipped on the icy bricks.

He ran on, the map flapping in one hand, the doll thumping his heaving chest with each gasp for breath. A witch's black cat hissed him from the summit of a ramshackle board fence, and a Chinese lounging upon an old divan and smoking what appeared to be an opium pipe smiled benignly.

He turned a corner and confronted a dead end.

"You want leave?" the Chinese asked.

He looked over his shoulder. "Yes. I—got—get—out—ahere."

The Chinese rose, smoothing a drooping mustache. "Okay! You come."

A slanting door opened into a cellar. When the Chinese had shut it behind them, it was pitch dark save for the tiny crimson glow from the bowl of the pipe.

"Where are we?" he asked.

"Now noplace," the Chinese told him. "In dark, who say?"

The sweet smoke of the pipe battled the mildewed air. He could imagine it curling around him like a white snake, a pale Chinese dragon. He tried to refold the map, conscious that he was doing it wrong; after a moment he shoved the clumsy packet into a side pocket.

"Paradise maybe. Hell maybe. Who say?"

He said, "I could, if I had a match."

The Chinese chuckled like the rattling of nine ivory balls in the mouths of nine ivory lions, and he felt a hard square box pushed into his hand. "There match. Strike. You say."

He had shaken his head before he realized the Chinese could not see him. "I might start a fire."

"Then Hell. Strike match."

"No," he said.

"I strike," the Chinese told him. There was a dry rasp and a flare of light. They were standing near a pile of mattresses. Barrels, bins, bags, boxes, and tall stacks of books crammed the cellar. There were floor joists an inch or less above his head. "Paradise? Hell?" the Chinese asked. "Now you say."

"Paradise."

"Ah! You wise! Come upstair, drink tea. Police man look outside, no find."

He followed the Chinese up a flight of steep steps, through a hatch in the floor above, and into a cluttered shop. Scarlet paper lanterns daubed with black Chinese characters dangled from the ceiling, and long scrolls hung on nails in the walls showed tigers as sinuous as serpents.

"You want sell? Sheng buy. You want buy, Sheng sell," the Chinese told him. "Not tea. Tea for nothing, make friend."

Again a match flared, and gas blossomed violet above an iron ring in a tiny room behind a bead curtain.

"You've made a friend already," he said.

"What you want, come Sheng. Good! You want, Sheng got. No got, Sheng get. Sit down?"

He sat in a flimsy bamboo chair that appeared to have been intended for a child. Though it had been cold outside, he found that he was perspiring.

"Tea, grocery, firework, medicine. Many, many things, very cheap."

He nodded, wondering how old the Chinese was. He had never met a Chinese before who had not spoken idiomatic American. If anyone had asked (though no one ever had) he would have answered readily that there were hundreds of millions who did not, who in fact knew no language but their own; now he learned that knowing and understanding are vastly different things.

The Chinese knocked out his pipe, refilled it, and lit it again on the violet gas tongues. After a token puff or two, he set a dented copper teakettle on the gas ring. "Sheng say Paradise, Hell? You say Paradise. Why you—what wrong?"

The doll had moved.

. 3 .

The Parade

Gingerly, he took the doll from his pocket. Its
legs, he felt certain, had been straight before.
Now one was slightly bent at the knee. Its face
had been calm and serious—perhaps he would have said blank
if he had not loved that face so much. Now the lips were slightly
curved.

"Ah, you admirer of goddess!"

Half unconsciously, he nodded.

"That good! I see?"

The Chinese held out his hand, and somewhat unwillingly he
passed the doll over.

"Oh, very beautiful! Legs long, feet small!" The Chinese
tittered. "You do not like Sheng have. Sheng understand."

Only when it was back in his pocket was he willing to admit
that he had feared he would never get it back at all.

"Soon Sheng show. First tea." A white smoke-dragon from the pipe mingled with and fought a savage steam-dragon from the teakettle. Seething water rained into a teapot, followed by a mummified snow of fragrant leaves.

"Soon," Sheng said. "Very soon. Like pot? Very good, very cheap. Nankeen yellow, hundred year make. Have more."

He nodded. "How did you come to this country, Mr. Sheng?"

The Chinese smiled. "Build railroad. Young man, think far away, all better." A thin hand pulled reflectively at the long mustache. "Go home, rich." The Chinese sighed.

"Do you still want to go home?" He found himself suddenly fascinated by this lean, brown, middle-aged man's history. It was as if he were seeing his own future in some strange Eastern glass. "You agreed that your basement was paradise."

"Paradise of young man. So he dream. Work railroad. Tear shirt." The Chinese paused reflectively. "No needle. Ask men, have needle? Piece thread? No have . . ."

"Yes?"

"Go to town. Saturday. Buy thread. Ask needle, store man no sell. Sell paper, twenty needle. Sheng buy. Say, you want needle? Cost dime. So Sheng here." The hand fluttered tapered fingers at the little shop, then swooped to pick up the teapot. Perfumed liquid splashed into the cups. "Sheng paradise."

"I see."

"Now dream new paradise, many children, many sons, pray for poor Sheng. Young Sheng dream so, this Sheng not. Law Heaven—one paradise each man."

He nodded, sipping the scalding tea and wondering just how his search for Lara could have gone so far astray as quickly as it had.

Without rising, the Chinese stretched a long arm to one of the shelves and took down a lacquer box. "Now Sheng show. You want much touch, okay touch. Sheng like better you no touch."

He nodded, setting down his cup. The lid of the box slid in grooves in the sides. Vaguely, he recalled seeing a box of marbles that had opened like that in Antiques. Inside the box was a doll, elaborately dressed, no longer than his hand.

"This Heng-O," the Chinese explained. "Also same yours."

He bent nearer to look. It was indeed the same face, as though an Oriental had sculpted Lara, unconsciously adding the racial features such an artist would feel normal and attractive. Her robe was real silk, a costume that might have been worn by a minute empress, aswim with embroidered birds and strange beasts.

"She's very beautiful," he told the Chinese. "Very, very beautiful."

"It so." Silently the lid slid shut again. "Moon full, she stand here. Joss burn. Only can do that. Sheng funeral rice steam on Sheng grave, she see me, smile, say, 'You burn joss for me.' Happy forever."

He nodded again and drained the last of his tea, grateful for its warmth and cheer. For a moment their eyes met, and he knew that the Chinese was his brother, despite the differences of half a world—and that the Chinese had known it even in the alley.

"I've imposed upon your hospitality for too long already, Mr. Sheng," he said. "I should be going." He rose.

"No, no!" The Chinese lifted both hands, palms out. "No go before Sheng show stock!"

"If you really want—"

The impassive face split in a broad grin. "You see many things. Tell friends. They come, buy Sheng, sure Mike!"

He tried to recall his friends. There was no one. "I'm afraid you're the only real friend I've got, Mr. Sheng."

"Then live too much by self. You look!" It was a deck of cards.

"Magic charm, bring friend! Learn poker, bridge, rummy. Go 'round, 'I want play, no one play.' Soon many friend!"

He shook his head. "It's a good idea, but I'm too shy."

The Chinese sighed. "No charm for shy. No liquor license. Like get mail?"

"Yes, very much."

"Good! Mail good shy man. Magic charm!" The Chinese held up a shriveled, flattened root.

"Will that really bring mail?"

"Yes! Mail root," the Chinese said. (Or perhaps, "Male root.")

It seemed crisp and thin between his fingers. In the dim light, he could have sworn he held an envelope. "I'd like to buy it," he said. He owed Sheng something anyway for rescuing him from the police.

"No buy. Free! Next time, buy." A slender thread of red silk held the dried root. "Put 'round neck. Wear below shirt. Plenty mail."

He did as he was told. A rhythmic booming, muted yet deep, sounded outside. He wanted to ask what it was, but the Chinese spoke first.

"Look see!" A tight roll of paper unwound to reveal the sketched figure of a man, half life-size. "For burn on grave. Then got good servant next place." The Chinese grinned again. "You die real soon?"

"I hope not."

"Then no need. Later, maybe. How 'bout horse?" It was a stocky, tough-looking animal sketched in bold strokes.

"I've never ridden one," he confessed.

"Next place learn. Plenty time."

His eyes caught a thick sheaf of fifty-dollar bills banded with brown paper. "You shouldn't leave these lying around, Mr. Sheng."

The Chinese laughed. "Toy money! On grave burn, next place plenty rich! You like?"

He carried them to a dusty little window. They were real bills, nearly new. When he slid back the paper band, Grant's face was sharp and bright.

"You like?"

The band read PUROLATOR SECURITY. Beside the words was a Chinese character in black ink, and the figure 10 cents.

"Yes," he said. "I like this very much. But you have to let me pay for it." He produced a dime, feeling very much like a thief. The Chinese accepted the coin without looking at it, and he put the sheaf of bills into the topcoat pocket opposite the map.

The street outside was not the one from which he had fled down the alley; but though it was smaller and narrower, lined with parked cars and sooty brick buildings, there was a parade. Drum majorettes strutted and twirled, bare legs shaded blue by the winter wind. Soldiers in brilliant green jackets shouldered and unshouldered short rifles; politicians grinned and waved, presenting one another with candy and cigars. Trumpets brayed. Towering floats crept forward like so many colorful juggernauts, clearly unstable, swaying like jonquils while lovely girls in flowers, feathers, and sequined gowns danced alone or with each other.

A bass drum thudded in rhythm with his heart.

A little crowd of men and boys, with a few women, followed the final float, possibly a division of the parade in their own minds. It struck him that if the police were still looking for him—though it seemed unlikely they were—this straggling group offered the best means of evading them. He joined it, pressing toward the middle and front until he was walking so close to the float that no one on either sidewalk could have had a clear look at him.

A skater in a pink tutu twirled almost at the edge. When she saw him, she stopped and smiled, pointing toward three iron steps that descended the back of the float.

He thought she was inviting him to join her and called, *"I don't have skates!"*

She nodded, still smiling, and indicated a door wreathed with roses.

For a moment he hesitated. If he climbed up the steps, he would be exposed until he had passed through the doorway. Once inside the float, however, he would be completely screened from view.

The skater smiled again and beckoned. She was blond and blue-eyed, apple-cheeked in the cutting wind.

As he mounted the steps, the crowd he had left behind him whistled, clapped, and cheered. The watchers on the sidewalks cheered as well, and one of the dancers ignited the fuse of a firework. It erupted in a glory of golden sparks just as the skater opened the rose-wreathed door for him.

"In a second," she said. "I have to take my skates off."

He found himself in the back of a camper. There were two wide bunks, one above the other, swiveling seats, a small sink, and a bureau with a washbasin set into its top. The driver, a middle-aged woman, did not turn her head to look at him; but he saw her eyes in the rearview mirror—eyes that watched him, so it seemed to him, far longer than was safe.

The ceiling was uncomfortably close to his head. He sat down and tried to look around him, but the sides of the float darkened all the windows. He could still hear the cheering of the crowd outside and the booming of the fireworks.

The door opened. The skater came in softly on stockinged

feet. Her fingers brushed his face, lingering upon a cheekbone. "I'm not one of those people who put a gun to your head," she said. "If you should change your mind . . ."

He said, "I like it here."

"Good. So do I." She wore a blue silk pullover trimmed with white fur at the cuffs and collar; it slid over her head with one smooth motion, revealing a narrow bra of peach lace. "Would you like me to undress you? I know that some of them— whatever you want. Whatever you've been thinking of all these years."

As he rose from his seat, he listened to his own voice as he might have heard someone else speak. "I've been thinking about Lara."

She paused, hands at the buttons of his topcoat. "Lara?"

"I love her," he said; and then, "But you're not her, and I really didn't know it was going to be like this." He took a step backward.

Her mouth fell open. For a moment her face was a tormented mask of disbelief and disappointment. Hate burned them away as fire scours a forest; her blue eyes blazed and flashed.

"I'd better go," he said.

A drawer under the sink rattled; she lunged at him with a kitchen knife. He stumbled to one side, and it stuck in the flimsy inner wall. Without thinking, he hit her wrist with one hand and pushed her away with the other.

The door opened easily, and by merciful miracle it opened outward. He fled, oblivious of the circle of ice that had been her rink.

His legs flew from under him, then the end of the float itself. For an absurd instant he felt he was falling off the world, flying out into space. The black pavement struck him like a fist.

· 4 ·

United

As from a great height, he looked down upon an endless plain of snow. It was nearly featureless, yet lit by a slanting sun so that such features as it possessed cast long shadows to eastward, their shadows more distinct and more visible than they. Night came quickly from the north, devouring the shadows, transforming the plain into a featureless darkness lit only by the memory of light.

"He's closing his eyes, Dr. Pille." (A woman's voice.) "As I see." (An androgynous voice, followed by footsteps that were merely padded and neither loud nor soft.) Day came again, and quickly.

"Are you awake?"

He said, "I think so."

A middle-aged woman in a white cap bent over him; the plain of snow receded, shrunk to a ceiling.

"That was a nasty bump you got there."

"What happened?" There was a dull throb at the back of his head.

"You fell down in the street."

"And I had the wildest dream," he told her. "Lara was just a little doll, and I showed her to an old Chinese. Can you give me something for this headache?"

She nodded and pulled a cork from a brown bottle. "Here. Smell this."

It had the odor of spring, when new green growth duels with melting snow in the rain-washed air. The throbbing sank, almost vanished.

"What's that?" he asked her.

"Just aspenin. Your nose may not work right for a while." She rose. "Everything okay now?"

He nodded, bringing back the ghost of the throb. "When can I get out of here?"

"Maybe tomorrow. Dr. Pille will see you again, and he may have you released. He may want to keep you for a few more days. Press the call button if you need me."

She was gone before he could ask her another question. He sat up, finding that he was sore everywhere. The room was tiny, with just space enough for the narrow hospital bed, a dwarfish white-enameled chair, a white-enameled night table, and a white locker. The walls were white, too, and the floor was white tile.

Gingerly, he swung his feet over the side of the bed. The locker probably held his clothes, with the doll Lara—Tina. He laughed.

A dream! It had been a dream, and nothing more—the mental health clinic; the dolls' infirmary; the strange, high shop that sold maps of elfland; the odd parade—all dreams.

But Lara?

Had Lara, too, been only a dream? If that were so, he did not wish to wake.

No, Lara was real, a real woman with whom he had talked and walked beside the river, ate and drank and slept only yesterday. Or perhaps, on the day before yesterday. Perhaps he had lost an entire day already, here in the hospital. Lara would be worried about him, back in that drafty old apartment. He ought to call, ought somehow to comfort her.

Yet it had been summer, surely, when they strolled beside the river. He recalled the smell of flowers, of green leaves; they must have been there. It was winter now, or was it?

Unsteadily, he went to the window. The hospital's little patch of lawn was pale with snow; dark figures bundled in wool, wrapped in mufflers to the eyes, picked perilous paths down an icy sidewalk. The street was gray with slush; even the brick-red, clanging trolleys were roofed with snow.

The white locker was locked, and he had no key. He rattled the locker door until a black man in a white uniform looked in at him. "You! Get back in the bed!" The black man pointed a finger.

He said, "I want my clothes."

"You get them when you get out. Till then, they stayin' locked up safe." The black advanced menacingly. "Now get in the bed or you don't get no chocolate puddin' for dinner. Want me to have to give you a shot? I got a needle 'bout as sharp as the end on a nail." Without touching him, the black man crowded him back until he sat once more upon the bed.

"Who do I have to see to get that opened?"

"Your doctor." The black man retreated to study the chart hanging from the foot of the bed. "He Dr. Pille. He make his rounds tomorrow. Till then, you stay in the bed 'less the nurse say you can get up."

"All right."

"You in for a sex change, huh?"

He jumped to his feet.

"Whoa-o! What I tell you? It don't say nothin' like that here. Just a concussion, and multiple bruises and stuff. Now you stay in the bed if you want puddin'."

When the black man had gone, he considered getting out of bed again. There seemed no point to it. The locker was locked, and he had nothing with which to break into it. The key was no doubt in some drawer in the nurses' desk. Still, he could call Lara and tell her he was alive and not seriously hurt.

There was no telephone on the night table. He looked about for the call button that would summon the nurse and discovered a remote control for the little TV high in one corner of the room; he switched it on, but nothing whatever happened.

The call button dangled from a white cord at the headboard of his bed. He pushed it and heard an indistinct chiming, as of bells on some far-off, fog-shrouded coast. Telling himself that he had done all he could at the moment, he lay back listening to the bells, his hands behind his head.

A gray radiance had enveloped the TV screen, flickering, waxing, and waning—lingering and at last growing brighter. Diagonal lines crossed the screen slowly, through a storm of snow. Lara's face fluttered behind them like an overexposed photograph, then vanished.

"AND IN THE CAPITAL, THE PRESIDENT HAS—AS SHE THREATENED EARLIER—VETOED THE FAMILY MAINTENANCE—"

He found the Volume Down button.

"—bill that would have permitted involuntary sterilization of mothers of twenty-five or more children. A spokesman for—"

He was sure it had been Lara, perhaps on another channel, a channel with almost the same broadcasting frequency. This was Channel One. He tried Two and Thirteen, and got nothing. When he returned to One, mixed teams were playing some complicated game that involved the kidnapping of opposing players.

Restlessly he searched the other channels, finding only a lecturing teacher and soapy lovers engaged in the usual debate, enlivened now by contemporary role reversal.

"Don't you see I want to make the way we feel about each other immortal, Beverly? Our love marching down the endless track of Time, showing the whole darn selfish human race that there are higher values than self."

"No, Robin. You want to end our love forever."

Slowly it dawned on him that he was in another city. At home there would have been eight working channels. He turned the lovers down to inaudibility, found the complex game again.

The nurse bustled in carrying a big vase of roses. "That was lucky! You rang for me, and I have these to deliver. I get to kill two birds with one stone. Aren't they lovely?"

He nodded. Red, yellow, white, and pink roses, and roses of a dozen colorful mottlings, cinnabar shot with bronze, old gold touched with flame, seemed ready to spill—almost to leap—from the bowl.

"There's a card table up in Furniture with a picture like that on it," he said. "I've never seen a bouquet like that in real life. They're always all one kind."

The nurse looked arch. "Your little friend doesn't believe in ho-hum arrangements, it seems. She went all out. Naturally, with her money . . ." She set the vase on the tiny white table, a few inches from his head. A minute card dangled from one of the handles of the vase on a gold thread.

He said, "I was wondering if you could bring me a phone. There's somebody I ought to call."

"Ahh!" Cupping spread fingers over her formidable breasts, the nurse inhaled deeply. "Don't they smell lovely! Of course there is. I'll get you a phone right away. You know, we would never have guessed you knew somebody like that."

"Like Lara?" Who but Lara would have sent him flowers?

The nurse shook her head. "No, no! The goddess." Seeing his startled look, she added, "The goddess of the silver screen— isn't that what they call her? I'll get your phone."

As soon as she was gone, he turned on his side to examine the card. There was a border of gold surrounding a completely illegible monogram. He opened the card and found a photograph of Lara and the name "Marcella" printed in florid gold script.

Lara was a movie star—a star called Marcella. The nurse had looked at her picture and recognized her.

Yet he rented movies two or three times a week, and watched still more movies on Home Box Office; if Lara had been so much as a featured player, he would have recognized her at once. Nor did he recognize the picture inside the card, save as a picture of Lara—even her hair style was the same.

His bruised muscles ached. He rolled onto his back and saw that Lara's face was once more on the screen; he reached for the remote control, but as soon as he moved his hand Lara shrank and vanished. Although he pushed the On button again and again, her face did not return. No button on the remote control made the set respond, and at length he pulled over the dwarfish chair and stood upon its seat to turn the knobs. Nothing he tried brought light to the screen again. He recalled a term from his days in Home Entertainment; there was no *raster*.

By the time the nurse returned with a telephone, he was back in bed. "I really hate to keep bothering you," he said, "but my television seems to be broken."

She tried the remote control without result. "No trouble. I just call the service. They'll bring you a new one tomorrow."

He felt a distinct thrill of triumph as she bent over to plug his telephone into the jack. "One more thing," he said. "Would you please read my diagnosis from that chart down by my feet?"

Like the black attendant, she lifted the chart from its hook. "Concussion, multiple bruises, alcoholism."

"Alcoholism?"

"I don't diagnose," she told him briskly. "Your doctor does that."

"I'm not an alcoholic!"

"Then you shouldn't have much trouble getting Dr. Pille to change your diagnosis. Do you drink?"

"Occasionally. It isn't a problem."

"Maybe the doctor sees it as more of a problem than you do. Particularly when he has a patient who falls down in the street and gets himself a concussion."

"It really does say alcoholism?"

"I told you. Want to see it?"

"But it doesn't say anything about a sex change?" That had been a lingering fear.

The nurse chuckled. "Somebody told you that. That's what we call alcoholism sometimes. It cuts down on the testosterone in men. Your beard stops growing, and you hardly ever get bald."

When she had gone, he reached for the telephone, but his

hand was shaking so badly he drew it back. There was no mirror in the room. He got up anyway, feeling vaguely that there had to be one somewhere, and was startled to see his own drawn face reflected in the dark window glass.

The short winter day had ended. Outside, cars as high and awkward as Jeeps crawled along the street with blazing lights. Pedestrians were individually invisible; but it seemed to him that some black fluid, as thick and slow as heavy oil, flowed and swirled at the edges of the traffic.

And it came to him that this viscous ichor was perhaps the reality, that the faces and figures to which he was accustomed might be as false in essence as the photomicrographs printed in the newspapers on slow news days, pictures that showed human skin as a rocky desert, an ant or a fly as a bewhiskered monster. This was how God saw men and women; who could blame him then, if he damned them all or forgot them all?

"I know what ya thinking."

He turned quickly, more than half embarrassed, at the sound of the voice. An extremely erect little man with a head like a polished ivory ball was looking through the doorway. He noticed with some relief that the little man wore hospital pajamas like his own.

"I was thinking about mail," he lied. "Today somebody gave me a charm that's supposed to bring you mail, and it seems to me that maybe I've been getting it."

The little man stepped inside. "Let's see it."

"I meant these roses. And something I just saw on TV, but I can't show you that."

"Ya charm. Let's see it."

He shrugged. "I can't show you that either. It's in this locker, I suppose."

"If Joe was 'ere, 'e'd bust open this tin box for ya like dynamite." The little man rattled the door.

"Is Joe the attendant?"

The little man grinned and shook his shiny head. "Joe's my fighter. I'm a fight manager. Joe, he's strong as a couple of bulls. 'E'd tear this tin box apart for ya if I told 'im ta."

"I doubt if the hospital would like that. Anyway, that's where I think my charm is. I don't really know; they've never given me an inventory or anything."

"Joe's 'eavyweight champeen of the world. I used ta 'ave a couple other fighters, Mel and Larry. Only when Joe won us the champeenship, I dropped 'em. I made sure another manager took 'em on, a good manager. They understand. They know I'll give 'em a break whenever I can. 'Ere's my card." The little man's hand went toward the place where the breast pocket of his suit coat would have been, had he been wearing a suit instead of his hospital pajamas, and came away empty. The little man grinned again, this time sheepishly.

He sat on the bed and waved toward the chair. "Why don't you sit down? I had an accident, and I guess I'm still a bit shaky; besides, we might as well sit if we're going to talk."

"Thanks," the little man said. "I like ta sit around and gab—makes me feel like I'm about ta cut a deal for Joe, ya know what I mean? So listen up! We gotta have a 'undred thousand up front, or we don't play."

He said, "You'll get it, don't worry."

The little man nodded. "That's the way, pal. 'Ey, I got ya name from the chart on ya bed. I'm Eddie Walsh, President, Walsh Promotions." Walsh's hand was small, cool, and hard.

"Pleased to meet you. Where are we anyway, Eddie? What is this place?"

"United," Walsh told him. "I thought ya was thinking of getting out." Then, seeing his look of incomprehension, Walsh added, "The United General Psychiatric Hospital, they call it. This 'ere's the good wing."

. 5 .

North

He lay on his back with his hands clasped behind his head once again; this time he was trying to sleep. The ward, or wing, or whatever the hell it was, slept already. Occasionally he heard the soft footsteps of the rubber-shod nurses; even more rarely, the shuffle of a patient's thin slippers. He was thinking about the world.

Not the world in which he now found himself, but the real world, the normal world.

There, Chinese-Americans spoke ordinary English and became nuclear physicists; the girls on floats did not invite men into their floats. In the real world, he thought, alcoholics did not get private rooms. Probably.

Most significant of all, in the real world streetcars had been done away with long, long ago, their very tracks entombed in layer upon layer of asphalt. True, it hadn't made sense to do away with them. They had been cheap, energy efficient, and nonpolluting. Yet they had been done away with, and a hundred harmful gadgets had been allowed to stay—that was the way you knew it was the normal world.

A trolley car was going past the hospital now. He heard the faint clang of its bell, and he knew that should he go to the window he would see its single headlight, shining golden through the falling snow.

The room had no door, and some feeble illumination entered from the softly night-lit hallway outside. Its sudden darkening made him sit up in bed.

A man was standing there. For a moment he thought the man was Walsh. But Walsh had been smoothly bald; this silhouetted man, although not much taller, had a luxuriant head of tousled hair.

"You're awake," the man whispered.

"Yes," he said.

"I wanted to tell you—we have a kind of bush telegraph. Each one tells one. Know what I mean?"

"I think so."

"That way, whatever one knows, we all know. It's the way we stay alive here. That Gloria Brooks, she did it to Bailey tonight. Billy North went to Al's room to bum a smoke, and he caught her at it. Each one tells one."

He nodded. "Okay, I'll tell somebody. Who should I tell?"

"I saw you talking to Eddie."

"Okay, I'll tell him. Where is he?"

"Down the hall to the first turn, then two or three doors down."

"Okay," he said again. By the time he sat up the man was gone.

35

As he told himself, he had not been sleepy anyway, and he had been getting more and more depressed. A dozen times he had reached for the telephone; a dozen times he had pulled back his hand, telling himself that he would wake up Lara, that she would be angry with him; he knew that the truth was that he was afraid she would not be there, that there would be no one there, no one in the apartment at all. That there had never been anybody in the apartment but himself.

His chart said *alcoholism.* He remembered drinking a lot a few times, and he had drunk too much last night with Lara. His mother had said his grandfather had drunk a lot. Before he had died, he had seen a little boy with golden hair—a golden-haired boy no one else had ever seen. Was Lara like that? He tried to recall the golden-haired little boy's name. Chester? Mortimer? She had said that his grandfather had mentioned it often in the months before he died, but it was gone now, gone utterly; nobody else had ever seen the little boy after his grandfather died.

Had anybody else ever seen Lara? Would anyone else ever see her if he died tonight? He did not intend to die tonight, yet he felt that this night would never end, that the brick-red trolleys would run on through the dark and the snow forever and ever.

Faint lights burned yellow-green in the hall. *Chartreuse,* he said to himself, and wondered if he were indeed an alcoholic, if naming colors for drinks was not some sign of his alcoholism, a vice he concealed even from himself. They had—once—had him in some kind of program at the store, hadn't they? Had it been an alcoholism treatment program?

"Down the hall to the first turn, then two or three doors down."

But was it two? Or three? He decided to try two first, and discovered that it was in fact no doors down, that all the rooms were as doorless as his own. Brass numbers on the wall beside each doorway told him that the second was 86E. A brass track below the number should have held a slip of paper with the occupant's name. It was empty, though he could hear the soft sighing of the occupant's breath within.

Briefly he considered the possibility that the occupant of the room was a homicidal maniac. This was some kind of mental hospital, after all. Walsh had said it was the good wing; that sounded encouraging.

He had not realized how dim the room would seem after the lights of the hall. The window looked out on a new scene, much darker than the busy street outside his own. He decided it was probably a park—a park full of large trees whose tops were as high as the windows on this floor, whatever floor this might be. The breathing of the occupant was as regular as the slow tick of a grandfather's clock.

"Walsh?" he whispered. "Eddie?"

The occupant stirred in his sleep. *"Yes, Mama?"*

It was not a propitious beginning.

"Eddie, is that you?"

As though at the flick of a switch, the occupant was awake and sitting up. "Who are you?"

He gave his name and, idiotically, tried to touch the other man's head.

At once his wrist was caught in a grip of steel. "What are you doing here?"

"I don't know," he said desperately.

"You know!"

"I fell. I got onto a float with this skater, and when I was coming out I slipped on her ice."

The grip relaxed ever so slightly. "You didn't make it with her." It was a statement, not a question.

"No."

"That's why, then. It's a trick that they use to put more pressure on the rest, see? If you start and then you think my God, I'm going to *die*, and you back out, they say you're crazy. Same thing happened to me."

He said, "My chart says alcoholism."

"You're lucky."

"Would you please let go of my hand?"

"No. And if you don't keep the other one to yourself, I'll take it too."

He groped for a way to prolong the conversation; it seemed dangerous to let it lapse. "I don't think alcoholism's lucky."

"Could have been acute manic schizophrenia. How'd you like that? Know what the stuff they do to you for acute manic schiz does to you? Do you?"

"No," he said. "No, I don't."

"Drives you crazy. Want to read what it says on my chart?"

"Sure, but I'll have to turn on the light."

"I'll tell you. Acute manic schizophrenia. Ask me the President's name."

"Okay," he said. It seemed to him that the room was colder than his own had been; he shivered in his thin hospital pajamas. There was an odor like almond blossoms.

"Go on, ask! 'Who is the President of the United States?'"

Obediently he said, "Who's President of the United States?"

"Richard Milhous Nixon!"

"Now how about letting go of my wrist?"

"You admit, you concede, that Richard Milhous Nixon is our President?"

He hesitated, fearful of some trap. "Well, they still call him President Nixon on the news."

38

There was a long silence, a stillness that throbbed with the blood in his ears.

"He isn't President any more?" the occupant of the room whispered. "But he was?"

"He was, sure. He resigned."

"For the good of the nation, right? That would be just like him—give it up if he had to for the good of the nation. He was a patriot. A real patriot."

He said diplomatically, "I suppose he still is. He's still alive, I think."

There was another long silence while the occupant digested this fact. He heard someone walk past, shuffling down the hall, passing the doorless doorway; he wondered if he should yell for help, but he did not even turn his head to look.

At last the occupant said, "Why didn't you give it to that skater?"

"I don't know."

"Tell me!" The grip on his wrist tightened again.

"It just didn't seem right. I've got a—" he groped for a word. "Somebody I care a lot about."

"Girlfriend or boyfriend?"

"My girlfriend; I'm not gay. Lara. I'm looking for her." Unable to help himself, he added, "She was gone this morning when I woke up."

The occupant grunted. "And you know about the President. Tell me something—how about yesterday morning? Was she there when you woke up then?"

"Sure," he said. "We had breakfast together, then I went to work and Lara went to look for a job."

"You were shacking up."

That was an old term, and it struck him that the occupant

was older than he had thought, ten years older than he was at least. He said carefully, "We've been living together for the past few days. With no job, Lara couldn't pay her rent." The memory of his message, which had been driven from his mind by the occupant's grip on his wrist and all the talk about Nixon, returned. He said, "I was supposed to tell somebody that Gloria Brooks did it to Al Bailey tonight. Billy North went into Al's room to borrow a cigarette, and he caught her at it."

The palm of the occupant's hand slapped his right cheek with a forehand, twisting his head so far that the returning backhand struck him across the lips.

"My name's William T. North," the occupant told him softly. "You refer to me as Mr. William T. North or Mr. North. Get it?"

He jabbed for North's face with his free hand, and though he could not get much weight behind the punch, he felt North's nose give under his knuckles in a satisfactory way.

"Say, that was all right." North's voice was so calm they might have been discussing the weather. "I'd break your neck for you, but they'd put me in the violent ward. I've been there, and it's no fun. Besides, I've got a little thing cooking. You want out of here?"

"Not without my clothes."

"Right. Absolutely right. In hospital rags they'd spot us in half a minute, just in time to keep us from freezing to death. But if you could take your clothes?"

"Hell, yes."

"Can you drive?"

"Sure," he said. It had been a long time—he was not sure just how long—since he had driven.

"Now I'm going to let go of your wrist. If you don't want to get

40

out, all you've got to do is duck through that door. But if you want to come—well, you've got some guts and you're from C-One. That counts with me."

There was a delay, almost as if the hand that grasped his wrist were arguing with its owner. Then it loosened, released its grip entirely, and drew away.

"Thanks," he said.

"Step One: you must learn how to open these lockers. You can practice on mine, using my equipment; but you're going to have to get your own and open your locker yourself, understand? I'm not going to do it for you."

"You said I came from C-One," he said. "What did you mean by that?"

"C-One's the place we're trying to get back to—President Nixon, and all that. Now listen. Here's my pick."

A small, stiff piece of metal was put into his hand. It had a small bend at one end, a much larger one at the other.

"These lockers have very simple locks. Have you seen one of the keys?"

"No." He shook his head.

"They're flat pieces of steel with one jagged side. The notches along that side are just to go around the wards of the lock, get it? When you use a pick, you bypass all the wards. The thing that does the business is the tip of the pick. All you have to do is get the tip of the pick where the tip of the key would be and work it around. Try it."

It was remarkably easy. He seemed to *become* the bent wire, encountering the unyielding wards, and then, at the very back of the lock, something like a ward that gave to his pressure.

"That's copper wire from a wall plug," North told him. "Find one that's got nothing plugged into it. There's a wall plate held by a little screw; you can unscrew it with any piece of thin, flat metal. Pull the plate off. The plug's held by two long screws. Take them out and pull the plug out. Don't touch anything metal while you're doing it, and work with your right hand only. Keep your left stuck in the shirt of your PJs, so you won't forget and use it—that way a shock can't go across your heart."

He nodded, fairly sure he knew what would happen if one did.

"There'll be two wires on the plug—a red one and a black one. The red one should be live; don't touch it. The black one should be return. It'll be insulated, and you touch it only by the insulation. That's what's black; the inside's copper. Pull it out as far back as you can and bend it back and forth until it breaks. Then bend the part next to the plug back and forth the same way. When you've got your wire, put the plug back like it was and screw on the wall plate again. Then wipe the floor—there'll be plaster dust on the floor. Meet me in the rec room after lunch and I'll tell you the rest."

"All right," he said.

When he returned to his own room, he was exhausted and very sleepy. His cheek still hurt where North had slapped him. He rubbed it and discovered that his lower lip had split. A thin trickle of blood had run to his chin without his being aware of it. He groped for the light switch so that he could examine his face in the mirror, but there was no light switch.

He considered opening the wall plug, but he had no piece of metal to turn the screw, and he would not be able to distinguish the red wire from the black one in any case.

Determined at last, he picked up the telephone. Slowly, counting holes in the old-fashioned spinning dial, he entered the number of his apartment.

For a long time the earpiece buzzed and clicked. There was a twitter of bird-like voices, the voices of Japanese children, or of music boxes tuned to speak. At last a man's deep voice asked, "Kay? Ist dis you, Kay?"

"I'm calling for Lara," he said. He gave the address. "I think I must have the wrong number."

The man announced, "Dis ist Chief of Department Klamm, Herr Kay," and he slammed down the receiver.

· 6 ·

The Club Fighter

He woke up wondering where he was. For a brief moment, the bed was almost his bed, the room nearly his apartment. Groping for the control of his electric blanket, he found a telephone.

It did not come rushing back to him. Rather it arrived in bits and pieces, like the guests at a masked ball, like dancers all dressed as dreams. It worried him that he could recall the dreams so very clearly, and the waking world not at all; he sat up in bed and saw the dim hallway outside.

Vaguely, he wondered what time it was. Down the hallway, very far down it, he could see a brightly lit nurses' station. He discovered slippers beneath the bed.

"Can't sleep?" the nurse on duty asked. She seemed neither friendly nor unfriendly.

"I just wanted to know what time it was."

"What most of them do," the nurse said slowly, "is turn on their TVs. Then they can tell what time it is from the shows. Or sooner or later they'll give it."

"Mine doesn't work."

The nurse considered this for a while, then looked—slowly—down at the desktop. He saw the brass back of a small clock there. "Eleven thirty-five," she said.

"I would have thought it was later than that."

"It's eleven thirty-five," she repeated. "It gets dark early, this time of year, and we put you to bed early."

As he returned to his room, it occurred to him that North was probably asleep again. North had put the pick on the table beside his bed.

As quickly and as quietly as he could, he turned the corner instead. A big, blond man in a dark overcoat was lumbering down the hall toward him. He went into North's room, pretending that it was his own.

North was no more than an indistinct pile of bedclothes, a scarcely audible breathing. On tiptoe, he crept to the table and ran his fingers over its surface. The pick was gone.

There was a small, shallow drawer. Carefully, he pulled it out. His fingers discovered a clutter of miscellaneous objects—a little book that felt like an address book, a pen, paper clips, a hex nut.

There's nowhere else, he thought. And yet there was—the windowsill. As he turned to examine it, his hip bumped the open drawer ever so slightly. There was a faint, metallic tinkle, and North groaned softly, as though in the grip of a painful dream.

He knelt, sweeping the tiles with his fingertips. The pick lay in the angle between the nightstand and North's bed.

As he stepped into the hallway, he noticed the light was on in the room next to North's; curious, he stopped to look inside.

The big, blond man he had seen in the hallway was on one of the tiny hospital chairs, holding a cloth cap. Walsh was sitting up in bed, looking alert and cheerful. "Come in, come in!" Walsh called. "I want ya ta meet Joe."

Hesitantly, he stepped inside.

"Joe fought tonight. Ya see 'im on TV? It was beautiful, just beautiful! Third round KO."

"My set's broken."

"Right. Sure. Ya told me, right. Well, let me tell ya, *I* watched 'im. I seen every second of it. I was cheering for 'im like crazy." Walsh laughed. "No wonder they got me in 'ere."

"I'm sorry I missed it."

"Joe didn't miss 'im, let me tell ya." Walsh's small fists made boxing motions: one-two, one-two. "Joe, show 'im ya face. See? 'Ardly marked 'im."

There was a shadowy blue bruise on the big man's jaw. "One time he got me pretty good," Joe said. The voice was as big and as slow as the man, yet not deep, almost threatening to rise to an adolescent squeak. "He was a good fighter, a real good boxer. I had the reach on him."

"Joe, 'e wasn't fit to get in the ring with ya." Walsh frowned. "That's the trouble with managing the champeen. Ya can't 'ardly match 'im in 'is own class."

Joe said, "I've got to go now, Eddie. The little woman's waiting."

"Come tomorrow—ya listening ta me? Ya'll 'ave plenty time 'cause I don't want ya ta do no roadwork, understand? Too cold. Maybe ya could work out on the light bag a little, skip a little rope. But mostly ya oughta rest up from the fight. Get back ta training the next day."

"Okay, Eddie."

"Jennifer don't never go ta see 'im fight. She's always scared

46

'e'll get 'urt. She watches the TV and 'as 'is dinner ready when 'e gets 'ome."

"I see," he said. "Eddie, I was supposed to tell you Billy North caught Gloria Brooks doing it to Al Bailey." Doing what, he wondered; Walsh might tell him. "North went to Al's room to borrow a cigarette."

Walsh nodded. "Yeah, I bet 'e did, the mooching bastard. Ya know," his face began to crumple, as a child's does when the child is told of some tragedy too big to understand. "I always liked Al." Two fat tears coursed down Walsh's cheeks. "That bitch!"

Joe stood. "I'll see you tomorrow, Eddie. That's a real promise."

"Fine, Joe. Ya my boy."

He turned away, ready to follow Joe out the doorway. Walsh called him back. "Stay 'ere a minute, won't ya? I need ta talk ta ya."

"All right," he said. "If you want me to."

Joe gave him what might have been a significant look. The big, scuffed shoes made no more noise than a cat's paws.

"Wish we could shut the door," Walsh whispered when Joe was gone. "Stick ya 'ead out and take a look."

He did. "All clear."

"Fine." Walsh snuffled. "I wanna tell ya about Joe. I know ya gonna say ya can't do nothin' about 'im. I just wanna get it off my chest."

"Sure," he said. To his surprise, he found that he liked the little man. "Sure, Eddie. Go ahead."

"Joe's married ta this Jennifer. Ya 'eard us talking about 'er."
He nodded.

"She's twenty, blond, a real looker. And sweet, ya know 'ow they are? Butter won't melt inner mouth. She tells Joe they'll wait till she's thirty-five. Gives Joe fifteen years. 'E goes for it. Ya know 'ow kids 'is age are, they don't think thirty-five ever comes. Say, ya ain't married yaself, are ya?"

"No," he said. "Not yet. Maybe never."

"That's the way, pal." Walsh paused. "See, I don't know if Jennifer's letting Joe alone. That's what 'e says, but can ya believe 'im? Ya seen Joe. 'E don't never notice nothing till ya 'it 'im with a two-by-four. Joe ain't dumb—that's what people think, but they're wrong—but 'e don't notice. 'E's busy inside. Ya know what I mean?"

"Sometimes I'm that way myself."

"So I pray ta God Jennifer's gonna get 'it with a truck. But if something like that 'appens, Joe . . ."

He thought of the way he would feel if something happened to Lara, and he completed the sentence: "Might kill himself."

Walsh nodded. "Not with liquor or jumping out a window— Joe ain't that kind. But 'e might 'ole up where 'e could be by 'imself with nobody ta bother 'im. Out west someplace, I guess. 'E wouldn't never fight again."

He recalled that the red-faced man had said that Overwood was at the foot of the mountains, and asked, "Would Joe go to the mountains, you think? Somewhere around Manea?"

"Yeah." Walsh nodded gloomily. "That's just what 'e might do."

The light went out.

Walsh's gritty voice came through the darkness. "Joe's at the reception desk. They switch it off from there."

As his eyes adjusted, he made out the dim outline of the doorway. "I'm surprised they let you have visitors this late."

"One of the guys that works 'ere's Joe's 'andler," Walsh said. "'E knows I gotta see Joe after the fight."

He hesitated, but there seemed to be nothing more to say.

The little copper pick felt hard and heavy in his hand. "Well, good night, Eddie."

"G'night."

In the hall he saw (with a shock of déjà vu) Joe walking noiselessly toward him. He started to speak, but Joe raised a warning finger, and he did not. When they were some distance down the hall, Joe guiding him gently but firmly by the arm, Joe said, "Would you like some coffee? Or pop? They've got pop."

He asked, "Will they give us some this late?"

"It's machines. W.F. will let us in."

Joe opened a door that appeared locked, a heavy metal door marked C, with a large lock clearly intended to keep people out. They went down flights of narrow concrete stairs, landing after landing, and through a second door into a wide, empty room where orderly rows of battered wooden chairs and tables stretched into the darkness. One corner of the room was lit, and the black man sat in that corner, still wearing his crisp white uniform, a cup of steaming coffee before him.

Joe waved to him, then fished in his pocket for a scuffed leather coin purse. "I'm going to have a cream soda," he said. "What would you like?"

"Coffee, I guess. Cream and sugar."

"All right." Joe selected two nickels from the purse and snapped it shut. "You can sit down with W.F. if you want to. I'll bring them."

He nodded and did as he had been told, wishing he had seen the nickels better. They had not looked quite like the nickels to which he was accustomed.

W.F. said, "What I tell you 'bout gettin' out the bed, man? *Woo-oh!* You ass mud now." He had an infectious smile.

"You'll have to turn me in, I guess."

"You guesses? What you mean, *guess?* You *know* I do! Goin' to be KP for you *all* year. You get dishpan hands clean up the elbows. The women see you, they think you a hundred years old. Leave you alone *for sure.*"

He nodded and said, "At least I ought to be able to rip off some chocolate pudding."

W.F. chortled. "You all right! No wonder Joe like you so fast."

He glanced over at the big man, now moving slowly from one machine to another, a red bottle in his hand. "Is Joe really a prizefighter?"

"Don't you know? I his handler. You see me on TV?"

He shook his head.

"Hey, man, you miss a good one—we the main attraction. Hey, Joe, tell him you the main event."

Joe, coming toward them with the bottle in one hand and a steaming cup in the other, shook his head. "Last prelim." He looked apologetic. "Five rounds to a decision."

"Only you didn't *need* no la-de-da five rounds. You KO'd him in the third."

Joe slid the coffee cup over, and slowly, heavily, seated himself in one of the battered wooden chairs. "That's what I wanted to talk to you about. Eddie thinks I'm the heavyweight champion of the world."

"I know."

"I'm not. Probably I never will be."

He nodded. "I never thought you were, Joe."

W.F. put in, "But you goin' to be the main event next time, if that sweet Jenny know her stuff."

Joe nodded slowly. "Maybe."

"Maybe! You means for sure."

"Jennifer's been managing me since this happened to Eddie. Eddie's still my real manager. He'll take over again when he's feeling better."

"Eddie used to handle Joe hisself," W.F. explained. "Then he come here, and there wasn't nobody 'cause Jenny don't want to do that. So I says I would. Won't take no pay—I sees all the fights for free, and everybody see me on TV 'cause one channel broadcasts. Sometimes we on the sports on the news, when they don't have nothin' else to show. Everybody say, *Whoo!* Look at ol' W.F. swing that towel. Besides Joe usually win, and I like that."

He said, "It's nice of you to stand by Eddie. Nice of you both."

For the first time, Joe had raised the bottle to his lips. It was large and flaunted its name—Poxxie—in raised lettering on the glass. Joe poured most of its poisonous-looking scarlet contents down his throat, which he seemed able to open and hold open, like a valve in a pipe. "I couldn't leave Eddie when he thinks I'm the champion. I don't want you to tell Eddie I'm not the champion. It upsets him."

"I won't."

Joe belched solemnly. "And if you can help him . . ."

Moved by he did not know what spirit, he said, "I think the best way to help him might be for you to become champion. Then he'd be well."

W.F. crowed, "What I say? You one smart dude. Right *on!*"

Joe shook his head. "I don't think I can do that."

"I doubt that any champion thought he could do it before he did it."

The very slightest of smiles touched Joe's lips, a smile that could not have been seen at all were it not for the impassivity of the wide cheeks and heavy chin. As if to remove the last droplets of Poxxie, a large dark overcoat sleeve rose and scrubbed at that infinitesimal curve; yet the smile remained.

Without in the least intending to, he yawned.

W.F. said, "Guess I better get you into the bed. You did the job, and you about fagged out, I think."

"I'll be all right," he said. He sipped his coffee, finding that it tasted even worse than it smelled. A moment later, W.F. was tucking a blanket around his shoulders. "You gets chocolate puddin' *every* meal," W.F. said. "Even for breakfasts."

· 7 ·

Lara, Tina, and Marcella

The ringing of the telephone beside his bed woke him. Groggily, he answered it. "Hello?"

A woman's voice: "Here, Emma, give me that!"

"Lara?" he asked. "Is that you, Lara?"

"Darling, it's me!" (Surely that was Lara's voice, Lara composed and gracious.) "I hope—I really *do* hope—I haven't roused you from a sound sleep, darling. But I just got back here—you know how it is—and dear, precious Emma had sat up. And there was absolutely *nothing* for her to do but this, so I said call the damned place and see if they won't let me talk with him, there's a darling, and she did and they would. But not till the poor old dear had talked herself positively *blue,* didn't you, Emma? While it got later and later and later and later. What time is it there, darling?"

He said, "I don't know."

"It's after one here, and all I've done is come home and call you. Except that I had a bath and a drink first." Lara giggled. "Sounds as though I drank the bath, doesn't it? No, Emma mixed me a toddy and made it strong enough to knock down a mare. I can say that now, darling, because she's gone. Did you get my flowers? Are they pretty?"

"Yes," he said. "They're lovely. Thank you."

"They should be, darling—they cost like gold. But I'm immensely glad you like them."

He decided to come out with it. "You're Marcella too."

"You mean besides all those perfectly awful bitches I play? Yes, there's a real Marcella too—a real Marcella still, though sometimes I have ever so much trouble getting in touch with her. Besides, it's so much fun being a bitch, though one doesn't like oneself half so well afterward. But darling, I want you to know it's horrible, horribly dangerous, my talking with you, knowing you're in that *awful* place, because I'm so *tempted* to be bitchy with you. Why couldn't you be good? But I'm coming to see you just as soon as I can. Perhaps then we can find a door out for you together."

There was no good-bye, only the terrible finality of the handset set down in the receiver. He hung up too and put his hands behind his head, as he always did when he had to think. Maybe Lara would call back, as Marcella or somebody else. As Tina? The Tina doll had been modeled on someone, surely—on a real woman who called herself Tina and was actually Lara. Or rather, who was really the woman he knew—who he had known—as Lara.

He stepped from the van onto ice, and his feet flew from under him. He jerked awake.

He had been sleeping, then; sleeping and dreaming. Perhaps even Lara's call had been a dream. He got up, found the pick he had taken from North's room, and opened his locker. His clothes were just as he remembered them. The charm Sheng had given him hung from a hook in the locker; the Tina doll was in the breast pocket of his jacket. The badly folded map was in one pocket of his topcoat. He took it out, but the room was too dark for him to read it.

As he replaced it, it met with some obstruction. He pulled it out again and thrust his hand into the pocket. A small box had appeared there—by magic it seemed, by the rankest sorcery. It rattled softly. One questing finger discovered a tiny drawer and pushed it open. There was a second, louder, rattle as small objects fell from the drawer to the floor. Matches, of course.

He squatted, found one, and struck it on the side of the box, producing an impressive flare of sulfurous light. A fat dragon writhed with astounding flexibility upon a paper label, floating upward, as it seemed, to kiss or perhaps to devour a Chinese character of astonishing complexity.

Afraid that a passing nurse might see the light, he blew out the match.

They were Sheng's matches; he recalled them now. As he and Sheng had gone through the basement of Sheng's shop, the Chinese had handed him this box of matches and urged him to strike one. When he had refused, Sheng had struck a match from another box. He must have put this one in his pocket.

He swept up as many matches as he could find and restored them to the box. Thrusting his head and shoulders inside the locker so that it would contain the light, he struck a second match and examined the doll.

It was Lara, beyond a doubt. Perhaps its hair was a shade less red—though by the light from the match it was hard to be sure; girls—women—often changed their hair colors anyway. And the cheekbones might be a bit less pronounced, but it was Lara. The flame reached his fingers, and he blew the match out.

After replacing the doll and the box of matches, he closed the locker door, wedging the burnt matchstick under it to hold it shut. Should he return the pick to North? For a moment he debated it with himself. It was certain North would notice its absence, but he did not know what North's hiding place had been; North might notice that it was out of place just as easily.

Furthermore, he could not go with North now.

He tilted the vase and slid the pick beneath its base, got back into bed and pulled up the sheet and the thin blanket. As if the tilting of the vase had released them, the perfumes of the roses seemed to fill the air. He found that he could tell one from another, though he had no idea which belonged to which blossom.

One seemed darkly amber, languid, sultry and freighted with spice. Another, light yet evocative of ripe pears and apples, suggested a pink flower. Between these two, sometimes subtle, sometimes wanton, danced a third, insinuative of no color, but daring, seductive, and ravishing. By one of those insights that come when we are near sleep, he knew that this was Lara herself, the first Marcella, the second Tina.

As though his guessing the secret had ended the game, Lara appeared to take him by the hand. The matchstick dropped to the floor and the door of the locker flew open. Beyond it spread a garden filled with sun and flowers. At its center, in a small lawn, stood a stone arch draped in wild profusion with roses: yellow, pink, and white, and a hundred other colors, tinctures, and mottlings. For some reason the sight of this arch filled him with a cold terror, like the dread inspired by the sight of a scalpel in a man about to be operated upon.

Seeing his fear, Lara released his hand and went into the

garden alone. Horrified yet fascinated, he watched her as she crossed the little lawn, passed under the arch, and vanished.

Though Lara was gone, he could not bring himself to enter the garden or to close the locker. A playful breeze teased the garden, ruffling its gay beds of tulips and swaying its bowing lilacs. Red and yellow birds fluttered through the air, singing as they flew, sometimes perching on the stems of the roses that shrouded the sinister arch.

When he had waited for a long time, so long that his arms and legs had grown stiff and cold, Tina emerged from the arch; her features—delicate and childlike, yet Lara's—belied her jutting breasts. Smiling and extending her hand to him, she crossed the lawn. At his touch she became Marcella, blond and elegant, bright with diamonds and swathed in mink. He was so startled by the transformation that he jerked his head out of the locker and slammed the door.

He sat up in bed, but the slamming of the door continued relentlessly, as though ten thousand schoolboys were selecting books, rejecting them, and choosing new ones, forever. Intense light flashed starkly from the curtained window.

Shivering in his pajamas, he watched a winter thunderstorm. Snow and hail filled the air, vanished, and returned triumphant. Thunder rattled the frozen limbs of trees, and lightning played among the towers of the city; by its fevered illumination he saw that they were of shapes never seen in his own, nor in any other city with which he was familiar: pagodas, pyramids, pylons, and ziggurats.

"*You* get back in the bed!" W.F. said behind him.

"I was just watching the storm."

"I *know* what you was doin'. Get in the bed this minute, and you can tell me all about it. If you don't," W.F. sounded

— 57

threatening, "you don't get no 'nanas with your Corn Flakes in the mornin'. Pretty near mornin' *now*." W.F. strode into the room. "Now *get* back in there!"

Obediently and even gratefully he climbed back into bed, drawing up the warmth of the blanket.

W.F. tucked him in, then bent over the roses, sniffing at one, then another. "You lucky you got these, you know? Joe like flowers so much he got me likin' 'em too. When he's home with that Jennifer, that's about all he do, is work with those flowers. He got a li'l greenhouse."

He would have returned to the locker and its haunted garden if he could. Instead he found himself at work, confronted by an angry-looking woman who told him, "I want to buy some furniture. Show me furniture, young man."

The aisles of Furniture had become deserted highways lit by the level radiance of a setting sun and stretching for hundreds and perhaps thousands of miles, lined with brass beds, bookcase beds, and big waterbeds, all of which he showed the woman; there were gateleg tables too, cute dinettes, and formal walnut dining room ensembles. When they had seen innumerable beige sofas and cozy wingback chairs, they came at last to a Chippendale writing desk. He pulled out a drawer to show her its green baize lining and found that it contained an unopened letter sealed in red wax imprinted with a heart.

Aware that the woman strongly disapproved of what he was about to do, he nevertheless took out the letter and broke the wax, which snapped like glass.

The snap was also the flicking of a switch. The infinite furniture aisles and the finite world were plunged alike into night. A woman stood in the dim doorway; from the gesture she made of thrusting her purse beneath her arm, he knew that the snap he had heard had been the sound of its clasp.

He sat up, but the woman had already turned away. For an instant her face was lit by the hall light, and he saw that she was Marcella, the woman whose picture (but it was Lara's) was on the card that had come with the roses, the woman he had seen in the garden. He sprang from the bed and rushed down the hallway, but she was gone.

When he returned to his room, North was sitting in the tiny chair beside the bed. "Hello," North said. "Thought I'd have to wake you. What's up?"

"I had another visitor."

"Anything to do with our plan for tomorrow?"

"Today, you mean. It must be a long time after midnight. No, it isn't."

"You got your locker open. I checked. That's good, that was the test. What we're going to do—"

"I'm not going," he said.

There was a long silence. At last North said, "You think you've got a better way now."

"That's right."

"I need somebody to drive me. You're the only one around."

He asked, "Can't you drive?"

"Hell, yes. But I'm not going to."

He hesitated. Marcella (who might or might not be the same as Lara, though he was sure she was) was going to try to get him out. But would her chances be worse if he'd gotten himself out before? "All right," he said. "But there's a price."

"Name it."

"You're from the real world—the world where Richard Nixon was President. So am I. But I think you've been in this one a lot longer than I have. How long?"

North shrugged, his shadowy shoulders almost invisible in the faint light. "I've lost track."

GENE WOLFE

"More than a year?"

"Sure."

"Then I want you to answer three questions for me, openly and honestly. Three questions about this world. Will you do that?"

"Shoot."

He hesitated. There were so many questions, and some of them were questions he had to ask himself. Did he want to go home? Or to find Lara? He asked, "Who is the woman they call the goddess?"

"Hold it," North said. "I can't answer questions that don't make sense. Do you mean the real goddess?"

"When I first got here, I bought a doll. The clerk said it was the goddess at sixteen. I mean whatever goddess he meant."

"All right, that's the real goddess. Only she's not real. She's just like Christ or Buddha, you get me? She represents the God-damned feminine ideal or whatever. There's a big place out west that's sacred to her—ten thousand square miles, they say. Nobody can live out there. Nobody's even supposed to go into it."

"No one ever sees her?"

"That's your second question?"

"Yes," he said.

"Sure, people see her. They see ghosts and flying saucers—all sorts of crap. She's supposed to go around looking for her lost lover, some guy she ditched thousands of years back." North paused; it was impossible to make out his expression in the faint light from the doorway. "If you ask me, she's Mary Magdalene, and she's looking for Jesus. Anyway, sometimes they see him too—the lost lover."

"This is my third. What do they call him?"

There was a noticeable hesitation before North answered. "I

won't count this one. There's a bunch of names, and I've never paid much attention to them." Another hesitation. "Attis, he's one. He's got something to do with spring, and the harvest. Or he did."

"I still have a question left?"

"Right."

"Then I'll save it for later. Are you going to tell me how we're going to get out? Or do you want me to play it by ear?"

"I'm going to tell you. Just before noon they'll herd all of us into the rec room. It's called group recreation, but it's really a get-acquainted party and gripe session. All the staff will be there, so that's the best time for it. What we have to do then—"

The light came on.

· 8 ·

Indoor Moopsball

He had barely gotten into bed when W.F. carried in his breakfast tray. "You was pretty good," W.F. said, "so you get 'nanas with your cereal."

He said, "You work some awful hours."

"Not really. I work days. See, the first time I see you yesterday, I was 'bout to go off. Then I went to the arena to handle Joe. Then I come back with him, 'cause I live out this way. I had a little talk with Joe 'bout strategy an' all that after you gone. I always do it with him after a fight, but he won't do it *right* after. He want to cool down and think 'bout things hisself. So then I think why don't I have a look in an' see how everybody's doin'."

"You can't have had much sleep."

"Don't *need* much. Never have. I'll sleep good tonight, though."

"W.F.?"

"What?" Already at the doorway, W.F. turned to look back.

"Did you see a blond woman here last night? A visitor?"

"Somebody come while you sleep last night, huh?"

He nodded, then added, "Not really while I was asleep. I was awake, and I saw her just as she was stepping out into the hallway." He indicated the golden card attached to the roses. "This woman."

"Listen." W.F. stepped toward the bed again and lowered his voice. "Lots of dudes have some dreams like that. Don't matter—don't you worry 'bout it."

Breakfast was Corn Flakes with a sliced banana, milk, and coffee. He ate listlessly, trying to recall what he had eaten for dinner the night before. The only thing he could be sure of was W.F.'s promised chocolate pudding. Had there been potatoes? He seemed to remember green beans and a scoop of mashed potatoes with a half tablespoon of gravy.

Was this what patients did? He had not thought of himself as a patient before, but as a wounded animal, a lost adventurer briefly exiled from the fields of life. Perhaps no one thought of himself as a patient until he was well, or almost well. He'd had a concussion, after all—a bad concussion. Perhaps this was how patients felt, how patients lived, waiting from one meal to the next, marking their whole lives with soggy Corn Flakes and cold coffee.

He tried to finish the coffee before it got any colder and discovered that his hand was shaking too much to hold the cup. This was a mental hospital. He had a concussion—or was that just what they told you? He felt his bandaged head.

There was a knock at the doorway; a man in coveralls stood there, artfully pretending that there was an actual door before him—a door impenetrable to the human eye.

"Yes?" he said.

"TV repair. You have a broken set?"

He had forgotten about it. "Yes," he said again. "Or at least it was broken yesterday." He picked up the remote control and pressed the On button. Nothing happened.

The man had stepped inside. "No picture. No sound."

"That's right," he said.

"You didn't mess with the knobs, did you?" The man edged in the direction of the set, keeping an eye on him.

"I'm not crazy," he said. "I'm an alcoholic, a drunk. I fell down and hit my head. Read my chart. No, I didn't touch the knobs at all; there's nothing but that little chair to stand on, and it's on wheels."

Somewhat to his surprise, the television repair man did as he had suggested, bending to study the chart at the foot of his bed.

"Okay?" he asked.

"Okay." The man straightened up, smiling. "You know how it is—some of the guys in this place are really nuts. I guess it's worse for you, being in here all the time."

"I haven't met many of them. I only got here yesterday." It struck him that he did not really know whether what he had said was true or not. "Or anyhow, I only woke up yesterday."

"I had one guy try to jump me once. I had one guy tell me he was God." The man chuckled. "And he hadn't liked how the world was going, so he changed it. But he didn't like the new way either, and he wanted it changed back. He was real mad."

He smiled dutifully.

"There was a woman too that said she was a pilot. You ever hear of a woman that could fly an airplane?"

"Sure," he said.

"Maybe she was, then. Only she said she was way up above all the clouds, and she didn't know quite where she was, and she didn't want to come down through them because sometimes you hit something doing that. So she saw this little bitty hole in the clouds, and lights on the ground, and she went through it, and everything was different." The man chuckled again. "They used to have the women mixed in with the men, you know, what do some of these guys know? But one of the papers found out about it." Expertly the man lifted the television from its slanted bracket.

He had put the telephone in his lap. Without much hope, he dialed his apartment.

"Knobs don't work," the man said. "Now I gotta see if you got power. Some of the outlets here are bad."

Somewhere (where?) a telephone rang and rang again.

"You got power, so it's the main fuse. Power, no light, no sound, it can't be anything else." The man whipped out a large screwdriver and began to take the back off the set.

"Hello?" It was a harsh male voice.

"Who is this?" he asked.

"You called me. Who do you want?"

"Lara."

There was a long pause in which he heard faint music and children's voices, as though a radio were playing in the next apartment, as though the apartment were by a school (it was not) and all its windows were open in this bitter cold, admitting the sounds of the playground with the snow.

"Lara's not here. Who's calling?"

"Tell me who you are," he said, "and I'll tell you who I am."

"I see. Okay, I'll tell Lara you called. Where are you?"

He hesitated. He wanted to be found, but did he want to be found by this man? Would this man really tell Lara anything?

She had brought the flowers. No, she had sent the flowers, but she had come later; she had even spoken to him on the phone, because it had been Lara, surely Lara, on the phone—Lara forced to use another name. "Lara knows where I am," he said, and hung up.

"Yup, the main fuse," the television repairman said. "I'll have it working again for you in a jiffy."

For want of anything better to say, he said, "I don't suppose I could trade it for a color set?"

"Color? You mean colored pictures?"

He nodded.

The man's face closed like the shutting of a door. In the tone of an adult explaining simplicities to an infant, the man said, "You can't do that. Look here, the way these things work is that you've got a round screen coated with phosphors. When the electron beam hits them, they shine. If it hits them hard, they shine bright. If it isn't so hard, they're not so bright. That way you can have white, black, and various shades of gray on your screen. But if you wanted colors, you'd have to have a phosphor dot for, well, every color there is—blue, red, yellow, everything. They'd have to be put on real close together too, without them getting mixed up, and I guess you'd still need the regular phosphor for white. If it was ever built, a thing like that would cost a million dollars."

He said, "I thought I saw an article that said they had them."

The repairman tossed the burned-out fuse in the direction of the wastebasket in the corner. "Probably somebody playing guessing games. Or a real little one that some company's made to show they could do it. I think they'd have to put out their own signal, though. The regular signal wouldn't work."

66

He nodded and lay still for a moment, watching the man put the back on his set. He knew he *owned* a color television, a GE as bright as Lara's roses. He knew Lara had sent him the roses. He had *sold* color televisions, and he had seen Lara. His neck was still stiff from the fall, and it hurt to twist it to look at the roses. He decided he would sit up and hold the vase in his lap for a time, smelling the roses and visualizing how they would look on color television. When he picked up the vase, he saw a roll of bills beneath it.

"All set," the repairman said, displaying the black and white picture. "I'll put it back up for you."

While the man's back was turned, he grabbed the roll of bills and hid it under the sheet.

"Try out your remote."

He did, changing channels, turning the set off and on, and raising and lowering the volume. "Works fine."

"What'd I tell you? It was the main fuse, that's all. You got a voltage spike, and it blew to protect your tubes."

Recalling Lara's fading, shrinking face on the screen, he asked what could have caused such a spike.

The repairman sighed. "Probably some equipment somebody's hooked up wrong. A hospital's got a lot, X-ray machines and all that stuff. Big elevators—if you wire them up wrong, they can generate voltages of their own and stick them in the system."

"I see," he said. And then, "Thanks."

When the man was gone, he let his fingers toy with the roll of bills, counting them by touch. Exactly ten. He wondered how big they were, and whether they were all the same denomination. What did they look like? Money here was not like his own money; the reaction of the girl in the map store had proved that, and it had been confirmed by the bundle of money—money meant to be burned—in the Chinese shop. He moved one of the bills until its corner protruded beyond the hem of the sheet and glanced at it. One hundred.

A voice from the television said, *"Hello?"* and he glanced up.

It was a moment before he recognized his own apartment, but it was all there—his worn couch, the vinyl-covered armchair the store had let him have for thirty-two fifty after someone burned a hole in the right arm with a cigarette, the telephone stand he had positioned to throw a shadow on that hole.

A faint, metallic voice asked, *"Who is this?"*

The man on the telephone in his apartment was not himself. This man was older than he, big, tough looking, starting to run to fat.

He pressed a button to increase the volume.

"You called me, fella," the man in his apartment said. *"What do you want?"*

"Lara."

There was a long pause. The big man seemed frozen. Slowly the image faded, replaced by a huge can of dog food. *"It's all meat,"* said a new voice. *"Give your pet just one can and watch him go for it."*

He turned the volume back down and lifted his knees so that the bedclothes were between his hands and the doorway; the bills were all hundreds, nearly new. None of them was completely new and unwrinkled. He had not seen hundred-dollar bills often, but the old-fashioned scrolling of these seemed familiar and right. The face on each bill was that of a woman, elderly, kindly, and intelligent—a lady who might, he decided, be a teacher close to retirement at some pricey finishing school. A footstep sounded in the hallway, and he thrust the bills under the sheet again.

It was the nurse, smiling and humming to herself as she entered his room. "Good morning, good morning! How are you today? Enjoy your breakfast?"

He nodded.

"Then I'll just put it right over here on your little table for W.F., all right? How's the head?"

"It doesn't hurt much."

"Well, if you want some aspenin, just ask. I know you can get up and walk around, because you were up so much yesterday— yes, I saw you, naughty boy! So you can come to Group Rec. Dr. Pille will be there today, and we want to show him a whole bunch of sunny faces. I know you haven't been, so I thought you might like me to tell you about it."

He said, "What do we do? Play softball?"

"That's right. Only not in weather like this, of course. And not with a real bat, because someone might be hurt. But we have loads of fun. You see, the idea is for all of us on the staff to join all of you in recreational activities. That way, we get to know you better, and you get to know us better. Dr. Pille doesn't really have to take part, but he's such a good sport! So he comes whenever he can. Once he played run-sheep-run! But today we can't have outdoor activities because of the snow, so we'll have indoor moopsball. Won't that be fun?"

"I've never played it." Suddenly and irrationally, he was afraid that the bills were showing above the edge of the sheet. As unobtrusively as he could, he pushed them deeper.

"Then this is your big chance to learn, isn't it! Up and out of bed, and don't worry about your pajamas, everybody—I mean all the other patients—will be wearing the same thing."

He had an apocalyptic vision of someone straightening up his bed while he was gone, and slipped the roll of bills into the waistband of his pajamas.

The nurse whispered, "This is the day. William will give you the signal."

· 9 ·

Freedom

"*All right*," the new nurse said loudly, "I want you to divide into two teams." She plowed through them like a white hospital ship through a sullen sea, pushing patients and staff to left and right. He found himself in the group on the right, with North standing beside him.

"Now I'm going to appoint two captains," the new nurse announced. "Dr. Pille, will you be one?"

The man who nodded was a slender, smiling Oriental.

"And you, Mr. Walsh. You be the other."

"Sure!" Walsh called. "Come 'ere, ya tigers! Listen up."

"You must each appoint a wizard."

"Ya," Walsh said, and touched him on the shoulder. "Ya my wizard."

He asked what a wizard had to do.

"Put the whammy on the enemy. I'll be out there leading the

troops. Ya got magic powers I just invested ya with, kid."
Someone handed Walsh a red bat of soft plastic and a plumed
red plastic helmet. "Thanks," Walsh said.

"I'm not magic."

"Not before, maybe, but ya are now. Lookit their guy, he's
working already. Ya gotta beat his spells, so get busy." Walsh
turned away. *"I got three staff. Staff's all cavalry, got it? Cohn, ya
cavalry too! Cavalry, go get ya 'orses."*

The "'orses" were bright red and blue plastic tricycles. In the
center of the floor, a couple of patients armed with plastic
garbage-can lids and huge, soft plastic mallets were already
flailing away at each other. Between them was a gaily colored
plastic beachball, presumably the moopsball.

It was probably good therapy, he decided. How could you stay
mad at a nurse or a doctor you'd just banged on the head with a
plastic mallet? Nevertheless, he didn't want to play. He yawned.

As if picked out by a spotlight, he saw the face of the blue
wizard, the man Walsh had pointed out to him. It was a thin and
even skeletal face, on a head that appeared to have been shaved.
Its owner stood motionless in the midst of the hubbub, smiling a
little, arms extended, eyes fixed upon him.

My God, he thought, it's working! He began to dance as he
had seen Indians dance in movies, stamping his feet, pumping
his arms, patting his mouth as he yelled.

"Woo, woo, woo! Pawnee gitchya! Scalp 'um white man!" After
a moment or two, he noticed that several members of the blue
team had stopped playing to stare at him.

"Pretty soon they'll put the captain of the winning team up
on their shoulders and march him all around. Go to your room
as fast as you can and get your street clothes on. Come to Door
C. It'll be open, and I'll be right inside." It was North, fading
into the melee as he turned to look.

A red-helmeted mob surged about the wide plastic tube the blues had defended, red cavalry fending off blue players with padded broomhandles. Walsh, conspicuous in the plumed helmet, scored the goal.

The hallway was deserted, and he wondered whether North was ahead of him or behind him. Ahead, most likely. North had seen games before and probably had a better idea of what would happen when.

The roll of bills had slipped almost out of his waistband; it struck him that he had been an idiot to do that Indian dance when the money could have fallen out at every step. But it had not, and the dance had worked. He put the bills into his wallet in front of his real money, three singles, a five, and a twenty from the place North called C-One, the sane and sober reality in which Richard Milhous Nixon had twice been elected President.

There seemed to be no point in bothering with a tie—yet he did, knotting it swiftly but carefully before his dim reflection in the window. As he pulled it tight, he realized that in the depths of his soul he believed the last few days had been only a nightmare, that everything that had taken place since he had met Lara had been a dream, that he must soon wake up and go to work; and if he went to work without his tie, he would have to buy one in Men's Wear.

North was waiting, dressed in a neat blue suit. "Here's the keys. She says it's a chocolate Mink. Middle of the lot."

The keys shared their chain with a rabbit's foot. He put the whole affair in his pocket as they clattered down the steps. "Won't they hear us?"

"They're still whooping and hollering about the game. The thing is to get out fast before they stop."

Instead of turning off into the room in which he had drunk

coffee with Joe and W.F., they emerged into a snowy parking lot from what was clearly the back of the hospital. The brown car was bigger than he had expected—yet hunched-looking, with its short hood, high trunk, and roomy passenger compartment.

He twisted the key in the ignition, but in vain.

"I thought you said you knew how to drive."

"It won't start, that's all. Won't even crank." Prompted by a dim and almost racial memory, he stared down at the pedals. There were three, and a wear-polished steel button to the left of the clutch. He pressed it with his foot; the engine sprang to life.

"That's better," North said.

He nodded, wondering about the floor shift. It had been a long time since he had driven a stick, and that had been a short lever on the doghouse of a sports car. This was an ungainly rod topped by a knob of hard, black rubber. He tried out the gears.

"Get moving, damn it!"

"Do you want to get out of here, or do you want to have an accident?" The car rolled smoothly back; he clashed the gears a little shifting into first, but second and third were smooth and firm. "We're thieves now, I guess," he said as they turned out of the hospital's parking lot. "If we don't get sent back here, we'll be put in jail."

Edged into the corner, North grinned at him. "How do you think I got the keys? Or got that door unlocked? I got money too."

"How much?"

"None of your God-damned business. You got any?"

He said, "Same answer."

"You know, I kind of like you." North chuckled. "Which is too bad because I'm going to have to bust your God-damned snotty nose for you someday."

"I hope it's not before you're through having me drive for you. Can't you drive? You said you could."

"I've been through the FBI's chauffeur course."

He asked, "Then why'd you take me with you?"

"Because I felt sorry for you, you jerk."

He glanced across at North and saw that North was no longer grinning.

A street he did not know unreeled before them; it was wide, with two traffic lanes on each side of two sets of shiny trolley tracks. There were trees, bare and yet snow-laden, between the street and the sidewalk. He thought of the streets he had seen radiating from the intersection outside the mental health center. This was one of them, he felt certain. But which? It seemed to him that though all had run straight, none had run in a definable direction—neither north nor south, east nor west. And yet this street had surely run to North.

"Stop up there," North told him, "where it says guns. See the sign?"

"You're going to get a gun?"

"Stop or I'll break your God-damned neck."

North seemed to mean it. He pulled to the curb in front of the gun store and switched off the ignition. North got out, and he sighed with relief as he saw North walk past the show window and go into the haberdashery beside it.

He took out the Tina doll and studied its enigmatic smile for what felt like a long time, then pulled the charm Sheng had given him free of his shirt. It was a root, a dry, hard thing shaped like a tiny wrinkled man no taller than Tina's forearm.

A passing woman glanced through the window, and he realized how strange he must have looked to her with the doll in one hand and the charm in the other. She probably thought he was crazy, and if she called the police, she would find out she was right.

Except that even United had not thought him crazy, only an alcoholic. He was—supposedly—a drunk, and North was what? A schizophrenic maniac. Something like that.

He put the charm and the doll away and turned his attention to the passersby. At first they looked ordinary enough, though a little old-fashioned in their dress. He had seen pictures set in the thirties and forties, and he felt that these quiet, dark figures hurrying through the cold were costumed for just such a picture, girls and women and a few men, all in heavy coats that reached nearly to their shoe-tops, the men in wide-brimmed felt hats, the women and girls in head-hugging cloches.

Or that he was somewhere in Eastern Europe, where according to the evening news such clothing was still worn. One young man who passed him had a fur hat, and several women were wearing fur coats. Was there a place in Eastern Europe where they spoke English? A training city, perhaps, for Russian spies? Yet such a city should have been far more accurate. American clothes and American cars were not hard to get.

Three middle-aged women passed, each with an attaché case or a briefcase. It occurred to him that he had seen very few older men, and he began to count. He had counted twenty-three women and three men who looked middle-aged when North came out of the gun store.

"All set," North told him. "Let's roll."

"I thought you were in the other place."

"I was. I got this coat. Like it?"

It was single-breasted, of thick, brown tweed. "Sure," he said.

"I got to feeling a little chilly. Now I'm fixed." North unbuttoned the coat and the jacket beneath it, and spread them wide. There was a shoulder holster on each shoulder; the butt of an automatic protruded from each holster. "Nine millimeters. I was afraid they wouldn't have them, but they did. Okay, let's get rolling. We've got places to go and people to see."

He shook his head. "Not as long as you've got those."

"You're afraid of me. I guess that's only natural. Here." North dropped one of the pistols into his lap. "Now we're even. I'll give you the shoulder rig as soon as we get someplace where I can take off the coats. Let's roll."

He shook his head.

"What the hell's the matter with you? I've tried—"

He didn't want to pick up the pistol, but he did. "Here. Take it back. Take them both back to the store. They'll give you your money."

North's right fist crashed into his jaw, driving his head against the window glass. For a moment he saw intense flashes of pale yellow.

"Next time I hit you, it'll be with the gun, not my hand."

He tried to open the door, but North caught him by the arm. "You got a gun," North said. "Go for it."

He shook his head, trying to clear his vision.

"Go for it! It's loaded, ready to shoot. Pick it up and try to kill me. I'll go for mine. One of us wins."

"You're crazy," he said. "You really are crazy." He felt the checkered grip of the automatic pushed into his hand; North had it by the barrel, trying to make him take it. Instead he held up both hands as he had seen people hold up their hands in movies, as he had seen suspects hold them up on television. He hoped a passing cop would see them.

North said, "You got no guts. No guts at all. I thought you had some, but I was wrong."

"If it takes guts to shoot an empty gun at a man with a loaded one, you're right; I don't have a bit."

77

North jerked back the slide; a cartridge flew out, striking the windshield. North caught it, took out the clip, jammed the cartridge into it, and slammed it back into the butt of the gun. "Want to try again?"

He shook his head and turned on the ignition.

"Then get it in gear."

As they pulled away from the curb, he asked, "Where are we going?"

"A hotel to start with. I need more clothes, documents, newspapers, a base to work from." North snapped his fingers. "The Grand! Keep moving, I've got to get myself located."

He wondered—very much—what sort of work was to be carried out from that base. He thought it better not to ask.

The street lost its trolley tracks and became a boulevard flanked by imposing buildings of granite and marble, buildings guarded by snow-draped statues and in one case by a live sentry who might have been a United States Marine in dress blues. At last they were drawn into a traffic circle in which cars, small trucks, double-decked buses, and an occasional bike spun dizzily around a bronze general with a sword and a cocked hat. There was a moment of wild disorientation before he realized that the general, his rearing charger, and his pointing sword were all circling too, that the statue was revolving counterclockwise, like the traffic.

A small green car cut in front of them, and North reached for a gun.

"Easy," he said, and laid his hand on North's until the green car was gone.

"By God, I would have rammed the bastard," North whispered through clenched teeth. "Rammed him!"

"And the police would have got us. Where do I turn off?"

North said nothing, staring straight ahead. Cars, mostly

78

black, wove in and out. A policeman and a policewoman passed them in a black-and-white squad car. The woman glanced at them incuriously before her squad car moved off through the traffic.

His jaw still hurt; he rubbed it with one hand as he drove. "Keep circling," North told him. "It's one of these."

. 10 .

Hotel Room

There was a balcony whose smooth carpet of snow testified that no one used it in winter. He did, opening the French doors and stepping out in his topcoat to study the winter sea. The waves were of that nearly black green he had been told artists called *cannon;* they pounded at the deserted beach like sentient beings, like so many workmen who knew that the job would be finished at last, the final stones, the last grains of sand, washed to the bottom, and that until it was done they would get their pay.

Nearer was a windswept concrete seawall; nearer still, a narrow asphalt road spotted with ice. A paved terrace flanked by evergreens in tubs led from the road to the marble steps of the Grand, which was clearly a resort in summer and in winter nothing much.

Their room—North had insisted that they share a room—

was on the uppermost floor. It cost a modest twenty-five dollars a night; yet even so they had been able to get a weekly rate of a hundred and twenty-five. It was spacious, with a high ceiling; and thus far it had been always cold.

A lonely gull circled the freezing sea, and it struck him that North might well have tried to shoot it if North had been there.

And that the seagull might—if only it could—tell him what sea this was and whether his own land lay over it, though he was convinced that it did not.

But where? Or had he been given some drug that permanently distorted the way he viewed the world, so that in the city where he had been born they now saw him wandering, wide eyed, talking to phantoms? Was it, as Lara had hinted in her note, merely the other side of a special door that he must find? If so, was Lara here or there? For she seemed to be in both places, admitting a strange man to his apartment, appearing here in his dream and on television, though that had perhaps been Marcella.

Who was surely, certainly, Lara herself in disguise. What had she told him? *"Darling, it's terribly dangerous, my talking with you."* That had been a message; that had been a warning as clear as Lara had dared to make it.

"What time is it there?" So "Marcella" was—had been—far away in another time zone, and had come on a jet as soon as she had finished speaking to him.

Or she had wished him to think her far away.

Marcella was a star, Marcella appeared on television, was known to everybody. What was it the nurse had called her? A goddess of the screen? But Marcella had telephoned him, waking him from sleep, if the call itself had not been a dream.

He watched snow dance across the broad, bare flags of the terrace.

On the other side of the French doors, the telephone rang and rang again. He opened them, stepped into a room that now seemed warm, and slid them shut, latching them carefully.

The telephone rang a third time.

He looked around to see whether the French doors had sent him back to his own country, or perhaps whisked him to a place stranger even than Lara's. Other than the comfort of the room, nothing seemed to have changed, and he knew that it existed only in its contrast to the freezing wind outside. He picked up the handset.

"Mr. Pine?" It was the name he and North had decided upon.

"Yes," he said.

"Are you sharing your room with a Mr. Campbell, sir?"

"Yes," he said again. "Or rather, Mr. Campbell's sharing his with me. He paid."

"Our records show only your name, sir, although they show double occupancy. The other gentleman is Mr. Campbell?"

"That's right. Why are you asking?"

"Mr. Campbell is buying some things in one of the shops, sir," the clerk said, and hung up.

He hung up too, and switched on the television. Lara did not appear on the screen, though he had half expected her. He took the map and the bundle of currency from the pockets of his topcoat, pulled it off, and tossed it on the sofa.

As far as he could judge, the bills were perfectly genuine. The brown paper band with its stamped inscription, inked Chinese character, and ten-cent price was just as he remembered it.

He put away the bills and studied the map, trying to recall the topography of the United States and where such an area might fit into it. The girl in the map shop had mentioned some nearby town—or maybe it had been the red-faced man he had talked to in the street. He could not remember the name of that town, though he racked his brains for it.

No town of any kind appeared on the map, which he thought too much like a picture. There were mountains with snow-white peaks, and narrow valleys that seemed forbidding. A crude red array of walls and towers marked "Giants' Castle" was probably just a rock formation. He felt he had heard of it, or perhaps only of something like it, a Giants' Causeway or something of the sort.

The girl had mentioned a place called Crystal Gorge; he felt certain of that. He found it on the map—sparkling urns and statues on glass pedestals. Another place was called The Goddess's Pleasure Garden, and there was a gray stone arch in the center smothered in flowers. Recalling that arch from his dream, he shivered.

The door banged open, and North came in carrying boxes and a paper. "Here you go," North said, tossing a box into his lap.

He pulled the map from under it. "What is it?"

"Hat. I had to guess your size, but you can bring it back if it doesn't fit. You look funny without one. Everybody wears them here."

He refolded the map, opened the box, and pulled out a high-crowned snap-brim. He had never worn a hat, but he had to admit that North was right.

"Got you a new tie too, and a couple shirts. If the maid snoops around, we want her to find something."

"Did the man who was supposed to meet you come?"

"I'm saving that for last. Try on the hat."

He did, thinking at first that it was a trifle snug, then deciding it was a good fit. The tie was red silk with a yellow pattern that reminded him of scrambled eggs. Both shirts were taupe, one with a yellow stripe, one with a blue.

"Pure silk—silk's cheap here. I figured you for a sixteen collar. If they don't fit, leave the collar open. They look better like that anyhow."

"Sixteen should be fine."

"Now you get to read about us," North said, handing him the paper. "We made page one."

LUNATICS ESCAPE

Three patients escaped from the male floor of United General Psychiatric Hospital yesterday. Names are being withheld to spare the feelings of their relations, but Dr. Jonathan Pille, a hospital official, describes one as dangerous. "He is a male Caucasian of medium height," Dr. Pille told this reporter. "With receding dark hair, dark brown eyes, and a black mustache. We were treating him with electric shock and lithium, and we felt we were making progress. He was transferred from the Violent Ward to our General Treatment Facility ten days ago, but without treatment he is liable to relapse."

The second is said to be a short, slightly built man of forty-five, almost totally bald. He is reported to have an ingratiating manner, and to be capable of appearing fully sane for extended periods. He is not thought dangerous, but should be confined for his own safety.

The third is young, below medium height, with curling brown hair and brown eyes. He is reported to be friendly with the patient above, and it is believed they may be together.

The present episode is the only instance of escape from United General in the current decade. Security measures are being tightened.

North said, "Not a word about her, you notice? They're afraid they'll make them quit using nurses on the men's floor."

"The nurse who helped you? Maybe they don't know about her."

"Sure they do, if they've got any brains. Whose car was gone? Whose—" North bit off the sentence, struck by an idea. "That's Eddie Walsh. It's got to be."

"He wasn't with us."

North grinned. "But we left the door unlocked. Remember Door *C*? That was always locked. The guys had him up on their shoulders when we went out, and he must have seen us. Eddie's one sharp little bastard."

"He didn't have any street clothes. My God, he must have frozen to death."

"He took his chances just like we did."

If North said anything more, he did not hear it. He saw his mother's face and heard his mother's voice, the face and voice as each had been toward the end, when they were about to lose the house: *"I took my chances."*

"They don't carry much in the way of ID here," North said. "According to what he tells me, a driver's license will get you just about anywhere. Here's yours."

A square of stiff paper sailed through the air and landed in his lap. It seemed to him that a driver's license should be cased in plastic and carry a picture; this looked more like an elaborate theater ticket, although a name was printed on it (as if he himself were the show tonight) and there was a space for his signature.

North said, "I'm going to take a shower and change. You too, if you want to. Then we've got things to do."

He nodded, still seeing his mother's face, her face as it had perhaps been when she was much younger, on the television screen. Or Lara's. The woman turned and was only an actress who presented her back to him while the camera peered over her shoulder at the handsome, vapid man she spoke to. His mother had been Lara, he felt—Lara in a way that fluttered off when he tried to grasp it. Not quite the Lara who had lived with him, yet they were both . . .

He shook his head. Was it possible to catch insanity like measles? What was it anyway? Was anyone who denied the facts insane, like poor Eddie Walsh? He shook his head once more and picked up the paper, a tonic for the madness that threatened to drown him: *Section 1, Classifieds, Sports.*

Eddie Walsh's features threw him a cocky challenge from the sports section.

JOE READY FOR THE CHAMP

Popular pugilist Joe Joseph has concluded an agreement to fight World Heavyweight Champion "Sailor" Sawyer, Joseph's manager, Edward E. Walsh, announced today. "Joe's already the champ," Walsh cracked. "He's just going to defend his title." A date for the bout has not yet been announced, but under the terms of the agreement it must be held within the year.

Joseph has scored convincing victories in his last five outings, KOing Ben MacDonald in the third last night. The match with Sawyer will be his first appearance in a main event. Walsh, who has been hospitalized with a stomach complaint, is returning to his post to ready Joseph for the big fight.

He dropped the paper. Poor Eddie—they would find him now. Even doctors read the sports. He tried to remember the Oriental doctor's name but could think only of Sheng; the elderly Chinese had sold patent medicines in his little curio shop. Would it be possible to call Walsh and warn him? Surely he had already seen the story in the newspaper, yet a warning might do some good.

There was a thick gray-and-yellow directory under the stand between the beds, but no Walsh, Edward E., was listed there. He tried to remember the name of Walsh's company, the company that Walsh had named when they had first met. Walsh Promotions, that was it—and there it was in heavy, black type a little way down the column. He dialed the number.

No twittering voices this time. The telephone (he imagined a dingy little office two flights up in a brick building near a gym) rang twice, and a marvelously familiar voice said, "Hello?"

"Lara!"

"Yes, this is Laura. What can I do for you, sir?"

"Lara, it's me."

"I think you probably have the wrong number, sir," Lara said cautiously. "This is Walsh Promotions. I'm Laura Nomos, Mr. Walsh's attorney."

He drew a deep breath. "I think you're Lara Morgan."

She hung up. He dialed the number again, and the telephone rang and rang in the imaginary offices of Walsh Promotions; but no one answered.

North came out, fresh and pink now from the shower, still buttoning a blue-striped shirt. "You want to go to the john or anything?"

He shook his head.

"Then let's go."

"Where are we going?"

"Let's just say it's to a little meeting with some friends of mine, to discuss our strategy."

He stood up, smoothing his suit and straightening his tie, got his topcoat and made certain nothing had fallen out of the pockets. "Strategy for what?"

"For taking over the government of this crazy place, what the hell do you think? We need men, and some sort of guarantee that the army won't move against us." North picked up the two guns in their black leather holsters and buckled them on, one for each shoulder.

·|| ·

The Conspiracy

"Turn in the middle of the block," North told him.

He turned and drove down a narrow, twisting alley like the one down which he had run from the mounted policeman. Different in one respect, however, for it was now night, and the alley was utterly dark except for the headlights of their car. Cats with shining green eyes slunk to one side, and once he had to leave the car to move a fallen garbage can out of their path.

The alley divided, then redivided again and yet again; and though he saw wider streets at the ends of some of its branches, North always directed him away from them. Soon he decided that North himself did not know where they were going, that North had probably jotted directions on a slip of paper that could now, in the darkness, no longer be consulted; that some whim of insane pride prevented North from using the overhead light or striking a match.

At last they halted behind several other cars and edged past them on foot to reach a narrow flight of concrete steps that led to a metal door. North pounded the door with his fists until it was opened by an old woman.

"You need a light out here," North said.

"The bulb's out," the old woman replied. She seemed to be expecting them, and ushered them into a cramped room with grimy concrete walls.

A tall woman in a dirty white coat switched on several very bright lights there, lights so powerful that he closed his eyes for a moment. The tall woman inspected their faces and daubed them with powder. "I like that smile," the tall woman murmured, and touched his lips with scarlet salve, then held up a mirror so he could inspect them. He rubbed one lip against the other, trying to get off as much as he could.

"I thought—" he began.

"You don't understand how they do things here," North told him. "It wouldn't do for us to look as if we'd just walked in off the street."

"It certainly wouldn't," the tall woman agreed, and bustled about, touching their faces here and there with a pencil.

He heard voices from outside the room, and once there was a noise like the rumbling of distant thunder; girls and men passed to and fro, shadowy forms in a shadowy corridor. When the tall woman had nearly finished, he glimpsed the shambling silhouette of a bear.

"Here we go," North told him. "Just follow me."

The shadowy corridor led to a brilliantly lit room in which four men sat around a painted wooden table. One wore a rumpled uniform; two were dressed in suits, as if for work in an office; the remaining man, whose room it appeared to be, was in yellow pajamas and a maroon bathrobe. Half a minute or more had passed before he realized that the room was a great deal larger than it appeared, that only this end of it (which was perhaps much less than half) was lit, and that there were watchers in the darkness beyond the light.

The man in uniform spoke to North, briefly explaining what had been said before he and North had arrived. It seemed clear he wanted North to lead them, equally clear that he would resent any leader.

North said, "We can not only fight injustice; we can win. But only if every one of you and everyone involved in the whole movement is willing to do exactly as he's told, and suffer the consequences if he doesn't. A thing like this attracts a lot of dilettantes; but dilettantes are of no use to it. We must have disciplined men, and they must discipline themselves. Is there anyone here who wouldn't be willing to eliminate the man next to him if I told him that man had failed us?"

He started to protest, but the man in uniform was already replying: "There isn't one man here who wouldn't be willing to eliminate *himself* if he failed."

"A man like that would not have failed us," North told him. "A man like that is strong, and it is through strength—and only through strength—that we can win. You may think the government is strong and we're weak; but you're wrong. The government is huge and rich, but it isn't strong. Its massive limbs are bound by ten thousand cords, too fine for your eyes to see. They're tied by religion and morality, and by the need to look moral and religious even when real religion and actual morality point in the other direction. They're tied too by filthy businesses and rackets and hack politicians who've each bought their own little pieces of turf. When the government begins—too late!—to move against us, you'll see just how clumsy and ineffective it really is. And the stronger we get, the weaker it will be. Strength is God! What is God, but the thing that grants our prayers? It is Strength that grants all prayers, that makes it possible for a nation or a man to do what he wants."

There was scattered applause from the darkened part of the room.

"What about this man with you, sir?" the man in the yellow pajamas asked. "Can he be trusted?" Older than the rest, this man was thick-waisted and white-haired; his voice was deep and gelatinous, as if it proceeded from the bottommost cavities of lungs choked with fat.

"No! No man can be trusted. You know that better than any of us—but when we betray our trust we die. We have been taught all our lives—taught by them—to think of that as our weakness. I tell you that it is our strength! We are supernatural beings chained by beings merely natural, and we must not turn our backs on the hand of God within us. We are a sacred band of brothers, and when every one of us knows that, we will be unconquerable!"

A curtain of thick, purple plush fell between the lighted part of the room and the dark. From the other side of it came the noise like distant thunder that he had heard earlier. The men at the table rose, the two in suits taking off their hats and wiping their faces. A balding man in shirtsleeves looked into the room. "Curtain call! One bow, everybody. *One* bow."

North took his right hand, the fat man his left. The man in uniform took North's right hand, and the two who wore suits separated so that there was one at each end of the line. Like so many children playing a game, they went through a break in the curtain and bowed—North twice—to an audience they could barely see.

"It's working," North told him when they were back in the shadowy corridor. "You heard them."

"I thought you meant it. I thought you really were going to overthrow the government."

"We are. This is how you start getting your ideas across to people. It's the same where we come from."

The man in shirtsleeves appeared, waving a slip of paper. "If you want to sit out front, here's two together. Your next call's at ten sharp. I've written it down here."

North glanced at the paper and muttered thanks. "Come on, there's a passage around the seating area, where the fire exits are. I used to work here before they put me in that place."

Their seats were only three rows from the stage. He wanted to ask North if there was popcorn, though he knew that popcorn was only in movie theaters. Or at least that in the real world it was sold only in movie theaters. He felt that Lara was in the theater somewhere, and if he could only find some excuse to leave his seat he might meet her.

A slight, blond girl came on stage carrying a stool and an instrument that seemed to be a cross between an electric guitar and a balalaika. She sat down on the stool and played, singing a song about pirates; as she sang, three swarthy pirates danced silently behind her. One had a black patch over one eye, one a steel hook to replace a missing hand, and one a wooden leg; the one with the wooden leg accompanied her on the concertina and danced too, his leg beating the air like the stick of a witch's broom. When the pirate ship lay half a cable from its victim, the rolling of the broadsides filled the theater and the three dancers seemed to have become fifty.

"It was kind of sad, wasn't it?" North whispered. "Her out there all alone. They didn't like her much either. An act like that's better in a supper club."

A piano was wheeled on stage, and an old woman who might have been a scrubwoman anywhere played "L'isle Joyeuse." The name was lettered on a card. He closed his eyes to listen to the music, conscious that though he had done nothing but hang around the hotel room he was very tired. The dancing pirates became harlequins and harlequinas, their ship long-prowed and slender with strangely shaped sails. He had seen such figures and such a ship somewhere, perhaps in a picture or on a painted screen in Furniture.

Though he could not see her through his eyelids, Lara had stepped from the piano. He knew it almost at once, opened his eyes, and sat up; she had already left the stage. He stood up. When North grabbed his sleeve, he muttered, "I'm getting sick," and rushed down the aisle and into the empty passageway behind the exits.

To his surprise, it was empty no longer; a tall, unsmiling man was stationed before each of the fire doors. None spoke or moved to stop him; but he had the feeling they would, if he had tried to leave the theater.

He ran backstage instead, certain that Lara had gone there, exiting stage right or stage left as they said, and that she had not come down into the audience.

It was as dark as ever, though he felt that the melody of the old woman's piano, the shining, sparkling notes, should have illuminated it—for it seemed to him that the crystal prisms of some priceless old chandelier had been turned to birds, and the birds set free. Cheered by this light, by which he could almost see, he flung open a door and saw the bear. It rose growling on its hind legs, and though it was muzzled and chained, he felt a sudden thrill of fear.

"Here you are," the man in shirtsleeves said. "I thought you were going to miss your cue." He closed the door.

"No, no," he said. "I can't do that again." He tried to explain about Lara.

"You had a dream, my friend," the man in shirtsleeves told him. "That's all it was—Madame was playing out there, and you had a little nap."

He said, "Even if it was just a dream, I've got to look. Even if there's only one chance in a million, because it's the only chance I've got."

"No, even if it wasn't a dream, you have to go on tonight. Klamm's here—the President's advisor, one of the most important men in the whole country."

"Klamm?" he asked. "I talked to him once on the phone, but that man was German."

The man in shirtsleeves looked at him with new respect. "That's right, Klamm's German."

"I didn't think the President would have a German advisor."

North walked past them rapidly without looking at either of them.

"Klamm's an immigrant, but very high up in the government. Now you have to go on. He's in the box on your left."

He tried to protest, but the man in shirtsleeves shoved him toward the stage. "If I see your Lara, I'll send her on, make her part of the play. That's a promise."

North was already entering. He followed, trying to look like a plotter but feeling his face pale with shock. He had lost the gray hat somewhere; he could not remember where.

The stage had changed. The man in uniform lay on a cot covered with a thin blanket. "And so you see."

"I've seen it before," North said.

He wanted to look for Lara in the audience, for Klamm in his box, but the lights blinded him. He felt that his first impression had been correct, that they were in a basement room, that it was the theater that was illusion, not the play. I've been an actor in a play all my life, he thought, and not known my lines. The only difference is that I know it now.

North asked the fat man, "How long?"

The fat man shrugged. "Today, sir. Tomorrow perhaps, at the very latest. The immunological system goes, and after that it's just a question of what gets there first."

One of the men in suits asked, "Why, Nick? Why did you do it?"

"I'm sorry, David," the man in the cot answered. "I simply couldn't help myself."

North turned away. "And there was nobody to help him."

His eyes had adjusted to the bright stage lights. He could see the audience now, oblique lines of pale, blurred faces that stretched into the darkness, here and there broken by an empty seat. Standing (as always) at North's shoulder and pretending to watch the man in the cot, he studied the faces in the hope of seeing Lara's; and when he did not see her, he thought to look for Klamm in his box, though he could not recall whether the man in shirtsleeves had said it was to the right or to the left, or whether the directions had been given from the point of view of the actors or the audience.

Klamm was there, the only occupant of a box, a crag-faced old man with long, pointed mustaches dyed jet black and cheeks pulled flaccidly downward by the weight of years. The great man wore a dinner jacket with a white dress shirt and a white tie, and seemed to be sleeping with open eyes, staring straight ahead as if content to wait, cigar in hand, for taller actors or more lofty themes, though they might be never so long in coming.

"Salmon die after they've spawned," the fat man was saying. "Drones when they've fertilized the queen. In many species, the male spiders are devoured by their mates. At least we're spared that."

He had looked to one side for a moment, and in that moment Lara had entered Klamm's box; now she stood with a hand upon the old man's shoulder. She wore a gown of shimmering material that wrapped one breast in a prismatic highlight, a double rainbow—violet, blue, green, and gold. Yet he thought her own glorious hair more beautiful, a part of her person that in transfiguring her transfigured itself.

He took a step toward the wings, and because he had, he saw the men with guns before anyone else did.

· 12 ·

Children of the Dragon

A fter passing through his topcoat at hip level, the first shot killed the man who had been dying on the cot. North was firing at once, a gun in each hand. More police—if they were police—were coming from the other side of the stage. He saw a dot of blood appear on the fat man's yellow pajama leg and rapidly grow larger. The fat man stared down at it open-mouthed, clutched the leg in fat, neatly manicured hands, and fell slowly until the crash of his gross body shook the stage.

"This way," North yelled, and went straight back, smashing the concrete wall like so much painted canvas. Dodging to stay out of North's line of fire, he found himself face-to-face with a magician in immaculate evening clothes. With practiced grace, the magician threw open the door of a crimson and gold cabinet.

North darted in. He followed, feeling rather than hearing the door slammed after him. They fell through darkness, sliding down something too steep and too slick to hold. Later he would remember that he had been afraid one of North's pistols would go off when the slide ended.

Neither did, but he could hear shots and screams above, and running feet. There was a scratch and a flare of light; North held a silver cigarette-lighter. Like the visiting princess who must feel a single pea, they lay upon a pile of mattresses. All about them stood a shadowy crowd of barrels, shelves, and boxes.

With strong teeth, North was tearing the cellophane from a cigar. "Know where we are?"

He nodded. He had seen a paper lantern and recognized the place. "In the basement of the Chinese shop."

North bit the end from the cigar and spat it out. "Close enough. We're in the basement of the theater. That magic act was supposed to follow us, so he was setting up in back of our scenery. He makes stooges from the audience disappear in that cabinet."

He shook his head and climbed from the mattresses, which were grimy with dust.

"It's probably better to lie low for a while," North told him, lighting the cigar.

He already had a foot on the stair. "Go ahead and shoot," he said. "They'll hear it, and they'll know where you are. Or you can start a fight. I'll yell, and they'll hear that." He took Sheng's matches out of his pocket and struck one, just as Sheng himself had struck a match upon an earlier occasion that now seemed forlorn beneath an infinite drift of calendar leaves. A dragon of red and yellow fire appeared, emitting black smoke, illuminating their corner of the dusty basement. It appeared to wink at him, then vanished.

"God DAMN!" North said, picking up the cigar and swatting at sparks. "How'd you do that?"

"Have fun." He waved good-bye.

He went up the stairs and into Sheng's shop. Sheng and Dr. Pille were sitting in Sheng's back room drinking tea. "Nice see you again," Sheng said. "This sister's son. Doctor. Fine man. Like tea? Want buy something?"

Dr. Pille extended a hand. "We've met, more or less. You were only semiconscious at the time, though. Later I saw you in the moopsball game. You were extremely impressive."

"And now you'll take me back. Or try to." He pulled out the remaining chair and sat down.

"Not really." Dr. Pille paused. "That is, not unless you want me to."

"Maybe I do." He found he was rubbing his temples with his fingertips. "Everything's so crazy."

Sheng chuckled. "We joke for gods. Relax, enjoy, laugh too. Do not do mean. Mean not belong joke. Die, drink wine with gods, laugh more."

Dr. Pille said, "The pressures of life become too much for all of us now and then."

It occurred to him that North might come up the stairs at any moment and kill them all. It seemed there was not much he could do about it.

"You tell," Sheng said. "Nephew very wise. Sheng fool, but old fool, see much. Even fool learn at last."

When he did not answer, Sheng continued in a tone that was almost coaxing. "Say Dr. Pille. Your doctor. Sheng listen."

"All right. To start with, that name. What sort of world is it when you wake up in the hospital and they tell you you're being treated by Dr. Pille?"

The doctor smiled, hiding his mouth behind his hand. "Is

that all? You see, my family name is Di; but when I was in med school it struck me that it wasn't quite the thing for a young physician, so I changed it. I've often regretted that change, I admit; I fear I retained an undergraduate sense of humor when I made it. But now Pille is on all my diplomas and licenses, and it would be a great deal of trouble to change back."

"Am I really an alcoholic?"

"I doubt it. But if you think you might be, you'd better cut down on your drinking."

Sheng said, "Drink tea," and poured steaming brown liquid into his cup.

"If I'm not an alcoholic, why did you say I was when they brought me in? It was on my chart."

Dr. Pille looked grave. "The woman preferred charges, and my uncle here had asked me to look out for you. He had seen you fall, you see. Breach of promise is quite serious, as you must know. If I had said you were sound except for your concussion, you'd have been taken to another hospital, and eventually to prison. By classifying you as an alcoholic, I was able to keep you at United and keep you off psychoactive drugs."

"All right." He nodded; it seemed too much to assimilate all at once. "Mr. Sheng, I was in this theater. I went into a magician's cabinet, and I fell down what I guess was a trap door onto some old mattresses. But when the man I was with lit his cigarette lighter, we were in your basement."

"Building belong theater. Sheng rent store, good tenant, always pay. Theater not need all room underground, let Sheng store merchandise, give Sheng key."

Dr. Pille said something to Sheng in rapid Chinese, then asked, "Who is this man who was with you?"

"North."

"He's very dangerous. Are you aware of that?"

"Yes, I know," he said.

"If he's really in my uncle's basement, I must inform the authorities. You should have—"

At that instant there was an explosion beneath their feet, rapidly followed by another. A demon, an alien being, a thing of flame having nothing to do with the life of earth (that yet seemed to live), roared up the stair, crashed into a wall, and veered into the room where they were drinking tea.

There was a third explosion.

He was in the street, sitting up and drinking tea. No, coffee. A cop in a tight blue overcoat held the mug, a thick, cracked one of white china. A white-coated medic crouched on the other side.

"See?" the cop said. "He's coming around."

A building was on fire. Men from two fire trucks sprayed it with water. He asked, "Is Mr. Sheng all right?"

The medic said, "You were in the Chinese shop? Okay, that explains it."

The cop said, "They took him to the hospital already. He was pretty shaken up."

The medic said, "We'll take you there too as soon as we get another ambulance."

He shook his head. "I'm not hurt. Dizzy, a little, that's all. What happened?"

The cop said, "There was a panic in the theater next door. Some Feds tried to bust some of the actors, and there was a lot of shooting. Something started a fire—probably a stray bullet messing up the high voltage for the lights."

The medic said, "We thought that everybody got out of the theater before the fire got too bad. Then we saw you."

The cop said, "You're out at the Grand, right? We found your room key in your pocket."

He nodded.

"We found your car keys too, but I don't want you to drive tonight. If you don't want to go to the hospital, I'll get a cab to take you back to your hotel, understand? You can pick up your car tomorrow."

The medic asked, "Do you think you can stand up?"

He proved it by standing. His knees were a little weak, but he was able to walk. "I guess my coat's ruined."

"Yeah," the cop said. "You'll have to buy yourself a new one. That reminds me, I want you to check while Fred and I are here, so you'll know we didn't take anything."

Feeling foolish he got out his wallet and carefully counted the money while another screeching fire truck arrived; there was a bit less than one thousand dollars in bills that looked nearly real. The thick sheaf marked *ten cents* was still in his topcoat pocket, as were his map and the doll.

At a corner far enough from the fire that traffic flowed unimpeded, the cop helped him into a taxi. The cop told the driver, "You take him out to the Grand, you got me? Nowhere else. He's registered there, don't worry, and he can pay you. If he passes out or anything on the way, tell 'em when you get there."

"Okay," the driver said. "Okay." Then when the taxi's door was shut, "Ya know, I hate these runs. Ya don't hardly ever get no decent tip."

He said nothing. He was staring out the window at the fire and thinking of Dr. Pille and North. He had forgotten to ask if Dr. Pille was all right. He had been afraid to ask about North, but North had probably been in the basement when the fireworks went off; North was almost certainly dead. Striking the trick match had made North drop that cigar, and the sparks had set off the fireworks, so he had killed North. He felt no regret, guilt only about having none. After a time it came to him that North had been courting death, had wanted to die, and in the effort to die had raised every encounter to the level of a life-and-death struggle.

"There won't be nobody at the Grand wantin' to go to town this late. Grand's just about empty anyway. Have to deadhead all the way back."

He said someone would probably want to go to the airport.

"Ya kiddin'? They don't fly after dark."

He put away the hundred he had been fingering and asked how far it was from the Grand to the airport.

"Twenty, thirty miles. But I got to take ya to the Grand. That son of a bitch has ya name and my number."

"I was wondering if it was possible to go past the airport. I'd like to see it."

"Be way out of ya way," the driver told him.

"All right."

He remembered driving North to the Grand, but they had not come by this route. Or at least, he recognized nothing he saw, though so many things were covered with snow that it was hard to be sure. The taxi dodged down a narrow street lined with bleak buildings with blazing windows. A drunk slept (or perhaps a man lay dead) in a doorway. He wondered if the dead man was dead in both worlds. Had Nixon felt a twinge, had Nixon shuddered, when North died? Perhaps. For Nixon had been loyal, or at least so he understood. Loyalty had been that President's great, shining virtue, the thing that had made Nixon such a threat.

He said, "It's the things that are most right about a man that make him a danger to everyone else."

"Boy, you said a mouthful. The more man a man is . . ." The driver's fingers snapped, sounding as loud as a pistol shot.

"If you want to stop at a bar, I'll buy you a drink."

"Can't drink on the job, buddy."

The driver was silent after that, and so was he. Staring out of the window of the taxi, he tried to find a common thread among the things that had happened to him, but time after time lost his thoughts among the looming buildings, the mystery and magic of the city. He remembered another city, his mother's apartment and the way she had walked him to school every day in the first grade. There were bad men, she had said, in the city, who would steal little boys if they could. Perhaps they had.

Buildings spun by, then halted like Nazi soldiers, clicking their heels at the red lights. There were no freeways here, no overpasses, only narrow, twisting streets whose few inhabitants seemed sinister, and long, straight boulevards whose esplanades were buried in snow. He seemed to remember that Eisenhower had built the freeways, though he had been born during Eisenhower's term of office. Eisenhower had brought Nixon; Nixon had brought North. His mind filled with lurid pictures of North trapped in the burning basement, firing at the flames.

Two boulevards met at an acute angle, and he recognized an evergreen near a streetlight, broken under its burden of snow. He had gone up or down this boulevard. He muttered, "Down," to himself; it seemed to him that when he had seen the broken tree he had been going in the opposite direction, looking out of the opposite window, the window of the hunched little car that the nurse had given North. For what?

He pulled out the keys on the rabbit's foot and looked at them. The rabbit's foot had not been lucky for the car, or for the rabbit. Could the car have been a Rabbit? No, it had been a Mink—a rabbit would have gotten away even in that alley, run from the flames, bouncing over the trash cans and the broken, empty bottles, bottles emptied of cheap wine in which there was no Christ, wine grown in the California sun to be pissed away in a corner.

Did they have a California here? That had surely, surely been where Marcella had been when she called, where Emma was, Emma who drew Lara's bath. Emma stood at his elbow, and though he could not see her there, he knew her for a Nazi soldier, a transvestite of the S.S. He wanted to say, *"So, Colonel Hogan,"* but the words would not come. The drawer was open, and in it lay the unopened letter, the letter shut with red wax. He was afraid of the woman, of the man behind him.

Why, I'm back in that dream again, he thought, and maybe when I wake up I'll be asleep beside Lara.

A single book lay upon the desk, pinned there with a nail so it could not be stolen. The title was stamped on the black morocco cover in German letters of tarnished gold: *Das Schloss.*

· 13 ·

Grand Hotel

He woke when the taxi stopped, very possibly because the driver had made certain that the stop would wake him. "That's twenty-seven ten," the driver said.

He handed over thirty dollars and got out.

Instead of pulling onto the terrace, the driver had let him off at its edge. Snow still danced across the broad flagstones; it was a dance of ghosts, of whirling white shapes that advanced and retreated in profound silence. A distant clock struck once, the deep tone of its bell rendered thin and spectral by miles of snow-covered fields; a freezing wind touched him through all his clothes.

He could hear the surf, and he turned aside from the warmth and the bright windows of the hotel to go to it, propelled by an attraction he could neither understand nor resist. The sand was strewn with shattered ice piled higher than his head.

He climbed it slowly and patiently, gripping the slabs with stiff fingers, slipping and falling often until at last he stood at the summit and looked across the whispering dark. It seemed to him then that he was himself a creature of the sea, a seal, a dolphin, or a sea lion made human by some heartless magic, magic like that which had given the mermaid legs in the story that had made him cry long ago, cry at the thought of the little mermaid dancing, dancing with her prince in the big castle in Elsinore, dancing the minuet while at each moment the white-hot nails of the land pierced her poor feet.

And it came to him that in those days before television had wholly claimed him, he had received from the mouth of his mother all the instruction he would need to navigate this queer country in which he found himself; but that he had paid no heed, or at least not enough heed, so that he could not recognize as once he might have recognized all its ogres and its elves, the shambling trolls and the dancing peris. North had been a monster, surely; yet what if North had been a salamander, and the master of the flames? What if North were waiting now in the hotel, if North danced with impatience in the hotel this very minuet, waiting hungrily to fire?

Surely his mother had taught him a spell for salamanders?

Nor was she dead, as he had once foolishly imagined. He had always known that, in some deep part of himself that he had banished for fear it would make him strange to employers, to the various girls in Personnel, to the supervisors and submanagers who could no longer be called floorwalkers (not by him at least, not by any hourly employee) the floorwalkers he had so longed to be, though he had no college, though he was not considered— and had never been considered—managerial material.

His mother had never been the waxen thing they had buried. He wondered where she was and why she had not called or written, why she had not advised him in some way, though perhaps she had, perhaps it was her letter that lay in the green-lined drawer of the dream.

The snow clouds parted for an instant, and the moon touched the ocean. He, seeing that fragment of it tossing in the silver light, knew it and knew that in some previous life he had sailed there for decades; and that this previous life was returning to him. He remained poised upon the ice, but the knowledge passed. The moonlight upon the waves became only the moon on the waves, and he grew accustomed to the salt bite of the wind, so that he no longer rejoiced in its sting, but felt only its cold. And after a time he turned away from the ocean and clambered slowly down, often slipping, gripping the ragged ice-slabs with frozen fingers, and crossed the black road with its dancing ghosts, and crossed the broad terrace with its dancing ghosts, and went at last up the steps and into the Grand Hotel.

The hotel had double walls of glass, with a double door in each. Between the first glass wall and the second stood a lone bellboy, like a sentinel guarding a castle without a garrison, a last sentinel left behind by Caesar to watch over the Roman Wall or the Rhine. This bellboy looked at his burned and perforated topcoat and his seared face and said, "Can I help you, sir?"

"Yes," he said. "Yes, you can. At least, I hope you can." He wanted to tell this bellboy his room number, but he could not remember it, so he said, "There was a fire. In a theater and a Chinese shop."

The bellboy nodded wisely. "What theater was it, sir?" The bellboy had curly hair as blond as excelsior and wore his pillbox cap over one ear.

"I don't know," he admitted. "There was some sort of play, about a revolution."

"Ah, that'd be the Adrian, sir. Nice place."

"Not any more," he said. "It burned to the ground."

"Prob'ly the Government did it, sir. You know how they are."

He nodded (though he did not know) and asked, "Isn't there anyone at the desk?"

"Not this late there isn't, sir. I'm supposed to take care of it. I'll take you up in the elevator too, sir." The bellboy shrugged. "It's our off season, sir. You know how it is. If we had fireplaces in the rooms . . ." The bellboy shrugged again, a minute movement of thin shoulders beneath his skin-tight red jacket.

"My friend rented our room. I'd like to know how long it's paid for."

"I can look that up for you, sir."

He nodded, took his hotel key out of his pocket and handed it to the bellboy, who opened the inner glass door for him and showed him into the lobby.

At the desk, the bellboy opened an enormous book and paged through it. "Here you are, sir. That was yesterday, or rather the day before, the way it is now. For a week, sir, so you've got six more nights left, counting tonight."

In the elevator, he asked the bellboy where he could buy a new coat. He was fairly sure that North had bought the shirts, ties, and hats without leaving the hotel; perhaps North really could drive, but he had always been asked to drive, been ordered to drive.

He said, "I beg your pardon?"

"I was saying there's a place here, sir. In fact, they're having a big sale, because of it being the off season. In the lower level, sir. There's a barber shop down there too, and a billiard parlor. Lots of things."

"I'm sorry," he said. "I'm afraid I got lost in what I was thinking."

"It's natural you're shaken up, sir. You must have just barely got out alive."

He said, "I don't know," wondering if he was not in fact dead. He remembered hearing about Purgatory as a child; even then he had not believed it, but perhaps he had been wrong, as he had been wrong about things so many times since, wrong about a whole series of wrong choices that had seemed likely never to end—until at last Lara had chosen him. Did they have fires in Purgatory? No, they had fires in Hell.

He felt that the elevator had started too fast, wrenching and shaking him. And yet he had not noticed at the time, not noticed until its motion had become smooth, showing him all the floors, all the hallways of the hotel, its veins and nerves laid bare by this cage of wrought iron, which displayed to him water lilies and pyramids at one level, golden cattle and sheaves of wheat at the next.

And at every level, empty veins and silent nerves. This was what a scalpel saw as it sliced flesh, this sectioned view that could not live.

He had undergone several operations as a child, none since, and thus he found that his view of surgery was still a child's—you went to sleep in the daytime and woke sick. This had been the reality, this surgeon's elevator touring his body to learn how it was made; the wrought iron glared at him with the faces of jungle beasts, from the rolling eyes of a bull with the wings of a vulture and the bearded head of a man.

"Top floor, sir." The bellboy took out the key. "I'll see you to your room, sir."

"Do I look that bad?"

"I'll feel better if I do, sir." The bellboy hurried down the

hallway ahead of him. "Here we are, sir. Imperial Suite." With a
rattle of the lock, he opened the door. "You and your friend are
the only ones on this floor, but if you have trouble or anything
just call the desk. I'll hear the phone."

He nodded.

The room, which had been cold before, was frigid now. As he
got out his wallet, he tried to recall whether he had drunk with
the taxi driver; surely he had, or he would not have slept in the
taxi. There was nothing smaller than a ten, but he felt that the
bellboy deserved a ten after all they had been through together,
studying the great book, watching the sea, performing their
autopsy on the bellboy's place of employment.

"Thanks, sir." The bellboy coughed. "Sir, we have these little
braziers . . ."

"Yes," he said. "I'd like one, if I can have one."

"They've got to be ventilated, but those French doors will
take care of that, sir." The bellboy flashed a lopsided smile. "I'll
bring one up to you."

"Thank you," he said.

He was undressing when the bellboy returned. The brazier
was a tiny thing, yet far better than nothing. He put it in his
bedroom, and when he switched off the light, he found that its
copper sides were faintly luminous, aglow with warmth and
cheer.

When he woke in the morning, Lara was not there, and every
muscle ached. The back of his right hand had been scorched as
well as his coat sleeve, and the burn was crusted and painful.
The cologne and shaving soap North had bought were still in
the bathroom, but neither seemed the right sort of thing to dab
on a burn.

Medical was listed on the white plastic card that slid from beneath the telephone. He dialed, and was told that the doctor was not yet in, did not often arrive until later or never during this, the off season, and would (or perhaps would not) call him upon arriving at last. He could not remember his room number, but he said, "I'm in the Imperial Suite, on the top floor," and the disembodied operator seemed to understand.

It was only when he had hung up that he realized his call had gone through without difficulty, that he had not gotten the twittering voices or Klamm, and that someone—almost the correct someone—had in fact answered.

He resolved to call his apartment again, and at once began to look for something else to do, something that would postpone the moment when he would actually have to dial his own number. He had assumed that the little brazier had gone out, but a few sparks remained, sullenly crimson among the fluffy gray ashes. He added bits of charcoal from a copper can that had accompanied the brazier, then rinsed his fingers in the bathroom, avoiding the burn as much as he could.

His topcoat was ruined. His best trousers would have to be replaced too, but they remained good enough to wear until he got new ones. He dressed gingerly, careful of the burn and thinking more about breakfast than of the call and his apartment, feeling it would be wisest to put both out of his thoughts until it was time to telephone—to telephone and talk to somebody who was not Lara, or no one.

The telephone rang.

He answered. It was the doctor, as he should have guessed. "Understand you've a burned hand, sir."

"Yes," he said. "I don't think it's too bad, but there's a sort of scab on it." He decided not to mention the burns he had discovered on his face when he had shaved. The doctor would see them, and would treat them or would not.

"Had a bit of an accident myself. Come on down, sir." The doctor's voice sounded vaguely familiar. "I'll give you some salve and a bandage to protect the skin until it heals. I'm in the basement—the lower level's what they call it."

The elevator was a long while coming. He rang three times before he recalled that it required a human operator, who would certainly be annoyed. Today the operator was a morose teenager with pimples.

"Lower level," he said.

The passing floors that had appeared so forsaken the night before seemed equally deserted now. He felt that he himself was only a ghost, riding a ghostly elevator in a phantom hotel, that this building had fallen to the wrecking ball long ago, that it had been replaced by beach-front condos, silent and sourly white structures haunted by the worm, condos wrapped in white winding sheets of salt, themselves slated for demolition if only someone could be found who wanted the land, who would pay hard cold cash on the barrelhead for their destruction.

The lobby flashed by, empty except for a thin, bespectacled youth at the desk. They landed, helicopter-like, in a windowless cavern of boutiques, all of them shut and dark, each of them (to judge by appearances) more than ready to swear that it was never really open, had never been open at all.

"Which way is the doctor's office?" he asked.

The teenager pointed.

"And could you tell me how late they serve breakfast in the coffee shop?"

"Until they close," the teenager said, and slammed shut the wrought-iron door.

He reached the end of the row of shops and turned a corner. The cavernous space was even larger here, enlivened by shelving balconies. Dusty flags like stalactites hung from the ceiling; there were only two or three he recognized. Whose was that two-headed eagle? That griffin clawing the air?

"Up here, sir!"

A fat man in shirtsleeves, leaning on a crutch, was bending over a slender balcony rail to wave to him. He waved in return and mounted a short flight of iron steps that creaked and boomed dully beneath his feet, wondering whether there was an elevator someplace and whether the doctor (who it seemed should not have climbed stairs) had been forced to climb these.

The doctor's door was the only one that showed a light, an old-fashioned pebbled glass door with an oak frame. Plain black lettering on the glass: C.L. APPLEWOOD, M.D.

Inside there was no receptionist, no nurse. The doctor sat at a desk at the back of a long, narrow room, large of feature, heavy of jaw, and smooth of face, with the high Shakespearean forehead that white hair and encroaching baldness give all men, and an extra chin upon which to display a slick professionalism in shaving and the touch of fine white powder that bespoke the actor.

"Good, good!" The syllables were resonant and constricted. "Good to see you made it, sir! Wonderful! We all made it then, save for poor Daniel. Dead, sir! Yes, dead as a stone, and I could not have saved him, sir, nor could any physician since Hippocrates. They got him, sir! Settled poor Dan once and for all. They got me too, as you've seen. A bullet, a thirty-eight I suppose, through the fleshy portion of the thigh. Had they but nicked the femoral artery, sir, you should not see me here! I would be a citizen of a better sphere, with poor Daniel at my side. As it was, I was able to hobble away before the fire—as you, sir, were not I see—our bold Carlos having shot the rascal set to guard the stage door."

The doctor chuckled; the sound was deep and throaty, like the contented noise, half clucking and half crowing, made by a great rooster.

"And now, sir, if you'll excuse me for not rising, I'll excuse you from shaking hands. Let's see it."

. 14 .

The Sea in Winter

The coffee shop was empty. A black-and-white sign on a wooden stand read: PLEASE SEAT YOUR-SELF.

He did so, choosing a small table beside a high glass wall, like the wall of a greenhouse or conservatory. Beyond it stood a low cliff or bluff, or perhaps only one wall of the cavernous, flag-hung arcade he had left; beyond that lay a broad expanse of beach upon which the ocean had erected a duplicate of the quarry he had seen a few years before on a *National Geographic* special. Expressionless images leaned or lounged here and there among the shattered wrecks of others, some finished, some incomplete, some scarcely begun—all this executed in slabs of greenish sea-ice.

One watched him, a statue some distance down the beach and midway between land and ocean, staring insolently but silently as he took a napkin from a water glass and turned up an inverted coffee cup.

It was impossible that the police should have chosen such a strange means of spying on him, yet he felt they had. In some way they would be watching him, so why not this? Or if it was not really true, it felt true. Klamm and his men would try to account for everybody they had seen on the stage—for him, for North, for the two in business suits, for Dr. Applewood, and for the man in the army uniform. (But he was easy enough to account for—even Dr. Applewood had said so.)

And he, too, was readily accounted for. The cop had looked in his wallet, had seen his hotel key, had told the driver where to take him. They knew where he was, and they would surely send somebody to watch him.

"Would you like coffee, sir?"

The waitress was about twenty, very petite, with black hair cut short, hair that curved around her face like the wings of a soft, black bird, a bird determined to hatch that oval face—or if it was hatched already, to shield it from the harsh winds of this world.

"Yes," he said. "And some orange juice, if you have any."

She said, "I'll have to squeeze you some, sir," and winked.

He was too astonished to wink back; but he watched her as she trotted away. She wore polished black shoes with very high heels (because she's so short, he decided), a little white cap, and a black silk dress with a tiny white apron, like the maid in some old movie starring Cary Grant.

The steamy fragrance of freshly brewed coffee told him she had filled his cup, though he had not noticed. The coffee was as black as her dress, as black as her shoes, and he knew that he would never be able to see anything black anyplace again— coffee or the night—without thinking about her shoes and her dress. He added cream (which he seldom did), looked through the glass wall, and remembered nights with Lara.

A big white boat was passing the hotel, half a mile or less from where he sat; passing slowly, as though fighting a headwind with its engines almost idling. A teacher had read it to him in school: "As idle as a painted ship upon a painted ocean."

He felt sure Lara was on that boat, that white-painted boat that would have looked so much more at home down in Florida or a place like that, on the Gulf or the Pacific or the Mediterranean. He felt sure that it was Lara watching him through binoculars as he sipped his coffee, sipped the icewater that the girl in the black shoes must have brought him too, brought him icewater even though he had not noticed, brought him water even though he sat in front of water and ice that went on forever.

She brought the orange juice, placing it before him with a delicate hand tipped with long, crimson nails, a hand naked of rings. "What else would you like, sir?"

"Right now," he said, "I'd like you to sit down and talk to me."

"I can't do that, sir. Suppose the manager came in."

"It's lonesome here," he told her.

"I know, sir. You're the only guest—the only one in the whole place, I think."

"I'm surprised they keep it open."

"This is the worst time of year. Usually it's pretty good through Yule, and then it picks up again in March."

He thought frantically, groping for a question or comment that would hold her in conversation. "Do you drive out from the city every day?"

"Sure. There's nothing to do way out here." She glanced around to see whether someone was listening. "For us, I mean. There's things for the guests."

"What are they?"

"Oh, the spa, and indoor tennis courts and so on. We can't use them. What would you like for breakfast?"

He noticed sadly that she had dropped the *sir;* he was no longer a customer, just another unwanted boyfriend. He asked, "What's good?"

Under her breath: *"I am."* Aloud she said, "Why don't you have a waffle? The chef's a real master with them. We've got about a dozen different kinds."

"Whatever kind you think's the best."

She nodded. "I'll be along again in a minute to give you more coffee."

"All right. Hurry back."

She walked slowly away, writing on her order pad. When she had rounded the partition and was out of sight, he spoke to the expressionless face of ice on the beach. "Did you get all that? Are you going to tell them everything?"

It did not reply.

Dr. Applewood had not been worried about spying, or about hidden mikes or cameras. When he had asked about the theater, Dr. Applewood had actually risen and seized the back of one of the old wooden chairs: "Do you recollect our stage properties, sir? That was what I used, like an old woman with a walker, clumping and thumping across the floor!"

But why had the doctor come to the hotel today, come with a bad leg to a hotel with a single guest? For that matter why had she said he was the only one? North was still registered. In fact, North might come back to the room while he ate his waffle, might already have come back while Dr. Applewood was bandaging his hand. They had all gotten away except Daniel— that was what the doctor had said. Daniel had been Nick, but where was North? Would North phone? Probably not—the police might tap the wire, listen to any calls to or from the room.

He sipped his coffee, which was excellent.

If he had a coat, he could walk all around the hotel; there had to be a parking lot somewhere. If North had used the little car that he had driven, he would recognize it, and the keys were in his pocket.

But North had probably not used that car. It had probably been burned when the theater burned down—he, not North, had the keys. Yet it was still possible. North had given him the keys, never saying they were the only set; and nothing would be less like North than to give somebody else the only set, to let go of that kind of power.

Anyway, thieves could start cars without the keys by hot-wiring the ignitions. North, who had made a lock pick from the hospital wiring, would know all about that.

A man in a three-piece suit came into the coffee shop and sat down not far from him. When the waitress brought his waffle, he asked her who the man was.

"Probably some guest. I don't know—I've never seen him before."

"You said I was the only guest."

"That was yesterday, you and your friend. He probably checked in last night—I only got to work an hour ago."

"There's a fine for not knowing his name: you have to tell me yours."

She grinned. "Fanny."

"Really?"

"Would I fib about a name like that? I know yours. You're A. C. Pine, and you're in the Imperial Suite."

She had gone before he could reply. As he ate his waffle (he had missed dinner the night before, and felt as though he could eat five), he vaguely considered the initials. What did A. C. stand for? Soon, he felt, he might have to tell Fanny; and it would be better if he were not stuck with something like Abner Cecil. Abraham Clyde? Arthur Cooper? By the time he had finished his orange juice, he had decided he was Adam something.

The lower level was no longer quite so deserted as it had been. Several shops showed lights, and once he heard footsteps. The first shop he looked into was a beauty parlor in which an enameled blonde was painting her own nails while she waited for customers. "Good morning," he said.

She looked up without interest. "Hi, ya."

"Nice day."

"Is it warmin' up a little?"

"I don't know," he said. "I haven't been outside."

The blonde sighed, looked away, then back at him. "I have. Believe me, it ain't a nice day. That wind could kill ya."

"I wouldn't think you'd get much business, then."

She shrugged. "I might as well be here. It's the only shop I got."

"Suppose I wanted to change the color of my hair?"

She looked up, interested. "Do ya?"

"Not today. Maybe in a few days."

"Sure, I could do it for ya, any color ya want. Twenty'd cover it."

"That seems pretty high."

"Okay, fifteen. But that's as low as I'll go. Ya oughta see what the hotel charges me for this place."

"Then let's say twenty, and you promise to keep it strictly confidential. Is that a deal?"

"Ya got it. Hey, listen, I never talk about my customers anyhow."

"And now, do you—" He paused. Slightly to the left of the blonde's head was a poster advertising shampoo. The woman pictured there was Lara. "Could you tell me if there's a place down here that sells men's clothing?"

"There's three, but I don't know—"

The door opened behind him; the waitress—Fanny—came in, and she seemed at least as surprised to see him as he was to see her. "Hello," he said.

"Oh, hi." She stood silently while he looked from her to the blonde. At last she said, "Are you done?"

"I guess so."

"I thought maybe I'd get a perm. I'm off now till lunch."

The blonde told her, "Ya don't need one yet. Why don't ya let me just wash it and set it?"

He said, "Well, good-bye, I guess," and stepped out into the cavernous arcade. He had gone fifty feet before it occurred to him to return quietly to the beauty parlor and listen; for a few seconds he hesitated, vacillating. He had seen people—actors— do it on television and in pictures hundreds of times, and felt somehow that it could not possibly work in real life. The women would hear him, or they would be talking about nothing. But was this real life?

As silently as he could he retraced his steps, glad that he could see no one watching (though someone might be watching) and feeling extremely foolish.

"*. . . little halfwitted tease.*" That was the blonde. Fanny answered resentfully, but so softly he could scarcely hear her, "*I talked . . . at breakfast. I was supposed to check in. You know my orders.*"

He crept away.

The first men's store he came to was run by a woman, which surprised him. He bought a new hat and a heavy overcoat, and at her suggestion a wool sweater-vest to wear under his jacket. He ordered a new pair of wool slacks, too. She measured his legs, marked the seams with chalk, and promised that the slacks would be ready next day. She wore a tape measure about her shoulders like a sash of office, and her gray hair in a bun.

"Do you run this place?" he asked.

"Who else?"

"It must be lonely, especially during the winter."

"You want to rob me? Go ahead, there isn't a dime. I'll tell the insurance, maybe they'll give me some money. But if you hit me, I'll kill you."

He hesitated, aware that she was joking but unsure of how to respond.

She patted him under the arms. "That jacket don't have room enough for a gun. You want, I'll make you a better one. Fifty, a hundred dollars, depends on the material."

"I don't carry a gun."

"A strangler, huh?" She scribbled figures on a scrap of paper. "Seventy-seven for the coat, down from one sixty-five. Twenty-five for the hat. Fifteen for the sweater, but for such a good customer, I'm making it ten, there goes my profit. Also you've got to pay for the pants in case you don't come back for them. Twenty-three for your pants, with tailoring. Comes to—let's make it a hundred and thirty, here's handkerchiefs, package of five, real Irish linen. Go out and your nose'll run like the river. You get a free tie."

He said, "I don't want one. I've got plenty."

"Okay, I'll tell you what I'll do. Since you're my first customer today and I like you, I'm giving you this lovely all-wool muffler for half off." She glanced at the tag. "Fifteen ninety-five, one hundred percent pure virgin lambs' wool. For you, right now, today only, eight bucks."

"I'll take it, but I'd like a little information with it. Is there anywhere in the hotel where a woman can get her hair done?"

She shook her head. "There's a place, Millicent's, but Millicent ain't here, this is when she goes on vacation. She won't be open till the twenty-first."

"I think I saw her the last time I was here. Blond woman, thin, kind of a long nose?"

"Nah." The proprietress of the haberdashery was surveying his purchases. "That ain't her. You're going to wear the coat, right? And the muffler and the hat. Your slacks'll be ready tomorrow afternoon. What about the sweater? I'd wear that too, if you're going to be out much."

"I will," he said. He slipped off his jacket.

"Wait a minute, I'll cut the tags for you. Hey, you got a magic doll. My nephew had one."

He had laid his jacket on the counter. Tina appeared to be peeping from his pocket.

Not knowing what else to say, he said, "Would you like to look at it? Go ahead."

She stared at him. "You know, you're taking a chance, saying something like that. Lots of women don't like those things."

"Are you going to damage it?"

She shook her head. "No. Not me."

"Then why shouldn't you look at it?"

Gently, she slipped the doll out of his pocket. "My pop had one. Mom said it used to talk to him at night, when they thought she was asleep. I guess I know whose hair you wanted done, right? You ought to carry her in a box, that's what most of them do. I'll get a comb and straighten it out a little for you."

125

· 15 ·

The Land in Winter

Leaving the haberdashery he walked past Dr. Applewood's office, though it was on the upper level and he on the lower. No light showed through the pebbled glass door; he wondered whether the doctor had gone home or been arrested. It seemed quite possible that Applewood had been an informer—that Applewood had summoned Klamm and Klamm's agents, that the wound received in the theater had been an accident or a trick, and that Applewood had returned to the hotel that morning in response to instructions from Klamm or the police.

He considered trying the door, entering the doctor's office if he could, and searching the desk; but decided against it. It was conceivable—though only, he felt, barely conceivable—that they did not know about Dr. Applewood. If so, they would surely learn if he were seen going into the doctor's office or so much as touching the doorknob. It was conceivable that they had not known where he was—as now they clearly did—before he had gone into the coffee shop; but he doubted it.

In any event, he was already much too warm, bundled as he was into sweater-vest, overcoat and muffler. He wanted to get outside as soon as he could. Some distance beyond the doctor's office he discovered a short stair labeled PARKING; he climbed it and let himself out through a rusty steel door.

The wind the blonde had mentioned met him at once; it was not strong, but persistent and very cold. He felt that it was not a sea wind but a land wind; it lacked the flavor of the sea, seeming instead to have blown across lonely miles of featureless snow.

Nor could he see the sea from the place to which the rusty door had admitted him. A small lot, plowed clean of snow, lay before him. In it were four cars, all parked as near the door as possible. None was the hunched brown Mink whose keys were in his pocket, though two were very much like it. The third was a bright red convertible, hardly larger. The fourth was a black limousine with jump seats in the back, a car capable of carrying eight in some comfort. Beyond doubt, that was the car in which Klamm's agents had come—Fanny, the blonde to whom she reported, the new "guest" in the coffee shop, and perhaps Dr. Applewood as well. He found himself wondering who had driven. The blonde—she was the type who would always want to drive, who would never allow anyone else to drive if she could help it; she would be a fast driver, he thought, constantly burning rubber or slamming on the brakes, the kind of driver North would be if he drove.

He tried to open the limousine's door with the keys of the hunched car. Neither would work, or even enter the lock. To his surprise, the trunk was not locked. He opened it and found a litter of paper; someone had tossed a file folder into it, and the

motion of the limousine had emptied it. The wind caught
two sheets of paper and sent them flapping across the frozen asphalt like terrified chickens. He seized another before it could
make good its escape and glanced at it, then read it with fasci-
nation.

Name:	"Wm. T. North," "Bill North," "Billy North," "Richard North," "Ted West." Actual name unknown. Name first given is name most used.
Date of Birth:	Unknown.
Place of Birth:	Unknown, possible Visitor.
Height:	5' 11"
Weight:	170 lb.
Hair:	Dark, balding. Often wears mous-tache.
Eyes:	Blue.
Complexion:	Ruddy.
Scars, etc:	Burns, palms of both hands. Misc. small scars on forearms, may be fresh. (North is self-mutilator.) Tattoo underside of right wrist "RN." Often wears watch on this wrist to hide tattoo.

7/12/87 mem. Blue September. 12/11/87 chief Iron Boot.
Arrested 6/6/88 ngri., U. Gen. Psychiatric Hosp. Expert
shot, often carries two or even three guns. Expert knife
thrower, may have knife strapped to wrist, arm, or ankle.
Violent, uncontrollable temper. *Extremely dangerous.*

There was a picture of North (looking slightly younger than
he remembered) and a set of fingerprints. He put the paper back

into the folder and poked among the rest, wondering if he would find a similar report on Dr. Applewood or himself. He did not, but he discovered a sheet headed *Daniel Paul Perlitz* and stamped DECEASED. Dr. Applewood had called the man in uniform Daniel.

Suddenly afraid he was being watched, he closed the trunk. His uncomfortable warmth had vanished; he was chilled now as he returned to the rusted door, and eager to regain the warmth of the hotel and shelter from the wind. To reassure himself, he put his hand inside his overcoat and made certain his room key was still in the pocket.

The steel door was locked, and neither his room key nor the keys to the hunched brown car would open it. After a moment, he decided that the lot was probably reserved for employees and the concessionaires who leased the shops and offices of the arcade. No doubt they received keys to this door. He would have to walk around to the front of the hotel, and it appeared he might have to do it through the drifted snow.

Turning up his overcoat collar and adjusting the muffler (silently he blessed the woman who had persuaded him to buy it) over the lower half of his face, he circled the lot looking for a path cleared of snow. There was none, only the drive through which the four cars had come (now drifted half full wherever it ran at right angles to the wind) which appeared to wind away in the direction of a few scattered structures nearly at the limit of vision and almost lost in the white erasure of the snow.

The hotel spread long wings to either side. Not so long, perhaps, to someone strolling at ease down their corridors; and yet very long indeed for him, since he would have to walk twice their length through snow that in places rose higher than his waist. He tried it for a few steps, then abandoned the attempt.

Sooner or later, the drive would surely join the highway that ran beside the sea.

As he crossed the lot, he considered the shortcomings of his equipment. The coat, the sweater, and the muffler had all been wise investments; but he should have chosen a cap in place of his hat, a fur cap with ear flaps that tied under the chin, or perhaps one of the woolen hoods the haberdashery had called *balaclavas*—he had seen a display of them and paid no attention to it.

He needed gloves as well. It seemed incredible to him that he had not thought of gloves; his fingers were freezing, though he had buried his hands in the pockets of the overcoat. Most of all, he needed boots in place of his shoes; his brief attempt to walk through the snow had filled his shoes with snow, and despite the exercise they were getting his feet were freezing. Worst of all, they slipped again and again, the smooth soles of his shoes refusing to hold the nearly invisible ice that coated the asphalt in random patches, refusing to grip the packed snow.

He had left the parking lot and entered the drive when he saw Fanny's picture; he picked it up and discovered that he was holding just such a paper as had described North.

Name:	Frances Land, "Frannie Land," "Faith Lord."
Date of Birth:	7/9/64
Place of Birth:	Marea AX
Height:	5' 3"
Weight:	105 lb.
Hair:	Black, curling.
Eyes:	Brown.

| *Complexion:* | Fair. |
| *Scars, etc.:* | Six fingers on right hand. Glasses for reading. |

Associates members Blue September, Immortals, Iron Boot. Believed sympathizer.

Shaking his head, he crumpled the paper and tossed it away. He had been wrong, completely wrong, about Fanny. He corrected himself—about Frances. Like Dr. Applewood, Frances had been an associate of North's. No doubt it had been because several such people worked here that North had chosen to come here, to this God-forsaken resort hotel in winter, this huge old hotel so many miles from the city.

The blonde in the beauty shop had been someone from North's organization too, then, since Fanny had been ordered (by whom?) to report to her.

Or Fanny was—what did they call it? Somebody who worked for both sides. Somebody who pretended to work for one while passing information to the other. For if Fanny had not come in the limousine, how had she come? And if the limousine were not Klamm's, why did it have those papers in the trunk, papers from the FBI or the Secret Service—the Secret Police, whatever they might be called?

The drive was barely wide enough for one car, and the plow had thrown up snowbanks on each side higher than his head. He walked in a world of black and white, and it seemed to him after a time that he was no more than a bit player in an old movie, an old black-and-white movie. There was no color anyplace because the print had not been colorized yet and there was only the gray sky above, the blacktop beneath, and snow to either side. His shoes were black too, and the dark gray of his new coat looked almost black. Was it the beginning of the late movie? Or was it the end, when he (back in his apartment dully watching this old movie) would get up, yawn, and take his glass and the bottle off the coffee table, knowing how soon the lovers would embrace, the woman dressed as Liberty hold up her torch.

As he walked he looked from side to side, and after a time he realized he was hoping to find the other sheet that had blown out of the trunk, because it would have a picture of Lara. Two sheets had gotten away, one he had caught. The one he had caught had been North's; one of those he had not caught had been Fanny's—Frances's. Surely then, the third sheet, which he had neither caught nor found, had been Lara's, Lara last seen dancing across the asphalt, over the snow, dancing in the wind.

Its thunder behind him warned him just in time, and he dove into the snowbank on his left. The big, black limousine roared past, so close he felt its suction try to draw the shoe from one foot.

He climbed out. Not swearing, he was too happy to be alive—still alive!—to curse anything. A thin layer of ice had cut his left forefinger, and he sucked it as he dusted the snow from his coat with his bandaged hand. When he took the finger out of his mouth to examine it, blood welled from the cut and dribbled onto the blacktop and onto the white snow.

He had put the packet of handkerchiefs in the side pocket of his jacket with the map. He took it out and opened it, and wrapped his finger in one of the handkerchiefs.

If he had not been afraid of falling on the ice, he would have skipped. This (he thought) was why Cary Grant and Rosalind Russell, William Powell and Myrna Loy radiated so much happiness—so much delight in those creaking late-night movies, shone so brightly even in black and gray when they should have been dead. How happy they were to be still alive, there in the flickering celluloid, there on the cramped screens that had been tacked to the radios they had known, how joyful!

Just like him. He might be dead now at home, dead and rotting as he sat before the television in the chair he had bought so cheaply; but he was alive here, his crimson blood proved it, even if this was the last reel.

The drive mounted a hill and bent to the right. He heard a truck roar past—not only heard it, but saw it, saw at least its orange-and-green top above the crests of the snowbanks. Another hundred steps or so brought him to the point at which the drive left a two-lane road, also of black asphalt, that might or might not have been one he had driven along with North. He tried to guess in which direction the ocean lay, and guessed wrong; but after a walk of half a mile reached a point from which he could see both the hotel and his mistake.

He was about to retrace his steps when an old red pickup with chains came rattling down the road, driven by a middle-aged farmer. He flagged it down and explained how he had been locked out as briefly as he could.

The farmer chuckled and opened the door. "Guess you won't be goin' out that way no more."

He grinned. "Hell, no!" He felt he ought to be angry, but he was completely incapable of it. The old pickup had a heater that worked, and its hot breath on his feet was the promise of heaven.

"Don't many people stay in the winter," the farmer said. "My Junie works there sometimes, but come fall they lay her off. Didn't even know it was open."

He nodded and said, "It's pretty empty. I hope you're not going out of your way for me."

"Goin' right by anyhow. I'm goin' into town. Hotel ain't far, 'bout two, three miles from my place."

The road ended with a stop-sign at a somewhat wider road;

and after they had turned onto that, he heard the waves. Soon
he saw them as well, cold and green—and yet alive, the scales of
a watery snake coiled around the world, he thought, and not so
much malevolent as inhuman.

"Here 'tis." The pickup jolted to a stop. "Name's Grudy, by
the way."

"Green," he said, and they shook hands. "If I could pay you
something for this, Mr. Grudy . . . ?"

The farmer snorted. "Don't you even suggest it, Mr. Green.
I'd do it any time—so'd you for me, I'm sure."

He thanked the farmer again and climbed out, shutting the
truck's door carefully and waving while the farmer drove away.
As he crossed the terrace toward the brightly lit glass wall of the
hotel, he looked at his watch. It was eleven thirty-four; the
coffee shop would be serving lunch, now or soon. He would find
some way to speak to Fanny, who, even if she were a double
agent, might lead him to those who were not. Fanny could learn
no more by seeing him again than she already knew; but he
might learn a lot, including how to think and act like a
conspirator, which seemed to be the thing he needed most to
know.

There was no bellboy at the entrance this morning. A sign
that stretched across both glass doors announced: CLOSED FOR
THE SEASON. A single bespectacled clerk fussed with papers at
the desk. He pounded on the doors, but the clerk soon vanished
into the office behind the desk, never to reappear; and after a
time the lights in the lobby winked out.

· 16 ·

The Cop

S tudying the hotel from the terrace, he could not
see a single light. For a moment, he considered
breaking in—there were a hundred windows
available to him, or so it seemed. In the end he rejected the idea;
if there were no one inside, it would do him little good, and if
some of the staff were still there (if the clerk were merely waiting
in the office for him to leave, for example, as he suspected) he
would be arrested and put in jail—a jail where Lara could not
possibly be.

He returned to the road instead, confident now that a well-
dressed man would soon get a ride, that even a well-dressed man
with scorched cheeks and a bloody finger would not have to wait
for long. The statue of ice that had watched him eat his waffle
watched him again; it wore an expression of sullen satisfaction,
possibly because of the slight change in angle. The ocean spoke
to him as an angry mother berates her child; but though

he could hear the anger and rebuke in its voice, he could not understand what it was it wished him to do, what the waves thought he ought to have done.

It was half an hour before the first car passed, and it did not stop. After a second wait that seemed equally long, a large red bus lumbered by, its driver ostentatiously oblivious to the frantic figure not at an approved stop. On the television news, he had often heard about drivers who would not pick up even the dying, but it had not occurred to him before that many of these must have been company drivers forbidden by their companies to provide aid, or that this must have been concealed through some private arrangement between the companies and the news media.

He counted the waves as they spoke on the ice-locked beach; and when he had come to a hundred and seventeen, the convertible passed, driven by the bespectacled clerk. He stepped into the middle of the road to make it stop; but save for swerving around him, the clerk ignored him still.

Deciding it was useless, he turned away and trudged after the convertible, which soon vanished around a snow-blind curve. The bus had passed, and so it seemed likely to him that there was a bus stop somewhere along the road, a bus stop from which country people who did not have cars or trucks could reach the city—a bus stop, and perhaps even a bench. His legs trembled from all the walking and standing he had done that morning; his head, which had ached off and on ever since he had awakened in United, throbbed now with pain.

A car behind him pinged and chittered like a broken music box. He did not turn to look, sure that no matter what he did it would not stop and unwilling to step from the cleared strip to its snow-packed edges.

"You need a ride?" It was Fanny, calling through the open

window of one of the subcompacts he had looked at in the parking lot.

He tried to smile. "Hey, do I!" She might be Klamm's spy; but if Klamm and the police were against North, was that so bad? Like the doors of the car he had driven for North, this one had doors hinged toward the rear. He twisted the handle, opened the door, and got in.

"Didn't you have luggage or anything?" She sounded sincere and slightly stupid.

"Not much," he told her.

Her left foot depressed the long clutch pedal as she pulled the shift rod smoothly back. "I see. Well, I wish you'd stayed on. Anyway they would've called a cab or something for you when you checked out, you know."

"I didn't check out."

The clutch pedal came smoothly up; the engine hesitated as if ready to die, then caught hold. The little car shook itself and lurched ahead. "They said you did."

"They locked me out."

"You didn't pay?"

"We were paid for several days yet," he said.

"They wouldn't do that."

He shrugged, looking out at the snowy countryside.

The little car staggered into second. "Anyway, there went my winter job. This fall they begged me—I mean *begged* me—to stay on. Fanny, we're going to try staying open all winter— that's exactly what they said. Now I'm out of a job, and all the winter jobs are gone."

"Maybe that woman at the beauty shop could find something for you." He turned to look at her. "I was going to say, the one who did your hair, but your hair hasn't been touched."

"You noticed." When she had shifted into third, she patted

her hair. "Naw, she wanted to shampoo and set it, but it don't really need it. I don't really need a perm either—I knew she'd tell me that. I just wanted somebody to talk to. Where are you going anyway?"

"The railway station."

"You're blowing town?"

He nodded. "I'm going to Marea."

"That's good. I mean, things don't seem to be working out so good for you here."

"Will you drop me there?"

"Sure."

"Thank you." He hesitated. "I probably shouldn't mention this, but do you know the name of the man I was staying with?"

"I don't pay attention to that kind of thing."

"Yesterday morning we ate breakfast together in the coffee shop, but you weren't our waitress."

"You probably got Maisie, or maybe Edith. See, they kept three of us on, and we were supposed to work two days and off one, Maisie and Edith yesterday, me and Maisie today."

He told her, "The other man in my room was using the name Campbell, but he was really William T. North."

She did not answer.

He said, "You know people in the Iron Boot. You know who William T. North is."

"And you want me to put you on a train for Marea."

"That's right."

"Okay." She nodded. "But I was going to do that anyway— no, you're right, I wasn't. I was going to try to get you to come home with me. Do you need money? I can give you a little; I don't have a whole lot."

"No," he said. "I need to talk to Klamm before I go."

There was a long silence. Their road joined a larger one, a highway with four lanes. She watched the traffic and steered. With the accelerator all the way to the floorboards, her little car would do fifty-four miles an hour on the flat. He recalled that the brown Mink had been a bit better: nearly sixty.

At last she said, "Then you'll have to come home with me."

"You could drop me off at a hotel."

She shook her head. "Who've you told? North?"

"Nobody." He tried to think of a way to explain. "I wasn't North's friend; I don't think he has friends. I might be Klamm's friend, if I knew what you and Klamm are up to."

"You were with North at the Adrian."

"That's right. You saw us? Or did they tell you?"

"I saw you. I was in the audience. They—Klamm—thought they had everything closed, everything tight. The whole block was sealed off. But North's got more lives than a tomcat, and they wanted me to see him just in case. As it turned out they were right."

"North escaped? I was afraid of that."

"That's the way it looks. Several people died in the fire, but we've identified all of them now."

He thought for a moment. "Dr. Applewood—I know you must know about him. Dr. Applewood didn't seem to have much trouble getting out."

"Of course not. We let him out. We let all of them out, except for one who got killed by accident."

"Why?"

"What do you care?" She sounded contemptuous.

"Because I was one of them."

"That's right, you were. You're willing to turn against North?"

"I've never been for him. I was a sort of prisoner—his slave, if you want to put it like that."

"And you couldn't get away?"

"I did." He told her what had taken place in the basement. "That is, I got away from North. What I want to know is why you let me get away, and Dr. Applewood and the rest."

"Because you were all just low-level people. When you've identified low-level people, you don't arrest them. You don't want to. You watch them like we watched the play before North showed up. You let them lead you to the ringleaders."

He said, "That was what you did with me, wasn't it? I had my hotel key in my pocket, and this morning before I ate I went to Dr. Applewood to get this bandage and some salve for my hand. After breakfast, when I came down again to buy some clothes, the light was off in his office. I suppose the blonde in the beauty shop saw me the first time and came to listen outside the door."

Fanny shrugged. "I suppose."

"You don't know?"

She glanced at him, irritated. "You think she tells me everything she does? She's my boss, a lieutenant."

"I'm sorry," he said.

When she was silent he added, "It's just that this morning in the coffee shop I thought you liked me. When they shut the hotel and nobody would pay any attention to me until you came by to pick me up, I knew I'd been supposed to find that paper about you, and you were just playing a part. . . ." He let the thought trail away.

"Nature made women to play parts. When we stop, the show's over." She drew a deep breath, then let it out with a puff. "I did like you, and I still do. But as long as we know each other I'll always be playing a part, every few minutes and sometimes for hours. I can't help it. Anything else you want to know?"

"Yes. Last night at the theater—who was the woman in the box with Klamm?"

"His stepdaughter."

"What?" He realized his mouth was open, and closed it.

"That's his stepdaughter. Klamm used to be married, though obviously they never—you know."

He did not, but he nodded.

"Then his wife found a man who would. She and Klamm were divorced, naturally, but they're still friends—she's supposed to have been his favorite student when he was at the university, and I imagine their love was always a lot more intellectual than anything else."

The highway had become a boulevard. Fanny turned off it onto a city street lined with stores. "All this is just what I've heard, you understand—I don't know Klamm or his ex-wife personally. Anyway, he's been like an uncle to her children. That's what they say, but that one's the only one you ever see with him in public. I suppose she looks a lot like her mother did when she was younger; it happens sometimes." Fanny smiled bitterly.

"And her name's Klamm?"

"Certainly not. Her name's Nomos. Laura Nomos."

"Laura Nomos," he repeated. He had heard the name, he felt sure. At the theater? In the hospital? He could not place it. Had Joe mentioned it? He found he associated it with Joe.

"This morning in the coffee shop I thought you really liked me." Fanny was parodying what he had said a few moments before. "When I found out it was really Klamm's stepdaughter, I was just devastated. I mean I am." She sighed theatrically. "She's a lawyer, I hear. You could look her up in the Bar

Association's guide—see how much you learn by hanging out with a cop?"

The little car turned right, and though they were not going fast, the turn was so abrupt that its rear wheels skidded.

"Any more questions?"

"Are you taking me to see Klamm?"

She laughed. "I'm taking you to my place—maybe in a week you'll get to see Klamm. How old do you think I am?"

He hesitated, fearful of insulting her. "I'm not very good at this. Twenty?"

"Thanks. I'm twenty-two, and if I was a grade lower I'd be in uniform. My lieutenant reports to a captain who reports to a person who reports to a woman who reports to Klamm. We have to go up the chain of command, and we'll have to have something to say that will make Klamm think you're worth his time. Is there anything else?"

"Who is Kay?"

Her eyes left the road to stare at him, their expression a mixture of surprise and skepticism.

He explained, "Once I talked to Klamm on the phone, and he thought I was somebody called Kay. I've known women named Kay, but this was a man, I think. He heard my voice, and he called me 'Herr Kay.' That's a man, isn't it?"

"I suppose it is. But I haven't the least idea *what* man. Except . . ."

"Yes?"

"Sometimes Klamm himself is called Herr K. in the papers, from his initial and because he was born in the German Empire. But I don't see how it could be that if you were really on the phone with Klamm."

"I don't either. One more question. What's a Visitor?"

Her lips tightened. "And where did you hear about that?"

142

"Does it matter? I want to know what one is, because I think I may be one myself."

Fanny nosed her little car to the curb. "It'll have to wait until we get inside," she said. "Here we are."

· 17 ·

The Room

"Not what you expected, huh?"

It was not. Fanny's room was small and shabby, no bigger than ten by twelve. Electrical wiring had been strung across the ceiling, and lingerie (a black brassiere and two pairs of panties, one peach, one pink) dangled from it. He said, "Even for a waitress . . ."

"This is a little extreme? Is that what you think? Rest easy; the department didn't rent this place for me to go with the job. We aren't that thorough, and usually we don't have to be. This is where I live."

As though to prove it, she sat down on the bed. "If it had gone on longer, I might have picked up some extra money in tips when the weather got a little better. Well, it's over with now. Tomorrow I'll tell Blanche about you and get my new assignment. Sit down."

There was only one chair, a wingback upholstered in faded chintz. He sat, feeling the chair was too small for him, that it had been scaled for a child, that it had once been part of the furnishings of a doll's house—furnishings dispersed long ago, scattered through smoldering dumps, through Salvation Army stores until only this chair and the doll remained.

"You were going to ask me about Visitors," she said. "You even said you thought you might be one yourself. Why is that?"

"Because I don't seem to fit in here." He paused, laboring to box his feelings in words; and at last he muttered, "I never really know what's going on."

Fanny put her fingertips together, reminding him suddenly of the buck-toothed woman in the Downtown Mental Health Center. "Just what is it you don't understand? I'll explain if I can." She rummaged in her purse, took out a battered pack of Chamois and extended it to him. "Smoke?"

"No," he told her, "and that's one of them. Hardly anybody smokes any more, except maybe dope. But here almost everybody seems to smoke. Even Mr. Sheng, he smoked a pipe. Klamm smoked a cigar right in the theater. And once when I tried to call my apartment, I got Klamm. I was hoping that Lara would answer, and now I think maybe she was standing there beside him, like she was that night."

"You know Laura Nomos?"

He shook his head. "Lara Morgan—she used to live with me. I'm looking for her." He paused to savor the idea. "That's why I'm here." Just saying it made him feel stronger.

"You think Laura Nomos and this Lara Morgan are the same person?"

"I don't know. They look the same—not really the same but like they might be. Maybe this won't make sense to you, but we used to have a supervisor, Mr. Kolecke, in the department where I worked. He wasn't friendly like some of them are, and he wasn't always fair; sometimes he'd crack down on people pretty hard for something that wasn't their fault at all. But I think probably he got more out of the department than anybody else ever did.

"One day I saw him on the street, and he had a boy and a little girl with him. He looked so different I wasn't sure it was really him. I followed them a couple of blocks trying to make up my mind, and they went into the Art Museum. I went in too after a while, and he was explaining the pictures to them. Not just what a windmill was and so on, but who the artists had been and where they'd lived, and why they said they painted the way they did."

Fanny nodded encouragingly.

"Finally I just walked up to him and said, 'Mr. Kolecke?' You know the way you do. He looked surprised, then he called me by my first name. We shook hands, and he introduced me to the kids. It seemed funny I hadn't recognized him right away. But after I thought for a while I saw he hadn't recognized me either until I said something. I hadn't felt different just because I was out of the store, wearing different clothes. But I'd looked different to Mr. Kolecke—so different he hadn't known me until he heard my voice, and I think maybe that's the way Lara is for me."

Fanny asked, "Does your hand hurt?" He looked surprised, and she added, "You've been holding your wrist with your other hand."

"Yes, a little bit. Dr. Applewood bandaged it for me this morning. I burned it in the fire last night."

Fanny leaned forward to look. "Your bandage is wet. You probably got snow on it, and it melted in the car. You've cut your finger too. Let me see those, and I'll give you some dry gauze and some iodine."

He extended his hands. "What are Visitors? You said you'd tell me about them, but you haven't told me anything yet."

"This may hurt a little."

She tore the old tape away, and it did. With the bandage off, he could trace the angry outline of the burn through its smear of yellowish cream.

"Visitors are people who seem just to appear." Fanny went to the wooden cabinet over the little sink in the corner and got out a blue cardboard box of surgical gauze. "There's a place—or anyway, this is how it looks—that's a lot like our world, but not quite the same. Or maybe there are several places like that. Anyway, sometimes people leak through. Do you like to go to the zoo?"

He said, "Not in weather like this."

"I do, and in some sections they've got rows of cages side-by-side, just separated by wire. You know, I'm getting pretty far from what the manual says about this. Wait a minute, I'll read it to you."

She pulled a booklet bound in scuffed orange paper from a shelf over the table and thumbed through its pages. " 'Visitors: Disoriented persons without verifiable history. Visitors often proffer detailed accounts of supposed homes and past lives, but interrogation soon shows these to be fictitious. Visitors are without the rights of citizenship, and are frequently dangerous. Dangerous visitors are to be destroyed.' " She interrupted her reading to say, "That's North, or at least that's what we think now. 'Harmless visitors are to be put under arrest and brought before a superior or federal district court, which will arrange for institutional custody.' " Her voice hardened. "That's you, if you're really a visitor."

He said, "I'm not. I was only putting you on."

"That's what I thought. Do you still want to see Klamm?"

"I don't know. You know more than I do about all this. What do you think?"

"I don't know either," Fanny admitted; she shut the orange booklet and replaced it on the shelf. "Whatever else he may be—and some people hate him—Klamm's no fool. He could probably help you if he wanted to. I'd like to sleep on it."

He nodded. "All right."

"Just like that? Wouldn't you like me to drive you to the station?"

It was said lightly, but he felt there would be trouble if he agreed. He shook his head instead. "I'm tired and there's a lot more I should know—things you can tell me if you will."

"Not about visitors, I hope, since you're not one."

"No, not about visitors—although I'm still interested in that, particularly in where they come from. About Klamm. Is this where he lives? This city?"

"Sure, this is the capital. He has to be here for meetings with the President. Naturally he travels a lot, because of his position."

"He has a house or an apartment here?"

"A house, I think," Fanny said. "At least he used to. I saw a picture of him in the paper one time, taken out on his lawn. He grows roses, that's his hobby. I suppose that's why he kept the house when he and his wife split."

"Do you know where this house is?"

She studied him. "If you're thinking about seeing Klamm at his house, forget it. He's the President's security advisor, which means that a dozen different groups are gunning for him, including North's. He's guarded around the clock."

THERE ARE DOORS

"But he might talk to me, if I rang his doorbell. I don't want
to kill him, I just want to ask him a couple of questions."

"Well, I don't know where he lives. And I'm sure you can skip
looking in the phone book."

"You must have some idea."

Fanny shrugged. "There's a couple toney suburbs down south.
A big place like that would just about have to be in one or the
other, but I don't know."

"Where is his office?"

"In the Justice Building. I've never been there—I mean, I've
been in the Justice Building, but I've never been inside Klamm's
department."

"I'm going to try to see him tomorrow."

"Okay, if you want to. I'll give you a ride to Justice."

"Thanks," he said.

"Have you had lunch? I haven't even eaten breakfast. I was
supposed to after I'd waited on you, but I had to report first, and
they'd closed the hotel when I came back."

"I thought you told them to close it, so you could pick me up.
In the car you said they'd just decided to close, but that was
while you were still pretending to be a waitress."

Fanny shook her head. "We believed them, that's all. They
said you'd checked out. We should've realized it was a case of
men protecting a man, but we didn't."

"They knew they were protecting me by locking me out of
the hotel?"

"They knew we were there to watch you." She shrugged. "I
suppose they thought that if they locked up you'd go somewhere
else and get away, without having to be warned by somebody you
might finger if you were picked up. Anyway, when I got back to
the coffee shop, they said you'd gone and they were closing. I

149

asked why they hadn't told us, and they said they didn't know
where we were. It was all horsefeathers, but there wasn't time to
argue."

"That was why the clerk pretended he didn't hear me, then,
when I pounded on the door."

She nodded.

"But I didn't get away. You gave me a ride, and here I am."

"Thanks. I appreciate that, but it won't wash. You made me."

He was puzzled.

"You spotted me for an officer, there in my car. You could
have knocked me over with a duster. I still don't know how you
did it."

It was an invitation to boast; he knew it and declined it. He
said, "But when you drop me off, you'll tell somebody else, and
they'll follow me. Maybe they'll help me, just like you did when
you gave me a ride; but I won't know who they are. You'll tell
them when you plan to leave me at Klamm's office."

"I told you—see how much you learn by hanging out with a
cop?"

"Why?"

"So you'll lead us to North. You don't matter; there are a
million like you." Fanny paused to smile at him. "I'm assuming
you're not a Visitor, notice? I hope you appreciate it. Anyway,
there are thousands like you and Applewood and the rest.
North's different—different in a way that makes him terribly
dangerous, the sort of megalomaniacal leader who appears once
in a lifetime. North could wreck everything. I know this sounds
crazy, but he could end civilization. He could start the whole
human race on the downhill path."

He nodded and asked, "What does he want?" then answered
his own question. "Power—I saw enough to know that. Still,

you're wrong if you think I'm going to lead you to him. I'm not going anywhere near North if I can help it."

Fanny grinned, her piquant face to one side. "Slaves don't usually go running back to their masters—but now and then their masters come to fetch them, or send somebody they can trust. We get them up here every so often."

"Get who?"

"Runaway slaves and people looking for them."

It would not sink in, or perhaps he did not want it to sink in. "You still have slavery here?"

"Not *here*—it's a state option."

"Black people for slaves?"

Fanny shook her head. "It isn't really determined by race, it's a matter of legal status. But most blacks are slaves, yes, and most whites are free."

He said slowly, "In the world we were talking about, where the Visitors come from, everybody's free. Or so I've heard."

"That's the way it is here, in most states. But if a state wants it the other way, it can make slavery legal; then anybody who owns slaves can bring them there without losing them. It's good for the economy, but it's a little messy sometimes."

"The Civil War. You didn't have the Civil War."

"No, that was Britain."

"And men die young here. That's how it seems."

Fanny stood up and picked up her purse. "Nature played a dirty trick on the human race, Mr. Pine. She gave you men more strength than most women, and what's much more important, more drive, more ambition. But when you've fulfilled your biological destiny—when either sex has fulfilled its biological destiny, actually—it dies. That means sixty or seventy years for us, sometimes only fifteen for men."

"I heard once on the news that there are nearly a hundred and fifty women over sixty-five for every man."

She ground out her cigarette. "Who said that, Ken Rather? It's not really that bad, lots of men hold out for their entire lives, damn them. Now come on, let's go get some lunch before I start thinking you really are a Visitor. There's a nice little Italian joint, Capini's, a couple of blocks uptown."

. 18 .

A Table between Worlds

F anny had slurred the name, saying it quickly and carelessly, and he had thought nothing of it. It was not until they were inside that he realized it was the restaurant where he often ate, the place to which he had brought Lara.

One of Mama Capini's sullen sons showed them to a window table. He ventured to inquire, "Is your mother here?" but the son turned aside without answering.

Fannie asked, "You've been here before?"

"I think so," he said. For safety's sake he added, "These storefront spaghetti places all look about the same to me. It was good, though."

"You said you had money; so we'll split this, if that's all right with you."

"No," he told her. "I'll pay."

"I should warn you, I eat like a fire."

Looking at her small mouth and slender neck, he doubted it; and when the waitress arrived, Fanny ordered a pasta salad and tea. He asked if the fettuccine Alfredo was good today; assured that it was, he said he would have that.

"And I thought I was hungry." She lit a cigarette, using the kind of bulky, reliable lighter he recalled from childhood. "Can I ask why you keep staring out the window?"

He had been trying to read the winter-grimed license plates of passing cars, hoping they would betray whether they belonged to his own world or hers. "Just keeping an eye on traffic," he said.

"See anyone you know?"

He shook his head.

"When you lunch with a good-looking woman, you're supposed to look at her, even if she's not so stylishly dressed. You're even supposed to make conversation, when your mouth's not full."

"I think you're dressed very nicely," he told her. She was still in the plain black silk frock she had worn in the coffee shop, having removed only the little lace apron and cap. Her serviceable tweed coat was draped over the back of her chair.

"My all-purpose undercover outfit."

Mama Capini came bustling out of the kitchen and waved as she veered toward them. "Ah! It's you." Her smile showed a gold tooth.

Tentatively he said, "It's been a couple of days, I think." Did some other version of himself eat here too?

"What you think you say? Maybe a month. You gonna get real skinny." Mama Capini turned her smile on Fanny. "Look at him! Never eats right but here."

"I know. He had waffles for breakfast." Fannie shuddered elaborately.

"That's right, no good! Maybe I open in the morning, give him omelets and some nice prosciutto, fresh bread. Then I save his life."

He asked her, "Mama, do you remember Lara? The redhead I brought here?"

"Sure, I know Lara." The gold tooth flashed again. "Nice girl, too good for you."

He nodded. "I know, Mama. Has she been in here since she came with me?"

"Oh." Mama lowered her voice and glanced at the vacant tables around them. "Lara dump you?"

"I'm trying to get undumped. Has she?"

"Last night for dinner, but real late." Hopelessly, Mama spread plump, clean hands. "We're all out of tortellini."

Last night! He asked, "It was Lara? You're sure?"

"Course. I know her right away."

Fanny asked, "Was she with anyone?"

"You take him yourself. He don't look so bad. You make him forget Lara."

"I'm going to try. But was she?"

"Married couple, new married." Mama noticed his skeptical expression. "I'm tellin' you the truth. She's got rings and everythin'. They hold hands under the table."

Fanny said, "Describe them, please." From a corner of his eye, he saw that she had slipped a small notebook and a stub of pencil out of her purse.

"He's big! Bigger than Amedeo. She's a little woman like you, real pretty. Both got yellow hair, the man and the woman."

"How old?"

Mama shrugged. "'Bout the same as you."

"How were they dressed?"

"Man's got a blue suit. A tailor made it—he's too big for

Kopplemeyer's. But all wore out, should have thrown it out last year, you know? I see the suit and I think, bet Lara pays. But I'm wrong. He pays."

"How was his wife dressed?"

Mama looked thoughtful. "Got a red wool dress, nice dress, but off the rack. Red coat with a fox collar. You know her?"

Fanny shook her head. "How about Lara?"

"Fur coat, a nice one, a real mink, pretty dark. Gown for a ball, you know? *Zecchinos* all over, like a rainbow. Low in front. Green stones in a necklace, maybe real." Mama touched her graying hair, then her neck. "I should have seen he's goin' to pay, not Lara. Lara knows he's goin' to, so she brings them where you took her. Not too high, you know? Nice girl."

Fanny said, "You're a good observer."

"He brought her, then she brings this couple. It's my business, so I noticed."

The waitress arrived with their minestrone, and Mama rose. "Anything's not good, you tell me."

Fanny smiled. "We will, but I'm sure everything will be wonderful."

When Mama was gone, he said, "I have to make a phone call."

"Really? Your soup will get cold."

"No," he told her. "Not really. I'll be right back." He made handwashing gestures.

The restrooms were at the end of an alcove toward the rear, and there was a pay telephone between their doors. He went into the men's, relieved himself, and rinsed and dried his fingers as well as he could. If Fanny had followed him, she would probably have returned to the table when she saw him go in. The coins in his pocket were mostly those of the real world, of his own world—fraudulent-looking quarters with nickel faces and copper rims, pennies of copper-coated zinc. But Capini's itself was part of his real world too, and in it he should be able to telephone his apartment without difficulty and without getting Klamm or anyone else but Lara, if Lara were there.

One of Mama's sons came in and stood at the urinal. "Ya gotta make a phone call? I can give ya change."

"No, thanks," he said. "I've got enough."

On the other side of the door he put a quarter in the slot. The earpiece chimed once and reassured him with a dial tone. He wanted to push the buttons quickly; he made himself slow down so that he could be certain there had been no mistake.

He pressed the last digit, and the dial tone ceased. There was nothing, no sound at all. His quarter jingled into the coin return when he hung up. Reinserting it, he entered his number again.

Behind him, Mama's son said, "Can't get through, huh?"

He shook his head. "It doesn't ring."

"They shouldn't have let those sons of bitches bust up the Bell System." Mama's son turned away.

"Wait a minute. Can you break a fifty for me?"

"No problem. Come up to the register."

He followed Mama's son to the desk, slipping a bill out of Sheng's packet.

"Need singles?"

"No," he said. For a moment he held his breath. "Just a couple fives."

"Okay." Mama's son accepted the fifty, laid it on the cash register, and gave him two twenties and two fives; the twenties had Andrew Jackson's picture, the fives had Lincoln's. "Whatcha think about the fight?"

"What fight?" He had been studying the bills. Suddenly afraid he had studied them too long, he thrust them hurriedly into a pocket.

"What fight?" Mama's son sounded aggrieved. "Joe's gonna fight the champ. Don'tcha read the paper?"

"That's right," he said. "I did see that. Let's hope Joe gives him a hell of a match."

"Take it to the bank, pal. Joe's a customer, ya know. He was in last night with his wife and some other mantrap. Big as a house, but he don't throw his weight around. He's as nice an' polite as you or me."

He said, "I'll keep my fingers crossed," and went back to the table, where he sat with his head in his hands. There was an empty bowl in front of him.

"Yours was getting cold," Fanny said, "so I ate it." There was a full bowl before her, still steaming. After a moment, she picked it up and offered it to him.

"That's all right," he said.

"I was just trying to make a joke. Take it, it's yours anyway. What's the matter?"

"How long have you been eating here?"

"What?"

"I asked how long you've been coming in here. When we were in your room you said there was a good Italian place a couple of blocks away—something like that. So you've eaten here before. When was the first time?"

Fanny counted on her fingers. "Four days ago. Tuesday."

"And they took your money?"

"I didn't pay." She hesitated. "I was with a sergeant I know, a sergeant in uniform. We were hungry, so we decided to try it. He was going to buy, but one of the men who work here said it was okay, on the house. You know how they do for cops sometimes. Now if you want to stay at my place tonight, you'd better tell me what's up."

"We're in my world—the place the Visitors come from. Or if we're not, this whole place is a Visitor."

She stared at him in disbelief.

"I've eaten here two or three times a week for the past few years. Tuesday night I brought Lara here. Some of her power or magic dust or whatever you want to call it rubbed off. Were you here for dinner? What time?"

Fanny nodded. "About eight."

"That was when we were here. The store closes at six, and it takes me about an hour to get home on the bus. I came home, showered, and changed clothes. My apartment's a block and a half that way." He pointed. "I think if I leave here without you, I might be able to spend the night in my own bed. Maybe even if I leave with you."

"Then you'll have to put me up."

"Sure."

"Because I'm not leaving you. You're bait for North, and getting him means a promotion, probably two grades— Detective Lieutenant Lindy. It might also mean the survival of the human race, although that's strictly secondary."

"All right," he said.

"You're willing to help me?"

"Yes, if you're willing to help me. If I go home, that's the life I had before I met Lara. She may visit my world, but this is where she comes from. This is where she lives, so this is where I'll find her, if I find her at all."

The waitress halted at their table. "Don't care for your soup, ma'am?"

Fanny shook her head. "I let it get cold, but that's all right. Take it away."

When the waitress left, he said, "This is where I belong too, because Lara's here."

159

"Since you're going to help me and we're sharing info, the future detective lieutenant will share some of hers: your Lara is Laura Nomos."

"I know."

Fanny looked surprised. "I didn't, not for sure. Or not till a minute ago, when you were up at the cash register. How could you be sure? And what were you doing there anyway?"

"I saw her in the theater, just like you did. And it was Lara—I told you about Mr. Kolecke. In your room you said she was Laura Nomos, so the names aren't just a coincidence."

"Well, I thought you were wrong, that Klamm's stepdaughter couldn't possibly be ducking in and out of the Visiting World as if she were the goddess. But like you say, I saw her. And that Italian woman said she saw your Lara last night, dressed the way Nomos was in the theater, so that was confirmation. You're not crazy or nearsighted. Your Lara's Laura Nomos."

He nodded.

Fanny shuddered. "And if you're not crazy, you might be right about this restaurant, and I ought to be scared to death. This is your world?"

"I think so. North calls it C-One." He showed her the money and told her what had happened. "Do you have any large bills?"

"A twenty. That's the biggest."

"That should do," he said. "I want you to take it to the register and ask for two tens. Take whatever he gives you and bring it back here."

· 19 ·

Home Again

The waitress had brought Fanny's salad and his fettuccine, with the tea and coffee, while Fanny was at the register. When she returned she asked, "Aren't you hungry?"

"I'm starved," he said, "but first I want to see what you got."

"Two perfectly ordinary ten-dollar bills." She held them out. "You really are crazy, that's what I think."

He shook his head and forked up fettuccine.

"And I asked if you were hungry."

"I want to think," he told her, "and I think better when I'm eating." After another bite he asked, "Would you like a taste? It's really very good."

"Just to keep you happy." She took a forkful, followed by two more. "You didn't really get those bills you showed me from him, did you?"

He nodded, his mouth full.

"You're saying that man knows, that he's manipulating us."

He swallowed. "I don't think so. He talked to me about the fight, Joe's fight."

"Who's Joe?"

"A boxer. I met him once. Everybody says what a nice guy he is, and he seemed like one, the one time I talked to him. Do you remember what Mama Capini said about the people Lara brought here?"

Fanny nodded. "The big man and the blonde? Sure."

"Joe was the big man. Laura Nomos is Eddie Walsh's lawyer. Eddie is Joe's manager. All these people belong to your world, but Mama Capini doesn't." He sipped his water and went back to the fettuccine. "Joe paid for the dinner, remember? If it had been Lara—Laura Nomos—I would have understood, and maybe Joe used a credit card or wrote a check. But I don't think either one would be like Joe. He bought me coffee from a machine and got a soft drink for himself, and he took the change out of one of those little coin purses that misers use on TV. I bet he's had it since he was a kid. I think Joe would pay cash."

"And not look at his change till later?"

"No, that's just it. Joe *would* look at it. He'd count it, too. Probably Jennifer—that's his wife, the woman in the red dress—takes care of most of the bills, but he wouldn't want her to pay for a meal in a restaurant. That would embarrass him. So his change was right, in the right sort of money."

"Then they'd have to know, here in this restaurant. That's what I said."

He shook his head. "If he'd known, he wouldn't have talked to me about Joe. At first you don't understand what's happened.

162

Believe me, I'm speaking from experience. What happened to him and this whole place is that they were pulled across, somehow. They went through a door—except they couldn't have. One door couldn't take a whole building, could it?"

Fanny laughed. "I don't know what you're talking about. What's this about doors?"

"Lara told me, in a note. When you've been around someone from the other world, you see doors. Anything that's closed on all four sides can be one. It looks *significant;* that was her word. If you go through, you cross over. But then if you turn around to go back, you don't go back. It isn't a door anymore, for you. You have to back out."

He snapped his fingers, and Fanny said, "What is it now?"

"Why is it a door looks the same on both sides?"

"Do they? Beats me."

"Because it is. That's what makes it a door. Shut your eyes. Go on, this is a test."

She did.

"Now, you've eaten here before, and you brought me here. What's the full, official name of this restaurant?"

She considered for a moment. "There's a sign outside with brass letters. *Trattoria Capini.*"

He sighed and said, "All right, now open them again." He handed her a book of matches that had been lying on the table.

Fanny glanced at the cover. "'Capini's Italian Cuisine.' Okay, it's not quite the same."

He put down his fork. "This restaurant—I call it Mama's—is in my world. It's the place where I've eaten for years. The other one—the *Trattoria*—is in yours. Maybe the family name's being the same on both sides is a coincidence. Anyway, the door of the *Trattoria* is a Door. People from your world who've been

163

with people from mine can get into mine by walking through it, like you did when you came in with me, or like Joe and his wife—her name's Jennifer, I think—did when they came in with Lara. But things sort themselves out after awhile. People are pulled by their own worlds, which is why I'm back in mine now, I think. Money is really just pieces of paper. If it's from one world it pulls others from the same world. Things move in ways that sort them out."

Fanny said, "You're implying that a piece of paper has a brain. I don't believe you."

"No, I'm not. Let me tell you about something they showed us in school. They tuned two strings to the same frequency. Do you follow me? Not the way you'd tune a piano, but so they made exactly the same note. Then whenever somebody plucked one, the other would start to shake. Not because it had a brain—it just did."

"Then both worlds are only frequencies, and nothing's solid at all."

"I wouldn't go that far," he said.

"But I would. Isn't that how TV's supposed to work? You tune to a certain channel and get two signals, one for picture, one for sound. The station fudges the frequency of each just a little all the time, and that's what changes the picture and the noise from the speakers. When you change the frequency in your set a lot, it picks up a new channel, and the show you've been watching is gone. There's a new show, with different people."

He shook his head.

"Well, I think I'm right." Fanny signaled the waitress. "Please, could I have more hot water for my tea?"

He wanted to say that although her world might be nothing more than the note of a piano string, his own was real; but he

164

remembered its coins, the false faces and the brassy edges of them, and he felt that it had no more reality than her own, and perhaps less.

Fanny pointed a finger at him. "Now listen to me. Suppose you'd been watching TV for your entire life. Suppose it was the only thing you knew, and there were shows like *Sunrise*, *Sunset*, *Work*, and *Shopping*; and you were used to them and had never even thought about anything else at all." She paused. "What do they call that little screen at the back of your eyes?"

He shook his head again. "I don't know."

"The retina, that's it. Well, suppose somebody changed the show there."

"Are you testing me somehow?"

Fanny grinned. "Nope, just making conversation. You tell me that if we walk out the door backwards, we'll be in my world. And you want to be there with me, so you can find your Lara—who's really Laura Nomos. And I think what's going to happen is that we're going to back through the door and be on the sidewalk again, and then you're going to say, 'See, it worked!' I may be a sucker, but I'm not that big a sucker."

"I'm serious," he said.

"Me, too. And I think I know why your doors work. Suppose two channels show the same thing, but in opposite ways. Say the thing's a door—or anyhow a doorway—and the first channel shows one side at the same time the other channel's showing the other. Wouldn't their frequencies have to have come closer to each other? If there were a lot of channels, some would get so close they'd touch. Then you could turn the knob just a little and skip from one channel to the next, right? But if you wanted to go back, you'd have to turn the knob backwards. You couldn't just keep twisting it in the direction you'd turned it the first time and get back. So that's what we'll be doing if we back through the door, turning the knob back. But I'd feel awfully silly."

He said, "You're going to do it, aren't you?"

Fanny shrugged. "I didn't think you cared about me. Only about your Lara."

"Do I have to choose? Right now?"

She grinned again. "Yep."

"Then I choose Lara."

"Which means you're going to have to let me pay for my own lunch."

"Back out," he said. "I mean it. It may not work—Lara's note said you should do it right away, and we certainly haven't. But at least we won't be any worse off. You'd be as lost in my world as I was in yours."

"That's a myth," Fanny said. "Isn't it?"

"Isn't what?"

"The lost traveler who meets somebody, or finds a city that no one else can ever find again. I'm not so sure I'd mind being one, even if the Department thought I'd gone over to the enemy."

He said, "Those shows usually have sad endings." He had seen *Brigadoon* on HBO, and he tried to recall how it had ended so he could tell her. Nothing remained in his memory but the name and the swirl of plaid skirts, the skirling of bagpipes.

That isn't how it really is, he thought.

Fanny stood, taking her coat from the back of her chair. "Well, come on. Here goes nothing."

"Right now? We've got to get the check."

"Here it is." She held it up. "The waitress put it here when she brought the water for my tea."

He took it from her fingers (a bit too easily, he thought) and held her coat for her. He discovered that he did not really think backing through the door would work. He was home, in his own world once more after—what? A Saturday morning adventure? Some kind of a mental seizure? Things sort themselves out. He had said that.

His coat was on a hook near the table. It was, of course, still the heavy wool one he had bought in the hotel. Too heavy, probably, for the weather here. But the package of fifties he had bought for a dime from Mr. Sheng was real money now, as the still substantial remainder of the thousand he had found under the vase in his hospital room was not.

With a second bill from the packet he paid the new cashier, another of Mama Capini's sons, a little older and a bit bigger than the one he had met in the men's room. As a test he asked, "What do you think about the fight?"

"What fight?"

"Joe's fight. I thought Joe was a customer of yours."

The cashier chuckled and rang up their total. "You been talkin' to Guido. He's a crazy one, that Guido."

He started to return to their table, but Fanny whispered, "I left the tip."

"Backwards," he told her. "Remember, we've got to walk backwards." He took an awkward backward step toward the door.

"No," Fanny whispered. "I won't." She caught his arm and spun him around.

Desperately he began, "You'll be—"

"No, I won't. The joke's gone far enough." She tugged at his arm.

Lara was standing across the street, snow blowing past her face as she studied the restaurant. He started toward her, and as he did he heard Mama Capini call, *"Arrivederci!"* behind them.

At the edge of vision he saw Fanny look back, wave, and smile as she stepped through the door.

Then he was on the street, and alone. Snowflakes sparkled in the sun, blown from the rooftops by a spring wind. Lara had already turned away; as he watched, she vanished through the revolving door of a fur store.

Recklessly he dashed into the traffic.

Brakes squealed. A white truck like a huge refrigerator on wheels slewed sideways until it nearly struck his shoulder with its own. Triumphantly, he leaped across the curb and straight-armed the revolving door.

A sale was in progress; the furrier's swarmed with women, many of them accompanied by husbands variously impatient. He raced among them, trying to decide whether Lara had worn a hat, whether her lovely hair had been on her shoulders or piled upon her head to form the covering he half recalled having seen while Fanny faded like a cheap photo at his side.

Twice he pushed his way completely around the store. Women were everywhere, with and without hats; none was Lara.

In desperation he snatched away a clerk, rescuing her from an angry-looking customer with blue hair who was disparaging two coats to her in tandem. He described Lara as well as he could.

The clerk shook her head. "Have you tried upstairs?"

He stared at her.

"In the salon." The clerk lowered her voice. "The more expensive things are up there, and they get a better class of people."

A pokey elevator carried him to the second floor, wheezing like an asthmatic old man. Here the carpets were white and the lights seemed touched with blue. He located a male clerk and described Lara again, adding that it was extremely urgent that he speak to her.

The clerk asked frostily, "You don't by any chance recall the young lady's name?"

"Lara Morgan," he said. "She sometimes uses the name Laura Nomos."

The clerk did not turn a hair. "Then if you'll come with me, sir, I can examine the book for today and tell you whether she's been here."

They went to the back of the store, where a ledger lay open on a desk. The clerk studied its pages. "Ms. Morgan was indeed here today, sir. At eleven thirty." The clerk glanced at his watch. "It's now nearly eleven forty, so I would imagine she's left the store. Ms. Morgan left her coat with us for cleaning and storage, as I believe she always does."

A tiny flower of hope blossomed in him. He asked, "She'll come for it, then, in the fall?"

"Or send someone, sir, if she wants it taken from storage." The clerk flipped pages. "Here we are, sir. She picked it up last October. But it had been with us for twenty-six months, sir."

· 20 ·

His Apartment

The mailbox was full, and among its bills and ads he discovered a yellow ticket advising him that still more were being held for him at the post office. A little strawberry-shaped clock he had gotten in a drugstore clung to the door of his refrigerator, its display faithfully flashing the time and date—1:38, 4 15, 1:38, 4 15, 1:39, 4 15.

It was the middle of April; he tried to remember when Lara had left him, but could not. Her note lay on the coffee table, undated save for a light coating of dust. He read it again.

> Darling,
> I tried to say good-bye last night, but you wouldn't listen. I'm not a coward, really I'm not.
> If it weren't for the doors I wouldn't tell you a thing—

that would be the best way. You may see one, perhaps more than one, at least for a little while. It will be closed all around. (They must be closed on all sides.) It may be a real door, or just something like a guy-wire supporting a phone pole, or an arch in a garden. Whatever it is, it will look *significant.*

Please read carefully. Please remember everything I'm saying. *You must not go through.*

If you go through before you realize it, don't turn around. *If you do it will be gone. Walk backward at once.*

Lara

Her signature was exactly as he remembered it, its first *A* a continuation of the capital *L.* He did not read the postscript (which he called the *PS*), feeling that he would quite literally die, that his heart would somehow burst, if he did.

A paper lay under the coffee table. March 13th—thirty-three days since Lara had gone. A night in the hospital, or perhaps two. Say two nights in the hospital, a night in the hotel with North, a night in the hotel alone. That was four nights, for thirty-three days.

He switched on the television and chanced upon a feature story about the rush to file income tax returns. April 15th; this was the day you were supposed to file. Mechanically, he walked to the post office and got the rest of his mail. His form was there, and the store had sent his W2 already—it was in the pile of papers on the bedside table. The bed was still unmade, still rumpled from the night he had staggered into it with Lara and the day he had awakened alone.

He used the short form and had nothing to report but his salary; it was complete, sealed and stamped, in twenty minutes. He had not worn the overcoat when he went to the post office, and now he debated whether to wear it when he went out to mail his return. The packet of fifties was still in the right side pocket. He took it out, wondering what Internal Revenue would do if they knew he had it; no doubt profits had to be reported, even if they were the profits of buying several thousand dollars for a dime. The brown paper wrapper was still stamped PUROLATOR COURIER, still marked with a Chinese character and the symbols for ten cents by Mr. Sheng's industrious brush. Where was Mr. Sheng now? And his nephew, Dr. Pille? On a different channel, in another show.

Taking Marcella's bills out of his wallet, he folded them, bound them with a rubber band, and put them in the pocket of the overcoat. Slipping the paper wrapper from Mr. Sheng's fifties, he crumpled it and tossed it into a wastebasket, and deposited the fifties in his wallet.

He felt like an international traveler—like James Bond— felt that he should have a small but deadly automatic tucked away somewhere, and several passports. He laughed at himself as he hung the coat in the closet, draping the muffler over its collar while he resisted, always resisted, the impulse to take out the Tina doll and study it, to kiss it perhaps, and comb its hair as the woman in the haberdashery had.

"Too old to play with dolls." He spoke the words aloud, but softly.

Returning from the post office a second time, he felt cold despite the sweater-vest and stopped to buy a new topcoat. At his own store—the store where he worked, or at least where he had worked—he could have gotten an employee discount. But the topcoat was on sale, and his discount would not have made it any cheaper; the discount applied only to the full price, never to a sale price. His new topcoat was tan, like his old one.

Back at his apartment, he stripped the bed, showered, and changed clothes, discarding his scorched slacks. There was a musty shirt on the floor of his closet. He bundled it with the sheets and pillow slips, and the soiled shirt, socks, and underwear he had removed, and looked around to see whether Lara had left anything.

She had owned very little, now that he thought of it. Two dresses, but perhaps, since he remembered both as green, there had been only one, a single dress that could be worn differently at different times, with different pins and so on. He tried to recall what they said in Better Dresses—*accessorized,* that was it. It occurred to him that Lara would never have used that word and would not have liked it, and he realized that he himself did not like it now.

So that much of Lara remained with him. There was nothing else, not a scrap of clothing, not so much as a used lipstick or a comb. Had Lara smoked? No, it had been Fanny, she had smoked a lot, had been almost a chain smoker, he thought. The ashtrays in his apartment were empty, soiled only by dust.

He carried the dirty laundry to the basement and loaded it into one of the washers there, adding granulated detergent from a coin-operated machine. While the washer ran, he read a paper someone had left behind. Innocent people were dying in Africa. The comic page no longer carried *Lolly;* something new and ugly had been substituted.

The washing machine fell silent, displaying a sodden bundle of cloth. He stuck the bundle into a drier, set it on Delicate, and fed it quarters.

A syndicated columnist with a reputation for wit imagined her interview with the President following a nuclear holocaust. The crossword puzzle demanded seven letters meaning *bear.* The store was running a big sale on tape decks—his own department. Buy a tape deck at ten percent off, get your choice of any tape in the store for a dollar. He imagined they had been busy and wondered how they had made out without him. Discontinued home computers were on sale too, at forty percent of list.

He stuffed his dry laundry into a pillowcase and carried it back up to his apartment. One shirt and the socks were gone. He returned to the basement and checked both the machines; his shirt and socks were in neither. They had returned, he decided, in some way. North had bought that shirt and those socks in the hotel.

The sweater-vest was still hanging in the closet. So was the overcoat, crowded into the little alcove around the corner from the closet door. He could not find his hat. He had worn it in the car with Fanny, worn it to Mama Capini's; he recalled hanging it on a peg. But he could not remember taking it from the peg when they left. Had he had it on when he ran into the furrier's? He did not know, could not remember.

His watch said it was five o'clock. There was food in the apartment, but the things in the refrigerator had no doubt gone bad, sour milk, soft carrots. The margarine might be okay.

He decided he could not face the job of cleaning out the refrigerator (and the bread box, now that he came to think of it) that day. He would eat at Mama's, and perhaps—

Perhaps something might happen.

His necktie was draped over the lampshade. He buttoned his collar and knotted the tie carefully; he made it a rule never to leave the apartment without a tie—there was always a chance he would run into one of the supervisors. He put on his jacket and his new topcoat.

When he had gone a block, he saw a man's black sock in the gutter and stopped to pick it up. It was not one of his, but it reminded him that he had often seen clothing lost or abandoned, lying in the street. No doubt his shirt and his own socks were similarly lost and abandoned, lying in the snow of Lara's city, the city that was so much like, and yet so much unlike, his own. The socks would be separated, he thought; they would be miles apart. No one would get any good from them, unless perhaps a child took one to make a puppet, and a tramp who did not care whether his socks matched chanced on the other. The shirt had been a good one, a real silk shirt. He hoped someone found it before it got run over, before it became a rag like the rags he had passed so often without thinking about where they might have come from.

One of Mama's sons was at the cash register. He tried to decide whether it was Guido, the son he had talked with in the restroom; he could not be sure. All the sons had always looked much the same to him, glowering men with black mustaches that came and went like customers, full of meat sauce at one moment and gone the next.

"Sit anywhere ya want to," the son called to him. "It's pretty early yet."

He took the table by the window where he had sat with Fanny for lunch. If he had indeed left his hat on a peg in Mama's, it was gone now. He told the waitress, "I was in here around noon with a lady; she had a salad. I don't know what it was, but it looked awfully good. Do you remember us?"

The waitress shook her head. "I don't think I served you, sir."

"She was—" he tried to remember how old Fanny had said she was. "—about twenty-three. Petite, curly black hair."

"Probably Gina served you, sir. Gina looks a lot like me."

"Then would you find her and bring her over here?"

"We got three salads, sir." The waitress described them. "They're all pretty good."

"Find Gina," he told her.

She left looking sullen, and he studied the license plates of passing cars. It was getting dark, but he could read some of them, and they were perfectly ordinary.

He looked through the pockets of his jacket, moved by the feeling that he had forgotten something. There was nothing in either side pocket, and only a handkerchief—the red one he had carried there for months—in the breast pocket. His checkbook was in the inside pocket, and he pulled it out and examined it. The last check he had recorded there had been written on March eleventh. It occurred to him that he had paid for the doll by check, and that the amount of the check had been large; but he could not remember how large, and he was not sure a check could be presented for collection by a shop in another world, a shop in a dream.

". . . not here," the waitress announced to his elbow.

He glanced up at her. "I'm sorry?"

"I said Gina's not here. I looked all over." The waitress brushed a lock of hair away from her forehead and contrived to appear both hot and tired when she was neither. "Dinner's just starting, too."

"Can she do that? Just leave like that?"

The waitress leaned closer. "Gina's screwing Guido. She can do any damned thing she wants."

"Is Guido here?" He glanced toward the register. There was no one there.

"Nah, Guido's gone. He don't hardly ever stay for dinner. What'd you like?"

He ordered one of the salads, and she drifted away. After a minute or two, he returned his checkbook to his breast pocket, wondering what to do until his food came. He had eaten here for years, usually alone as he was now; surely he had done something. While Lara had lived with him, there had always been things to do, someone to talk with.

Mama Capini pulled out the empty chair and sat down. "Hey, what's the matter with you? You didn't get full at lunch? You should of said somethin', I'd have got you some garlic bread."

He asked, "Do you remember the girl I brought here for lunch, Mama?"

Mama kissed her fingers. "Sure. You gonna get married?"

"If she comes in, will you tell me?"

"Sure!"

"And remember Lara? Tell me if Lara comes in. Especially if Lara comes in."

"Sure. You lookin' for a date?"

"No, I'm just trying to find these people. And if the big man and his wife—that's the lady in the red dress—come in, let me know about them, too."

He dawdled over his salad for an hour and half, drinking an espresso and a couple of amarettos. He saw no one he knew, and nothing happened.

At last he paid the check. When he counted his change, it was just money; nor had he seen any bills with strange pictures in the drawer. The man at the register was the one who had told him Guido was crazy, bigger and older than Guido. As he trudged back to his apartment, he wondered vaguely where Guido had gone. Had Guido been drawn into the other world? If so, did he know it yet? Perhaps Gina came from there; if customers could walk through the door from another world, as Joe and Jennifer had, it seemed likely enough that a waitress looking for work might walk through it, too.

Back at the apartment he put on one of his favorite albums, but found that the music that had once charmed him was harsh and ugly now. He turned on the television. After an hour or so, he realized he had no idea what the show was or why he was watching it.

· 21 ·

The Store

He had forgotten how new the store looked, how shiny everything was. The walls were faced with limestone, and the company had them sandblasted every other year. The curving show windows had bright brass frames. Maintenance washed all those windows every morning and polished the frames until they sparkled like gold.

"It's not open," a fat woman told him. She was standing in front of one of the windows eyeing a sundress.

"I work here," he said, and hoped he still did. The store would open at nine-thirty sharp, but main-shift hourly employees were supposed to clock in by eight-thirty. It was three minutes after eight. He went around back and climbed the concrete steps to the employees' entrance, where Whitey watched to make sure no one punched in for someone else.

"Hi," Whitey said. "Have a nice vacation?"

He nodded. "Seems like I've only been gone for a couple of days."

It did, and yet it did not. Nothing had changed except for himself.

He resisted the temptation to have a look at his department and took the elevator to the administrative floor. Lie, or tell the truth? Tell them the truth, he decided; he was a bad liar, and he could not think of a story that would explain such a long absence anyway.

The next question was: Mr. Capper or Personnel? Capper was (or he had been) in charge of the department; with Capper on his side, Personnel would not be too rough with him. On the other hand, if Cap was mad—and there was a good chance of that—the personnel manager would resent his not having gone there first, and would probably kill any chance of transferring.

Besides, Personnel was easy to find. Cap might be in the office doing paperwork, but might just as easily be out in the department helping stock. Cap might not even be in yet.

Ella was at her desk doing her nails. She said, "Well . . . hello!"

There were folding steel chairs for job applicants. He sat in the one nearest her desk. "I'm back," he said.

"I see." Ella hesitated. "Mr. Drummond's not in yet."

"I'll wait."

"I carried you sick for a week." Although they were alone, Ella lowered her voice. "Then he made me start phoning. Once he even went to your apartment at night and rang your bell, but he said nobody answered."

"I was away. I got back to my apartment yesterday, and I could see I hadn't been there. Everything was dusty, you know?"

"You blacked out?"

"I don't think so. I can remember two nights, one when I was in a hospital and one—no, two—when I was in a hotel room." Not knowing what else to say, he added, "It was the same room."

Ella leaned toward him and held out her hand for his. He noticed then how much she looked like Fanny, though perhaps he was just forgetting what Fanny looked like. Ella said, "You've been gone over a month."

He nodded. "I think so."

Unconsciously he had extended his own hand, and when Ella touched it she felt his bandage. "What in the world happened to you? Your face too—you've got a burn on your cheek and one on your forehead."

"They've gone away, pretty much," he said. "They weren't very bad."

"Were you in an accident? What happened?"

He nodded again. "I was in this Chinese shop—Mr. Sheng's. He had fireworks stored in his basement, and something set them off. I think it was a guy named Bill North. Anyway, North was down there, and he's a cigar smoker." Though he felt it might be against his best interests, he grinned. "I was drinking tea with Mr. Sheng and his nephew, and a skyrocket came right up the stairs. It hit the wall at the top and came into the room where we were. It scared hell out of us. Then I guess some more must have gone off, because the next thing I knew I was in the street with my ears ringing and a cop and a paramedic bending over me. They said another ambulance had taken Mr. Sheng to the hospital, but—"

Drummond came in, nodded to Ella, raised an eyebrow at him, then smiled.

Ella said, "Good morning, sir."

Drummond went into the little private office behind Ella's reception room and shut the door.

Ella whispered, "I want to go in and talk to Dixie just for a minute. You wait here, okay?"

He nodded, studying her as she went into Drummond's office. She was a little bit heavier than Fanny, he decided. That was an improvement, if anything. And her hair was brown. He felt sure Fanny's had been black. Of course, no one was or could be like Lara, and he could never mistake any other woman for her. He had known right away that Marcella was really Lara, although Marcella had been a blonde, or at least had appeared to be. You could never tell, he thought, in black-and-white or in pictures drawn by a second-rate artist.

He glanced at his watch. It was eight twenty-eight, but he did not know just when he had come into the Personnel Office; it seemed to him Ella had been in the private office with Drummond a long time.

There was a drinking fountain in the hall outside. He got a drink, filling his mouth with icy water several times and each time making himself swallow it. He had the feeling that he did not always drink enough water, and ought to make himself drink more whenever he got the chance.

When he went back in, Ella was still in the private office with Drummond. He found *Time* in a pile of magazines on the end table and leafed through it. The President had reaffirmed his commitment to "ordinary Americans" and endorsed a reduction in Social Security benefits; the Near East seemed ready to explode. He wondered if it would help to send the President to the Near East, then tried to remember whether he had ever seen *Time* or a newspaper There. "There" was, he discovered, his private name for the other world, for the place where Lara was. He could not remember having seen one, although he could not be sure he had not—

Yes, of course, he had seen Walsh's picture in the paper. This was Here and that was There. He could not remember if the comics had been the same, or whether that paper had carried any comics at all.

The door of the inner office swung open, and Ella came out. She said, "Mr. Drummond will see you now." He put down *Time* and went in.

Drummond smiled and said, "Sit down. I'd like to start by admitting that most of this is my fault. I like to keep tabs on all our employees, and I certainly should have kept better tabs on you."

He sat and found he was facing a large bronze nameplate as well as Drummond. The nameplate read:

A. DICKSON DRUMMOND
Manager of Personnel

He said, "That's very nice of you, Mr. Drummond. Only it wasn't your fault, I know that." He counted silently to three and added, "I really don't think it was mine either. It just happened."

Drummond shook his head. "No, I blame myself. I was on the phone with your doctor a moment ago, by the way. She says it's been a long time since you've been to see her."

He tried to remember whether he had ever been to a doctor. Surely he had, but he could not recall the occasion. Dr. Pille had been his doctor in the hospital, but that was certainly not what Drummond meant. He said, "I guess it has."

"We want you to see her right away; let me make that clear. Not next week, not tomorrow, not this afternoon—this morning, as soon as you leave my office."

"I was hoping to get back to my department, sir. There's a sale, and they need me."

"And you can," Drummond told him, "just as soon as you get back from the doctor. Come up here, show me a note saying she's seen you, and you can get right back to work."

A great weight lifted from his chest.

"Your doctor will see you as soon as you get to her office—she doesn't take appointments. There's no reason you can't be back at work before lunch."

He nodded.

"She asked me to ask you whether by any chance you suffered a blow to the head."

He nodded. "I slipped on some ice and hit my head on the pavement."

Drummond smiled again. "It could've happened to any of us, couldn't it? That's all for now. You go over and see her, and don't forget to bring me the note."

He rose. "I won't, sir."

"One more thing." Drummond raised a finger. "While you were missing, I had Ella phone your number. She was never able to reach you, but on one occasion she got someone who said his name was Perlman, or some such. Do you know why he was in your apartment?"

He shrugged. "I guess he must have been from the building management company, sir."

When he was outside in the reception room again, he tried to remember the telephone calls he had made from United. The harsh male voice—had that been Perlman?

Ella asked, "Everything okay?"

"Fine," he said absently, suppressing the fact that he had to go see some doctor he could not remember. Had there been a doctor's bill in the mail in his box? Or in all the stuff that he had picked up at the post office? He had not paid a lot of attention to most of it; he could not remember that either.

"Ella, you said you called my apartment?"

She nodded.

"Mr. Drummond mentioned that, too. He said you talked to somebody named Perlman once."

Ella shook her head. "I never got an answer at all." She hesitated. "If you're going to be here in the store about noon, how about letting Personnel buy your lunch? Sort of celebrate your coming back."

"You didn't talk to anybody named Perlman?"

"I didn't talk to anybody," Ella said. She seemed suddenly depressed, for no reason he could see. "But I was out for a week with my back, and they got a temp. Dixie's been blaming me for her mistakes ever since, so she was probably the one that talked to Perlman. But if you ask me it was a wrong number."

There was an employee lounge on the floor below, a bare and frequently dirty room in which associates who brown-bagged ate their lunches. He fed coins into the coffee machine (recalling Joe in the basement of the hospital), found a clean chair, and sat down.

Doctors had to be paid. He got out his checkbook and read through the stubs. He had written no check to any doctor. None at all. Yet doctors were paid, by someone.

By the company's medical plan, then, very likely; but that was administered by Personnel. If he asked Ella for the number of his doctor, she would tell Drummond. He could not just start telephoning doctors. How many doctors were there in the city? Thousands, probably. He tried to recall what Drummond had said about this one: "Your doctor will see you as soon as you get to his office. He doesn't take appointments. There's no reason you can't be back before lunch."

No, that was wrong. Not *he*. It was *she*. *She* doesn't take appointments. The doctor was a woman. There might be thousands of doctors, but how many of those were women?

Fifty, maybe. And he wouldn't go to a doctor out in the suburbs.

There was a phone in a corner of the room, with a tattered directory on a shelf under it. He opened it to the physicians' listings and got out his pen.

Some of the doctors had provided only initials; he decided to consider them male for the purpose of his search. At least half the women were gynecologists or pediatricians; they could be eliminated too. He crossed off all those with addresses more than six blocks from the store and his apartment and was pleased to see that only three names remained. Pushing coins into the slot, he got out his wallet and checked the name he and North had chosen in the hotel. A. C. Pine—that was it. He laid the driver's license on the shelf.

"Dr. Nilson's office."

Did this doctor take appointments? He said, "This is Adam Pine. I need an appointment with the doctor as soon as possible—this morning, if you can arrange it."

"Dr. Nilson—" Faintly someone called, *"Lara! Lara!"* He could not tell whether the voice was male or female; it sounded far off and scratchy.

"Would you mind if I put you on hold, Mr. Green?"

She did not wait for his answer. Her voice was gone, and after a moment or two had passed, a piano began "Clair de Lune."

He waited, telling himself he would stand there all day if necessary. "Clair de Lune" ended, and something else began, a piece he did not recognize.

At last a new voice said, "Dr. Nilson speaking."

"I want to talk to Lara."

"To Lora? She just left."

"Then I want an appointment to see you as soon as possible."

"I don't take appointments—it's first come, first served. Come to my office. It's in the Downtown Mental Health Center, and I'll fit you in when I can."

He tried twice before he could get out the words. "I think you've treated me before. That you have a file on me." He gave his name.

Dr. Nilson's voice became warm. "Oh, of course, Mr. Green. Believe it or not, I was looking over your case the other night and hoping you'd drop in again. It's been more than a month."

He started, "If you've tried to phone—"

"I never do, except in emergencies. It's so much better if the patient contacts me because he wants to. Come this morning, won't you? I'll see that you get in."

"Yes."

"And now, if you'll excuse me—Lora's not here, and there's someone on the other line."

· 22 ·

His Doctor

The crisp air of morning had already been softened by the sun. He strode along with his topcoat folded over his arm, glancing into the store windows he passed. His department rarely got a window—windows went to the clothes people, mostly—but when it did, he was the one most often assigned to set up the display; he was professionally interested, or so he told himself.

As he looked, he wondered what to do with the money from Mr. Sheng's package. Prudence (his mother's ghost) advised him to bank it against a rainy day. Caution whispered that Internal Revenue might check his deposits.

How could he explain? And there would be no explaining the fact that he had not reported the income when he had filled out his 1040A. Instead he had asked for a refund, because he always had Accounting withhold more than he needed to cover his income taxes. No, he thought, even the IRS could not blame him for not reporting the money on that return; it was for last year, and he had bought the money this year.

Or had he? There had been something oddly old-fashioned about There, now that he considered it. Most of the buildings had looked old, and even the ones that had seemed new had been old in design, built of conservative brick, with windows that slid up and down like windows in a house. The cramped little cars had felt modern enough—old cars were bigger, with fins on their tails and doors as thick as a bank vault's. So There had modern cars, except for their long-handled gear shifts; but the TV had been all black-and-white.

He tried to recall the date on the paper in which he had read about their escape and about Joe's match with some other boxer whose name he could not remember. It was gone, faded to invisible ink.

Maybe he could take a Caribbean cruise, like on *Love Boat*. No, because you were supposed to fall for somebody, and he could not fall for anybody except Lara, and he had already fallen for her. He might think he had, as he had with Fanny, getting laid for two or three thousand dollars.

He laughed at himself. There had been a time when he had gone to singles bars one or two nights a week, a time that had ended when he realized the women were looking for husbands and not for love. (No, never for love.) If he just wanted to get laid, that could be arranged a lot cheaper.

Men in blue hardhats and International Orange safety vests were at work not far from the building. Hard-edged black wires traced languid curves in the street. He stopped a workman and rather timidly asked what they were doing, and the man explained that they were taking down overhead lines that had been replaced by underground cables.

He nodded, said thank you, and stood looking at the street, recalling the significant door that would not open for him again. A meter maid touched his arm and pointed out the Downtown Mental Health Center. "It's right over there, sir. Would you like me to take you?"

"No." He shook his head and realized with a start that he had been crying, bawling in public for the first time since he had been a small boy. Jerking the red handkerchief out of his breast pocket, he mopped his streaming eyes and blew his nose. When he felt presentable again, he went inside.

A board beside the elevators listed Dr. Nilson's office on the fourth floor. He discovered that he had known that already; no doubt it had been part of the listing in the telephone book. He rang for the elevator and went up.

There were three patients in the doctor's reception room: a thin and gloomy woman, a fat boy of sixteen or so who grinned at nothing, and himself. He chose a chair, necessarily between the other two, and wondered what they thought of him, how they would describe him. As a neat little clerk, perhaps—not that he felt so neat this morning.

There was nobody at the reception desk. The telephone rang six times as they sat waiting, but no one answered it.

When it had stopped ringing, he rose and examined the desk. Its top held a potted plant, a green blotter, and a silver ball-point pen embraced by a pink koala bear. The flat drawer under the desk top contained pencils, a ball-point office pen, a gross of paper clips in a small cardboard box, and some rubber bands. False drawer fronts on the left concealed an electric typewriter bolted to a swing-up typing stand. He lifted it to see whether there was anything hidden behind it, and the gloomy woman stared at him disapprovingly.

No wonder you're so down, he thought. You won't let anyone have any fun.

False drawer fronts on the right slid up to reveal bins for white and yellow paper, for stationery with the Downtown Mental Health Center letterhead, matching envelopes, carbon paper, and flimsy second sheets.

That was all. If the person who had used the desk had ever stored personal possessions in it, she had taken them with her. He reflected that even a desk dictionary might have revealed her name, scrawled inside the front cover. But the desk dictionary, if it had ever existed, was gone.

There was nothing beneath the blotter, no labels pasted to the telephone. The toy koala was cute and mute. He pulled out the stationery, the white bond paper, and the yellow paper, and ruffled through them, thinking vaguely that something might have been concealed there. There was nothing, and the carbon paper (all unused) and second sheets were just as sterile. The pen in the drawer was plastic, the kind given away by office-equipment dealers in search of business. GOOD TIGER INC, with an address and telephone number, took up half the pen's sides. The others read: DOWNTOWN MENTAL/HEALTH CENTER/ LORA MASTERMAN. He slipped the pen into his pocket and sat down.

A lanky woman with a wisp of beard marched out of the inner office, crossed the waiting room as if they were invisible, and went out. The buck-toothed woman with whom he had spoken the day he had discovered Lara was gone looked through the doorway, saw him, and said, "Please come in, Mr. Green."

The fat teenager stood up. "Now wait a minute!"

The buck-toothed woman told him calmly, "Mr. Green's

case is something of an emergency, Mr. Bodin, and I reserve the right to see my patients in whatever order I choose."

He said, "In a minute, he'll tell you I took this pen from your receptionist's desk, doctor." He held it up so she could see it. "I thought I might want to make some notes about what we said, and I forgot to bring one of my own."

"That's perfectly all right, Mr. Green. Won't you come in?"

Her office was smaller than Drummond's, and much plainer. He sat down when she did and asked, "What's the matter with me, doctor?"

"I really don't know, Mr. Green. That's what we're trying to find out."

"You've seen me before?"

She nodded.

"How often?"

"Does it matter?"

"It does to me. Very much. How often?"

She flipped through the file folder on her desk. "This is your eighth visit. Why is it so important?"

"Because I can only remember coming here once before."

She frowned. "Interesting. When was that?"

"March fourteenth. Do you remember what I asked you then?"

"I have notes from our interview. You were looking for a young woman called Lara Morgan. Did you find her?"

"No. Do you have a picture of Lora Masterman?"

"If I did, Mr. Green, I wouldn't let you look at it. Ms. Masterman no longer works here, and I wouldn't want her annoyed by my patients."

"She left you pretty suddenly," he said. "I talked to her when I called from the store. She put me on hold, and after ten minutes or so you answered. When I got here, she was gone."

The doctor nodded again. "It's true she gave no notice, Mr. Green. Nevertheless, her resignation is my problem, not yours."

"Tell me one thing, and I won't ask you anything else about her. Does she fit the description of Lara I gave you when I was here in March?"

"I must have your solemn word, Mr. Green."

"All right, I give you my solemn word that if you'll answer that one question I won't ask you anything else about her."

Dr. Nilson nodded. "Agreed, then. Let me read over what you told me." She scanned the paper before her. "You said that Lara Morgan had red hair and was about five feet, nine inches tall. You also said that she had freckles. She was wearing a green dress, silk or nylon, and gold jewelry. No, Mr. Green, the description doesn't fit Lora at all."

He leaned forward in the hard, wooden chair. "Is it just the hair color? Because—"

"Mr. Green, you gave me your word that you'd ask me no more questions if I told you whether Lora's appearance corresponded to the description you gave. I have told you: it does not. My time isn't unlimited, and there are patients waiting to see me—patients who were waiting before you came."

He nodded and offered her the Lora Masterman pen. "I have to have a note from you saying I've been to see you. Otherwise they won't let me come back to work. If you'll give me that, I'll go."

"Then I won't, at least not right this moment. You have no more questions for me, Mr. Green. At least, no more about Lora; so you promised. But I have several for you. My first was why you've come to see me today, but you've just answered that. The second is why you must have this note. You haven't been at work for some time?"

He shook his head. "Not since March thirteenth, the day before I came to see you last."

"You devoted your full time to your unsuccessful search for Lara Morgan?"

"Yes."

"I see." Dr. Nilson made a notation on her pad. "Prove to me that Lara Morgan exists, Mr. Green."

"All right, I will—if you'll prove to me first that Lora Masterman existed."

For a second or two Dr. Nilson glared at him, then a smile tugged at her lips. "You're either much worse or much better, Mr. Green, and I swear I don't know which. You're a conundrum wrapped in an enigma. Winston Churchill said that about Russia, I believe."

"Can you do it?"

"Yes, indeed. Quite easily, as it happens. We now have a full-time attorney here. About two weeks ago, he bought a new camera and went through the building snapping pictures to try it out. One he took of Lora and me was so good—at least, in his opinion—that he had prints made for both of us." Dr. Nilson pulled out one of her desk drawers. "I still have mine, right here."

She produced a brown envelope about five by seven, with the words CANDID CAMERA SHOPS across the top.

"Don't!"

"Don't what, Mr. Green?"

He did not reply.

"You don't want to see my picture?"

"There isn't any picture there," he said. "Or if there is, it won't show Lara. Lora." He did not know how he knew, yet he did.

"You're quite correct in thinking that it doesn't show your Lara Morgan, but it shows Lora Masterman and me. As a matter of fact, I was looking at it just a few minutes ago, after Lora left so abruptly. She was the best receptionist I've ever had."

She pulled a print from the brown envelope and held it up for him. In it, she stood in the waiting room, her hand upon the shoulder of a smiling, brown-haired girl seated at the desk. A modest plastic nameplate, barely visible in the lower right corner of the picture, read *Lora Masterman.*

"There she is, Mr. Green; no freckles, very little jewelry, no green silk dresses—or at least, I never saw her wear one—and no fur coat. Brown hair, not red. Brown eyes, not green."

He nodded slowly. "It's Tina."

"Tina?"

"Tina's one of the names she uses. I think that when she looks like that, she calls herself Tina."

"I see." Dr. Nilson gave the words no inflection at all. "Can you tell me why she changes her name?"

"No," he said. And then, "Maybe I can, a little. I've been thinking about her a lot."

"I can see you have."

He said slowly, "Have you ever looked at the sky at night, Doctor?"

"Yes, often. Not really as often as I'd like; there's so much light from the city that one seldom sees the stars. But last winter there was a blackout—perhaps you remember. I stood on my balcony until I was nearly frozen."

"And you know how far away they are."

"Vaguely. I'm not an astronomer."

"I watched Carl Sagan once, and he said most of them are so far away it takes millions of years for a beam of light to get from them to us, and light's the fastest thing there is. Haven't you ever wondered why God put them so far away?"

"I suppose everyone has, Mr. Green."

"And yet we have Visitors sometimes, and things from our world that just go away."

Dr. Nilson nodded. "Like the sign at the airport—arrivals and departures."

"I guess so. I've never ridden in a jet, or any other kind of airplane. But I know that people and things just vanish, and sometimes other people and other things show up here." He tried to recall what Fanny had said about the television channels but decided he could not explain it well enough. He said, "There's another world, just next door, if you go through the right door."

Dr. Nilson did something on the underside of her desk top. "Please go on, Mr. Green."

· 23 ·

Explanations

"Suppose that in that world there was a woman—a goddess, really—who wanted to make love to a man from our world."

Dr. Nilson smiled. "Why should she want to do that, Mr. Green?"

"Because in her world men die after they make love."

"Like drones, is that what you mean? I must say it would be a nice reversal; here so many of us die after rape, or even before it."

He said, "I don't understand about the drones."

"Male honeybees. Most bees are sterile females; they're the ones who do the work. A few are fertile females, I suppose they're called princesses. A few others are fertile males: drones. At the nuptial flight, the strongest drones mate with the princesses, who become queens. Then the drones die."

He shook his head. "It isn't really like that, there. The men do a lot of the work. The cop that talked to me at the fire was a man and so was the medic, and later the clerk who wouldn't let me back into the hotel. But when they make love, they die. Their immune systems collapse. A doctor there told me that—Dr. Applewood."

Dr. Nilson smiled again. "You mean they have doctors, just as we do? And policemen? I suppose they speak English?"

"Yes, at least in the part I visited. But they must have different languages in different places. I know there's a man who talks with a German—" Abruptly he fell silent.

"What is it, Mr. Green?"

"I just realized who it was I heard calling Lara when I was talking to her—to your Lora—on the phone. It was him. It was Klamm."

Dr. Nilson leaned toward him, her hands clasped beneath her chin. "Don't you realize, Mr. Green, that if there were a world like the one you've been telling me about, a world where men die after intercourse, it would have customs—a whole culture— quite different from ours?"

"They don't," he said. "It's a lot like ours." He paused, thinking. "I hadn't really worked it all out before, but it has to be. Because the worlds are so close, because it's so easy to go across. Suppose somebody there thinks up a new word. Pretty soon somebody switches over, maybe not even knowing that he did it, and hears the word and brings it back. Or maybe one of them comes here and uses the word. Probably a lot of customs that we think are ours are really theirs, like the groom wearing black at his wedding."

There was a discreet tap at the door. Dr. Nilson called, "Come in."

Two husky black men in the trousered white uniforms of male

nurses entered. Both were about his own age, and it seemed to him that their dark, serious faces contrasted oddly with their clothes. One carried a small canvas bag.

"I don't believe you'll have trouble with Mr. Green," Dr. Nilson said. "In many respects he seems quite rational, and it may be that he needs nothing more than a short rest."

When he stood up, a man took each arm. Something with Lara at its heart exploded in him, and he fought them as he had not fought since he was a boy, shouting and kicking. They threw him down. One held him while the other unzipped the bag and forced him into a canvas and leather straitjacket.

Her voice kind, Dr. Nilson said, "Mr. Green, I'm going to telephone Mr. Drummond, where you work. If you want to make a disturbance—to cry out for help, for example—you may do so. But it will make a poor impression on Mr. Drummond; I think you realize that."

She had picked up the handset and pressed numbers as she spoke. For a moment, the room fell silent as she listened to the instrument.

"This is Dr. Nilson, Mr. Green's doctor? May I speak to Mr. Drummond please? It's important.

"Mr. Drummond? Dr. Nilson. Mr. Green tells me you wanted him to bring you a letter to establish that he had seen me. I hope this call will do instead.

"Fine. I'm having Mr. Green hospitalized, Mr. Drummond. I don't believe that his problems are very serious, but after such an extended absence, I consider it advisable.

"I can't make a definite promise, Mr. Drummond. Perhaps around the end of the month, perhaps somewhat later.

"I don't know. My professional opinion is that he will be ready and able to return to work when he is released, but that's opinion, and not fact.

"Of course. Good-bye."

She hung up, and for the first time he was conscious of her perfume, a slight flowery fragrance more suited to a young girl. "Mr. Drummond asked me to convey his good wishes to you, and his hopes for a speedy recovery. You work for a very enlightened company, Mr. Green, one by no means oblivious, as so many are, to the demands of humanity. I hope you appreciate it. You will have heard me tell him that I believe your hospitalization need be only a short time, and that I expect you to be able to return to work upon your release. I said those things because you had wisely chosen to remain silent, a hopeful sign."

He said, "Thank you."

"I can't visit you every day in the hospital; my schedule is too crowded for that. But I will try to see you there three or four times a week. I hope to find you progressing, and I'm certain I shall." She nodded to the men, who helped him to his feet.

He said, "I don't think this is necessary."

"But I do, and you must defer to my opinion."

The words broke out, though he struggled to bite them back. *"This will keep me from finding Lara."*

"It will certainly prevent you from looking, Mr. Green. I hope that soon we'll be able to show you how pointless it is to look, just as it would be pointless to look for Cinderella."

One of the white-uniformed men said, "Come on," in a voice that was soft and even gentle. There was a tug on his arm.

He said, "All right," and as he spoke, the telephone rang.

Dr. Nilson picked the handset up. "Oh, hello, Lora . . . No, I'm not angry. I know how trying it can be."

They pulled him out of the office and closed the door firmly behind him. "Now *walk.*"

He did, down the stairs and out the back of the building. A small white ambulance—actually a van sporting red emergency lights—stood at the curb. One of the men opened the side door for him. He went in, and the man followed him. The other man got into the driver's seat.

When he sat down, the first man slapped him hard on his left ear, the blow like an explosion at the side of his head. "That's for kicking my knee," the man said. "I want you to know."

He could scarcely make out the words for the ringing that filled his head, but he nodded.

"We like it when they fight and yell," the man told him. "It's the yellers and the cussers that come out first—anybody tell you that. People like you still got some pepper in them, they don't just knuckle down, they say, hey, I'm gonna get *out* of this place. Only if you kick and hit, you're gonna get hit back."

He nodded again and said, "I understand."

"Only not 'cause I explained it to you. 'Cause I hit you, that's why."

"All right."

"Don't you kick me no more, and I won't hit you."

He asked, "Did you know Lora?"

"Dr. Nilson's receptionist? Sure."

"What was she like?"

The man shrugged. "White girl, so I didn't pay her a whole lot of attention. No big tits or anything like that. Once in a while you get white girls that like blacks, only not too often. We'd joke around a little. She wasn't stuck up."

"Was she beautiful?"

"She ain't gone."

"Yes, she is. She quit suddenly and cleaned out her desk."

The man looked skeptical. "Dr. Nilson had her on the phone when we left. Probably she'll come back."

He nodded and asked again, "Was she beautiful? Is she?"

"You want her to be, man?"

"I guess I do."

"Then she was. Like, big blues and one of those china-doll faces, you know?"

The driver said, "Green."

He answered, "Yes?" and the first man asked, "What you mean?"

"That Lora woman has green eyes, fool."

"Don't pay no mind to him," the first man said. "He's crazy. Now, you want out of that jacket?"

He had somehow expected that the hospital would be in the city. It was not, but in the suburbs, set among rolling lawns and beds of daffodils just coming into flower. The wind had a bite to it, yet was fresh and clean in a way winter winds never were. When he saw there were no bars on the windows, he said, "This doesn't look like a mental hospital."

"It isn't, man. It's just a regular hospital, and they do babies and triple bypasses and all like that. See, that way if people ask where you was, you can just tell them where like you was swearing in court, 'cause you might have had your appendix out. See?"

He nodded. They went inside, where one man talked briefly to a receptionist who motioned them toward an elevator. On the ninth floor (he was careful to note which button had been pushed) the same man conferred much longer with a nurse at a desk. When their conversation was over at last, the man said, "Now we gone take you to the lounge. I told her you'll stay there nice and not make no trouble. You do it, hear? 'Cause we got to leave you there and go on back."

He nodded again. He had nodded so often now that he had lost track of the number.

Although the lounge was clean, he missed the freshness of the spring wind. He tried to open both windows, but they would not open; when he examined their frames, he saw that the glass was very thick. There were seven varnished chairs in the room, and a low, varnished table supporting a stack of old magazines. After a time, it occurred to him that Lara's picture might be in one. He picked up a magazine and began to page through it.

He was on his third when a weary-looking bald man came in and sat down. "You like to read?" the bald man asked.

He shook his head.

"I do. I'd read all the time, if it weren't that my eyes give out. Then I have to go off and take care of my patients." The bald man chuckled.

"What do you read?"

"History, mostly. A little fiction. Of course I have to read the medical journals. We subscribe to *Newsweek, The New Yorker, Psychology Today,* and *Smithsonian.* My wife always reads them, and sometimes I do too."

He said, "I'd like to see some movie magazines. I don't suppose that impresses you very much."

"More than you might think," the bald man told him. "Most people don't read at all."

"Books always seemed like a waste of money to me."

"You're careful about money?"

"I try to be."

"But you're in the hospital, now. Hospitals are extremely expensive."

"The store's paying for everything," he explained. He felt a sudden thrill of fear. Was it?

The bald man got out a notebook and a Cross pen. "What day of the week is this?"

He tried to remember and could not. "Wednesday?"

"I'm not sure myself. Do you know the date?"

"April sixteenth."

"Do you know why the store's paying for your treatment?"

"That's the policy," he said.

"But why do they feel you need treatment?"

"Because I was gone so long, I guess. Nearly a month. No, over a month."

The pen danced over the notebook. Sunshine had come in the window; reflected on the pen's bright gold, it made it seem that it was the pen who spoke, and not the man. "I want you to cast your mind back, back for an entire week. Don't answer at once; shut your eyes and think back. Now, where were you a week ago?"

It was the day he had met Lara. "I was walking beside the river."

"In the park."

"Yes."

"Why were you there?"

"I'd brought my lunch. I ate it there on a bench, and I had fifteen minutes before I had to be back at the store." By way of explanation he added, "We're close to the park."

"You had worked in the store that morning?"

"Yes."

He was taken to a new room and made to undress and put on hospital clothes. A man in a white uniform took his own away in a wire basket.

After a while a nurse came in and gave him medicine.

· 24 ·

The Patient

There seemed to be things to do in the day room, but its games and pastimes were largely illusory. A cabinet on the west wall held half-a-dozen jigsaw puzzles, all with missing pieces—the basis for predictable jokes whenever someone got a puzzle out. The piano needed tuning; not that anyone in the ward could play more than "Chopsticks" anyway, though occasionally someone tried. The dog-eared cards in the drawer were short the ace, deuce, and four of hearts. The nurses guarded a container of Ping-Pong balls and usually said they were out of them to save trouble.

Or perhaps, he thought, they really were out. Perhaps the container was empty and had been so for years, as dusty within as without.

"Want to play some chess?"

GENE WOLFE

He looked up. The man with the board and box was short and middle-aged, with haystack hair.

"Some of the chessmen are gone," he said.

"We can use something else."

He nodded and went over to the table. They used checkers—two black checkers for the missing black pawns, and a red king for the missing white queen.

"White or black?"

He considered. In some vague fashion, the decision seemed enormously important. He studied the white queen and the black, trying to decide which was Lara. The white, of course. White for her complexion, red for her hair. "White."

His opponent spun the board. "Your move."

He nodded and pushed a pawn at random. The black queen's pawn advanced two squares. He moved his bishop. "Don't I know you?" he asked.

"I don't think so."

"Maybe we met awhile back," he said. He added, "Outside," though that did not seem quite right.

"Maybe," his opponent said. "I've been getting shock, know what I mean? It makes you forget stuff." He raised both hands to point to the inflamed marks at his temples. "You?"

"Not yet."

"But you're going to, huh?"

"I think so."

"It doesn't hurt. A lot of guys think it's going to, but it doesn't. Say, you've got the marks already."

When the game was over, his opponent sat at the piano and played an old-fashioned song, "Find Your True Love," singing to the out-of-tune music in a hoarse but not unpleasant voice. It was not until that night, when he lay in his narrow hospital bed with his hands in back of his head, that he placed his

206

opponent as the patient who had sent him to tell Walsh about—someone and someone else. He could not recall the names.

There was a woman with dyed hair and a long face who was deeply concerned about his attitude toward sex. There was an Indian who explained to him why it was so much easier to cure people who believed in demons. There was the tired middle-aged doctor, whose name he could sometimes remember, and there was Dr. Nilson, whose name he sometimes forgot.

Then there was grass to be cut and a garden to be weeded, lawns to be raked, and russet, brown, and deeply golden leaves to be burned. There was snow to be shoveled. They gave him a warm jacket and gloves for that, clothing donated by some kind person who had left empty .22 calibre brass in the pockets of the jacket.

Some nights he wondered what had happened to the hospital to which the van had taken him, and sometimes he felt sure he was back in United. Once he told a smooth Korean about United and Dr. Pille, and the smooth Korean, Dr. Kim, giggled.

There was an attendant who was kind to him but eventually, behind the boiler in the steam plant, wanted him to do something he did not want to do. It was then, while he was walking alone back to the main building, that it came to him that he was there for a memory that was, after all, no more than a dream.

At his next interview, he asked the Indian doctor whether they had ever found out what had happened to him while he was gone.

"Ah, but do not you yourself know?" the Indian inquired. "You can tell us, I think."

He shook his head and said it was all a blank, and watched

with satisfaction as the Indian doctor (also with satisfaction) made a note on his pad.

He had lost his apartment, but the store found him another one that was if anything better. His clothes and furniture had been put in storage, and it was pleasant to see the old things smile as they came out of their boxes and to arrange them in the new places. Because it was summer, he left some winter clothing boxed up. The apartment included storage space in the basement of his new building; he tagged the carton as the building manager instructed him, and together they put it into the storage room and relocked the door.

Some of the people he had known at the store had left; some remained. At Mr. Capper's urging—so he later learned—some of those who remained organized a welcoming dinner for him Tuesday night after work. His own dinner was free, the others chipping in enough to cover theirs and their share of his. It was not a big group as such things went—only a dozen diners and himself. Yet he was glad of it, and glad to find that he could remember the names of most of the people there.

At one point in the dinner, when most of them were through with their entrees and the waiters were waiting for the rest to finish so they could serve dessert, a woman who might have been Lara walked down the hallway outside their private dining room. It was as great temptation to say something or call out, but he did not. Later, when he excused himself to go to the bathroom, he kept his eyes open; but he did not look into the other private rooms, and he saw nothing.

The next day was his first real one back at work. He had been transferred out of Personal Computers—because personal computer sales were slacking off—back into Furniture and Major

Appliances. He was a little frightened until he dealt with his first customer, but she bought a sofa and a coffee table, and after that he was all right.

Bud van Tilburg was head of Furniture and Major Appliances, and thus his boss, whom he called Mr. van Tilburg and at whom he always smiled. It was not until several weeks had passed that he connected his transfer with Mr. van Tilburg's friendship with Mr. Drummond. Then he marched into Mr. van Tilburg's office and asked man-to-man if he was pulling his weight. Mr. van Tilburg punched up the figures for everybody in the whole department and showed him that he had outsold them all, had outsold the runner-up by well over a thousand dollars. "Getting you was the best break I've had in the past two years," Mr. van Tilburg said.

After that he tried even harder. When he had been in the department before, it had never occurred to him that you could learn about furniture just like you learned about computers and video games.

Yet it was so. There were various fabrics and stuffings, for example; and finishes and methods of construction. Not to mention the innumerable styles: Chippendale, Queen Anne, Early American, Traditional, Jacobean, Italian Renaissance and Italian Decadent, Henry IV, Louis XIII, and French Renaissance—on and on. He learned them all, checking books out of the library so he could study the pictures and memorize what the experts said about each. He learned to tell red oak from white, white oak from maple, maple from walnut, walnut from pecan, pecan from teak, and at last false rosewood from real Brazilian rosewood.

There came a day when he realized as he walked home that he

had sold something to every customer to whom he had spoken. It gave him a glow that lasted until he went to bed that night, and of which some trace remained even while he fixed his coffee and ate his sweet-roll the next morning.

He had to cross the park to reach his new apartment, but as far as he was concerned there were only two seasons—spring, during which the department carried lawn and patio furniture, and of course Christmas. Sometimes there were jonquils in the park, and sometimes there were chrysanthemums. Sometimes there was snow—no one ever seemed to shovel the park paths—and he wore the high, fleece-lined boots he had bought at discount in Men's & Women's Shoes and carried his working shoes in a brown paper bag.

Thus three Christmases came (in October) and went (in early December). One day in February he spoke for nearly an hour to a fat man of sixty or so who seemed to be interested in bookcases. The fat man left without buying anything, and as soon as he was gone Bridget Boyd came hurrying over from Small Appliances. "Do you know who that *was?*"

He shook his head.

"That was H. Harris Henry himself!" She sensed his lack of comprehension. "Our president, the honcho of the whole company. You must be in the stock plan."

He nodded.

"Then you get the annual report. Don't you even look at the pictures? You'd better start."

He decided he would not start; he had never felt the least inclination to read the thing, and now it was clearly too late. "You could have told me," he said.

"How could I? You were with him." She nibbled her lower lip. "If we ate our lunches together, I could fill you in on the Corporate Structure."

She pronounced it like that, with capitals, and he turned away.

A week later, an order came transferring him to Antiques in the uptown store. The new job carried a healthy raise but meant he had to ride a bus for twenty minutes, morning and night. In addition, he usually had to spend another twenty minutes waiting for a bus to come. The wait at the bus stop was miserably cold until April, and the buses were unbearably hot from June through August and most of September.

He liked the job, though he had immediately spotted several pieces on the floor as rank forgeries. When his customers asked about those he simply read the description on the tag, prefacing the reading with, "Well, it says." If he liked the customer, he might also shake his head slightly. Since the items in question were large and showy, they generally sold well enough even with his negative endorsement.

There was one particular piece he wanted himself, a small desk of unimpeachable pedigree that had begun its career nearly two hundred years ago in the service of a British sea captain. As well as he could judge, it had been built in India of native sandalwood, using milk-glass drawer pulls salvaged from a still earlier piece. Three of the drawers retained their original green-baize linings; and when he had nothing better to do, he liked to examine them, always feeling when he opened them he was going to find something in them that he had never found before, sometimes actually bending down to sniff the faded cloth. The old captain had kept his tobacco in the upper left drawer, he thought; the other odors were fleeting and deceptive —so much so that he was never certain he was not imagining them.

One night he dreamed he was actually sitting at that desk.

The floor moved beneath him, gently rocking, rising and falling with a motion he saw echoed ever so faintly in the well of black ink into which he dipped a feather pen. "My Dearest Heart," he wrote. "My good friend Captain Clough, of the *China Doll,* has promised to post this in England. She is a clipper, and so . . ."

There was a hail, and hurrying feet drumming the deck over his head. He sat up, and in a second or two he was laughing at himself, though there was something within him—some part that was still the old captain—that was not laughing.

The next day an ugly middle-aged woman made him show her the desk. "The chair's missing," he said. "It really ought to have the chair."

"That's all right," she told him. "I can get one made for it. It's simple enough."

He told her the price, trying to sound as though he thought it too high.

"Not bad," she said, poking and prying.

He lowered his voice. "They should take off three hundred in January."

The woman smiled, the smile of a cat that feels a bird in its claws. "Fine, have them send me a check."

When he had written the order and turned it in, he glanced up at the clock. The woman had used a store charge, and for a moment he dared to hope that the sale would not be approved.

It was ten till six, ten minutes until quitting time. Next week—only next week—the store would stay open till ten, and on alternate weeks he would have to come in at two and remain until ten. There would be temporaries who could not make change, and temporaries who had taken their jobs to steal. Not too many of either on his floor, thank God.

The first warning chime sounded.

At the second, he strolled into the Employees' Lounge to get some coffee. The windows were dark. He walked across to them, surprised that it had gotten dark so soon. They had gone off Daylight Savings, of course. He had forgotten.

People had been talking for weeks about what a beautiful fall they were having, about Indian Summer. It seemed to him, looking through the dark glass at the bent, hurrying figures on the sidewalk, that winter had arrived at last, and that it was likely to be a hard winter. He had a heavier coat, a long wool coat of a gray so deep it was almost black, put away somewhere. He reminded himself to get it out.

. 25 .

The Doll

The bus was as warm and stuffy as ever, and a brisk block-and-a-half walk from the bus stop to his building did no more than cool him off; by the time he had reached his apartment, he had wholly forgotten his decision. Next day the wind was gone and the weather was, or at least seemed, considerably warmer. The city was far enough south that really severe winter weather was exceptional.

Next week was the exception. Before it was over he had not merely remembered what he had meant to do, but actually cornered the custodian and demanded the carton he had left in storage.

"Got your woolies in it, huh?" The custodian chuckled. "Hope the moths ain't et 'em."

"That's right. I should have sealed it with tape."

The custodian nodded. "And sprinkled in some moth flakes.

That's what I'd a done." He was sorting through the two dozen keys he carried on his belt. "Here 'tis."

It would not fit the keyhole; he selected another. The third not only entered but turned the lock with a protesting click.

"When folks move out I always remind 'em about this place," the custodian said. "But if they got anything here they forget about it anyway. Lots of people have put stuff in here, but you're the only one I recollect that ever wanted something out. No." He paused, one hand on the knob, and raised a finger of the other. "Miz Durkin got that old dress of her sister's out, that she was going to give her friend. Only the friend didn't like it, and it went back the next day."

They entered, and the custodian pulled a string to turn on the light. The room was nearly full. "See what I mean? Pretty soon I have to throw a lot of the old stuff out. Only I don't want to—you know somebody's goin' to say I stole. 'Course I won't throw out anythin' that belongs to somebody still lives here."

He nodded, trying to recall the carton. Had it been from a grocery?

"Don't see it, huh?"

"No," he said. "Not yet."

"Might be in back of this, or under it. I just put this in about a month ago." The custodian tugged at a large suitcase, and after a moment he helped, moved by pity for the old man's feebleness. As they shifted the suitcase, it struck him that it had been a long time since he had felt pity for anyone except, perhaps, himself.

His carton had indeed been under the suitcase. He picked it up, thanked the custodian, and carried it to the elevator. While he waited, it occurred to him that the custodian had as much right to be considered an antique as the desk he had lost; that just as the desk had been older than most desks, so the custodian was older than most men. Yet nobody cared, no one would make the least effort to save the old custodian from the flames of the crematorium. Eventually, he thought, old people will be preserved like old furniture. Collectors will cry to think of the things we've thrown out.

The elevator doors opened, and he dropped the thought down the shaft while he got the carton inside and pushed the button. Now that he had the carton—it was one of the movers', of course—he was no longer certain it contained winter clothing, though he had no notion of what it might contain instead. He tried to recall the day he had moved from the YMCA. He had not owned an overcoat then, he felt sure; he had worn his windbreaker to work that winter, keeping his suit-coat in his locker.

When he shouldered open the door of his apartment, nothing seemed familiar; it was as though someone had moved his sofa and chairs, his very rooms, while he had been at work. His living room had doubled to become an *L*; his kitchen had grown as if its stainless sink and Formica counter had been mixed with yeast.

He put the carton on the floor. His fireplace was gone—he could not understand how that could have happened. He recalled lying there in front of the fire, drinking brandy with somebody, with some girl, a woman. Had the fireplace really belonged to the woman? No, not a woman—she had said so. Had she taken it with her when she left? That was impossible.

There had been another apartment, of course, an apartment in which he had lived before this one but after the *Y*. Strange that he could recall moving out of the *Y* so well but could not remember moving into this place at all.

He had been ill. He had forgotten that. Or to be honest, had been pushing that out of his mind. No doubt the company had transferred him to the uptown store so he would be among people who didn't know about his breakdown.

Not that they hadn't found out soon enough. He remembered the girl from Better Dresses asking him when he had sat next to her at the picnic. It had been a mistake; she had been like all the rest, a single woman looking frantically for the kind of man who would never consider her if she found him, a handsome, wealthy, athletic college man who was sensitive, intelligent, cultured, and completely blind to what she was.

He laughed softly to himself.

And yet was he any better? Yes, he thought. Yes, I am. I'm willing to admit what I am.

But what am I? Surely not God, and it was God who said, "*I am.*" He remembered that, but he could not remember how he knew it; it might have been in one of those Biblical epics, Charlton Heston turning back the Red Sea.

He hung up his topcoat, his jacket, and his tie and put on water for coffee; his feet hurt, as they did at the end of each day. While he pulled off his shoes, he found himself wondering whether there was any brandy left—not from then, not from that night. He could not remember when it had been, but it had been a long time ago.

The built-in cabinet in the living room held half a bottle of rum. He could not recall buying it and thought it might have been left by another tenant, but it reminded him of the captain he had been for one night, and the captain's desk. He stirred an inch of rum into the mug of instant he prepared for himself, on top of the cream and sugar.

The carton was tied with heavy cord. He carried his coffee back into the kitchen, got out the large knife he sometimes used to slice onions, and sharpened it.

For a moment he waited, fingering the edge, sipping his rum and coffee, smiling a little. There was a pleasant excitement in not knowing what might be in the carton or even if it was his at all. The custodian was old and might easily (he told himself) have fastened his tag on the wrong container. He looked through his tape collection for an appropriate one to put on the stereo, and settled in the end for *The Music of Christmas,* moved by a dim recollection of opening boxes beneath the tree as a child. Soon, very soon, the store would play carols all the time, and he would join the other retail-sales associates in complaining about them; but tonight it seemed to him that he should listen to Christmas now, that he should hear it again before the store destroyed it, with everything it had once meant.

> *Adeste, fideles,*
> *Laeti triumphantes;*
> *Venite, venite in Bethlehem.*

He cut the string and flipped back the cardboard flaps. A thick sweater-vest lay on top. He picked it up and admired it; it was of that light brownish tan they called camel, thick and soft, with a V-neck and buttons up the front—just the thing, he told himself, to keep the wind from his chest while he waited for the bus. As he searched it for its labels, he congratulated himself on remembering these things.

It was a Medium, which should fit him well. A second label announced that it was one hundred percent virgin wool, that it should be dry-cleaned only, and that it had been made in Toronto—that would be Canada, he thought. He carried it to the closet and hung it with his topcoat and jacket.

When he had pulled the sweater from the carton, he had been

careful not to look at the next item. Now he rubbed his hands in anticipation as he returned to it for his second discovery.

It was a pair of gloves, gloves of soft dark leather lined with fur. Never worn—the store's price-tag still dangled from the plastic cord that bound the two together. He cut it, pulled them on, and punched the air, although he had never boxed. They fit him perfectly, and he imagined himself playing the piano in them, although he could not really play the piano. The stereo had launched into *Silent Night;* he accompanied it on a magical instrument that always put the right keys under his fingers. It would be useless to put the gloves in the pockets of his topcoat, since he was hoping for a warmer coat from the carton. After considering the matter, he pulled them off and put them on the bar of the hanger that held his jacket.

Next was a long, knit muffler of bark brown, and under it the overcoat he had remembered. He took them from the carton, thrust his arms in the wide sleeves of the coat, and wound the muffler about his neck. Both seemed to exude palpable warmth. He went into his bedroom and stood before the mirror to button the overcoat, which fit just loosely enough for him to be sure it would be perfect with a jacket under it. While feeling its thickly napped material with his hands, he discovered that there was something in one of the side pockets.

It was a map. Too warm already, he took off the coat and laid it on his bed, seated himself beside it, and opened the map on his knees.

The area depicted seemed to be heavily forested and almost without roads, traversed mostly by narrow blue streams marked with rapid after rapid. Its highest elevation was Mt. Hieros; judging from its white center, Mt. Hieros was capped with snow. There was nothing to indicate where either the mapped tract or its mountain might be. Straggling letters stretching from one corner of the map to the opposite corner spelled OVERWOOD.

He shook his head, refolded the map, and tossed it onto his dresser for further study after dinner. He had not been to the Italian place in a long time. It had been conveniently near his old apartment—the neighborhood of his old apartment had returned to his mind vividly now—but it was ten blocks or more from this one, and he had not relished the walk. Now he found that he was not only hungry but eager to test his reclaimed winter clothing against the wind. He put on his second-best shoes, the sweater-vest, his jacket, and the gloves, added the muffler, and last of all wrapped himself in the long, dark overcoat.

Outside, the wind refused to cooperate. It had vanished with the daylight, leaving a clear cold night in which the air seemed to stand upon shelves of glass, like crystal goblets in Fine China. He hurried along admiring the ghostly plume of his own breath, his body warm, his cheeks nipped by frost.

Mama Capini was still there, and she remembered him, though he scarcely remembered her. She welcomed him back and presented him with a straw-cushioned bottle of Chianti on the house. He ordered lasagna, drank several glasses of the wine, and collided full-tilt with another patron as he was leaving.

The accident was only an embarrassment; he apologized, the stolid middle-aged man he had bumped told him to think nothing of it, and it was over. Yet it made him aware that there was something in the breast pocket of his overcoat, something long and hard and irregularly shaped. His first guess was that it was another bottle, his second that it was a gun; but it seemed oddly made for either. When he took off one glove and explored the object with his fingers, he felt fur, as though some small, unbending animal were standing on its hind legs in his breast pocket. In the glow of good food and wine it did not seem to matter.

The glow was largely gone by the time he had returned to his building, and he found he was as childishly anxious about the contents of the pocket as he had been about the contents of the carton. He laid the coat carefully on the sofa and stood what remained of the Chianti on the lowest shelf in the door of his refrigerator before he took out the oddly shaped object of which he had been so conscious on the walk home.

It was a doll. He carried it to the light to examine more closely; what he had thought fur was soft brown hair—real human hair, it seemed. Beneath the hair was a piquant face, at once beautiful and impertinent: a woman—a girl—with long legs and a slender waist, jutting breasts, rounded hips, and staring hazel eyes. She wore a belted, sleeveless smock of metallic green; it was her only garment, as he determined by an embarrassed glance.

Why had he owned such a thing? Or had he owned it at all? Although the coat and gloves had fit him, it seemed more than possible that they had not been his; he was of about average size, after all. He had never had a daughter, he felt certain. He had never even been married. Surely he would remember that.

No, how simple it was! He must have dated a divorcée. He had gotten the doll, probably in Toys at the employee discount, to give to her little girl; no doubt Christmas had been coming then, as it was coming now. Then he and this woman had broken off, and he had put away the coat without emptying its pockets.

He took the doll into his bedroom and laid it on the map—something else to think about later.

Much to his surprise, he did think about it later. Finding himself unable to follow the Midnight Movie, he brought the doll into the living room again and cradled it in his hands as though it were a child, haunted by the feeling that he too was on TV, that he owed his whole existence to some set playing to an empty room, that he and the doll were lost, were the lost children in the woods in the story his mother had let him watch when he was very small so long ago.

He snuffled and was ashamed, amused, and heartbroken all at once; without his knowledge or consent, his eyes had filled with tears. He pulled out his handkerchief, blew his nose, and wiped his eyes. But a tear dotted the green smock, another fell upon the graceful little legs, and a third plashed full in the doll's piquant face.

And the doll moved like a living girl in his hand.

. 26 .

The Mad Tea Party

He nearly dropped it.

"Hello." The doll sat up, or at least, sat up as well as it could, its hips resting in the palm of his left hand. "Hi, I'm Tina." The wide hazel eyes blinked slowly, then focused on his face.

One final tear fell, wetting Tina's hair.

"I belong to you," Tina said. "I'm *your* doll, and I can talk." Her voice was almost too high for him to hear, as high as the chirp of a cricket, he thought, or the twitter of bats. "If you want to have a tea party, I can help you set the table."

He nodded, more to himself than to her, and said, "Would you like some tea?"

"Yes, please," the doll answered formally. "I would like some tea very much."

He nodded again. "Can you walk?"

223

"I can walk, but it might be better if you carried me. You can carry me like a baby if you like." She seemed to sympathize with his expression of dismay. "Or I can ride on your shoulder. That's the best way of all. You see, if I walk we'll go pretty slowly, because my legs are so small. And if you stepped on me, I might break."

He nodded solemnly and put the doll on his right shoulder, where she held the top of his collar with one tiny hand. "Don't go too fast, and I'll be fine."

He said, "I'll try not to." He blew his nose again, being careful not to move his head, and wiped his cheeks.

"Why were you crying?"

"Seeing you reminded me of somebody else, of somebody I'd forgotten." He hesitated, not sure what he had said was fair to Lara. "Or at least that I'd put out of my mind." As he stood up, moving as slowly and smoothly as he could, he added, "Dolls don't talk here, or anyway, not as well as you."

There was no reply.

He went into the kitchen. Most of the water he had heated for coffee remained in the pan, but it was cold now and scummed with lime. He threw it out, put in fresh water, and turned on the burner again. There were tea bags in the canister, the remnants of a box of exotic teas he had bought (in Gourmet Foods, at the discount) for an assistant manager in Lingerie but never given her.

"I don't know if I've got a cup small enough for you," he said.

He settled on a demitasse cup, pushed the tea bag into it, and doused it with boiling water.

Tina said, "May I talk?"

"Sure, why not?"

"You said I wasn't supposed to. But I like just a teeny-weeny pinch of salt in my tea."

He passed the saltcellar over it. "That enough? You take sugar?"

"No, thanks," Tina chirped. "No milk either." She bounced from his shoulder like a tennis ball and stood, legs wide, on the dinette table to drink from the cup. It was as big for her as a wastebasket would have been for him.

When she put it down, it seemed to him that it was as full as it had ever been, but she patted her midriff and wiped her mouth on the back of one bare arm. "Now if you'll just leave it there, I could come and get some whenever I wanted to."

That seemed no crazier than talking to a doll. "All right," he said.

"And I won't have to bother you. I'm really not very good at doing things for myself. I couldn't have turned on the water like you did."

He nodded.

"Well, I can do things *a little.*"

He asked, "Can you tell me how a doll can talk?"

"Because I'm built that way. It's my insides." She patted her middle again. "But I can't add or subtract or spell or any of that other stuff. I haven't been to school."

He nodded again.

"I'd like some nice clothes. Have you got any?"

"Not that would fit you," he told her.

"I'd like a ball gown, just to start. And a vanity set, so I can do my hair."

"It's too late tonight," he told her. "I'll get you some things tomorrow." He was confident that tomorrow she would be gone, or at least inanimate and silent.

"And I'd like a bra and panties. I'd like two of each, so I can wear one and wash one."

"I'll see what I can do."

225

GENE WOLFE

"One pair could be fawn, and the other pair could be ginger. That way we could tell which I'd worn last. And a nightie. Can I sleep with you?"

"If you don't snore," he told her.

"I don't. You can't even hear me breathing." She threw out her chest as though to prove she did indeed breathe, tiny, conical breasts pushing impatiently against the metallic fabric of her smock. "Tomorrow night I'll put up my hair, if you get me rollers. It would be better if you carried me, remember?"

He asked, "What if you want some tea in the middle of the night?"

"I won't," Tina chirped. "But if I did, I could come out and get it without waking you up. You wouldn't have to worry about stepping on me then. Besides, I can move faster now."

He picked her up and replaced her on his shoulder. "Is that what you work on? Tea?"

"Sometimes silly children want us to drink more tea than we can hold."

"I won't do that," he promised. He recalled something a bartender had once told him, and added, "If you don't want it, don't drink it."

"I like you. We're going to have a lot of fun."

"Not now," he said. "Right now I'm going to take a shower, and then I'm going to bed."

"I could have a bath in the washbowl while you're taking your shower."

"All right."

"All you have to do is turn on the water for me. Not very hard. Not very hot, either."

"All right," he said again. He pulled up the chrome handle that stoppered the bowl, and adjusted the hot and cold knobs to produce a thin stream of tepid water.

226

Tina hopped from his shoulder. "Can I use your soap?"

"Sure." He took off his shirt and tossed it in the hamper as he always did. Tina had skinned out of her metallic green smock; she had no pubic hair, but her breasts were tipped with minute pink nipples.

He turned his back to remove his trousers, and when he went into the bedroom to hang them up and get his pajamas, he debated putting on the bottoms before he returned to the bathroom. It would be useless, since he would have had to take them off again immediately.

Tina had worked up a fine lather in the washbowl. He asked if the water was too hot.

"No, it's fine. Could you give me a drop of shampoo?"

He did, tilting the bottle just enough to pour a single emerald drop into her cupped hands.

As soon as he closed the shower door, he felt certain she would be gone when he came out. Perhaps the basin would be full of water; perhaps not. He made the spray colder and revolved beneath it, grunting because he wanted to shout.

"I'm going to use one of these little towels, okay?"

"Sure." His next appointment with Dr. Nilson was Tuesday. Five days. He wondered whether he should call her now; she had given him her home number, though he had never used it. As he thought about that, the memory of a disheveled man in hospital pajamas playing an out-of-tune piano returned with such force that he seemed to see and hear it, seemed to feel the unyielding wood of the bench upon which he had once sat.

> When you find your true love,
>   When you see her eyes,
> When you've left your new love,
>   At the end of lies . . .

Tina was singing as she dried herself, singing in a voice sweet and yet so high that at times it soared beyond audibility, singing to the tune of the cracked old piano someone had donated to the hospital. No, he could not call Dr. Nilson. He couldn't even mention Tina when he went on Tuesday.

He reached for a towel.

In bed Tina said, "I can sleep on top of the covers. But it would be better if I slept under them. I'd stay warmer."

He lifted the blankets for her, and she snuggled beside him. After a time he said, "How old are you, Tina?" He could just see her in the faint light leaking past the blind.

The doll turned over and yawned theatrically, an elfin hand covering her mouth, a tiny arm stretching above her head. "How old are *you?*"

He told her, then added a year. "My birthday was last month. I'd forgotten."

"That's *old.*"

"I know," he said.

"I don't think you're *that* old. I'm not."

"I didn't think you were."

"What did you get for your birthday?"

"Nothing. I really didn't pay any attention to it."

"Didn't Mama and Daddy give you anything?"

He shook his head. "My mother's been dead for a long time, and I haven't seen my father for ten or twelve years."

"But he still loves you."

"No, he doesn't. He never did."

"Yes, he does."

"Tina, you've never met him."

"I know about Daddies, though. And you don't."

"All right," he said, strangely comforted.

228

"What did you give him for *his* birthday?"

The question surprised him; he had to think for a moment. "Nothing. I never do."

"You could give him a big kiss."

"I don't think he'd like that."

"Yes, he would. I'm right and you're wrong."

"Perhaps," he said.

"Next birthday, what would you like?"

He told her about the desk.

"I think you should get that for your next birthday. I'll tell Daddy."

"It's been sold already."

"Maybe the lady would sell it, too."

He nodded to himself. "Maybe she would. Would you like some more tea, Tina?"

"Yes!"

He threw back the covers, rose, and switched on the light. By a route he could not quite follow, Tina leaped from the bed to the dresser. "Is your tea set in here?"

"I don't have a tea set," he told her. "Not yet, anyway. I was looking for this check book."

"I can't read. I haven't been to school."

"I'll read it for both of us," he said. "I've got thirty-two hundred dollars. That's more than the desk cost."

"You should have bought it."

"You're right. Now let's have some tea and talk about it. Do you think she'd sell it at a profit? Where do you think it ought to go?"

"Not facing the TV." Tina hopped onto his shoulder. "So you'll do your school work."

"Not in a corner," he told her. "I hate things in corners. Against the window."

"All right!"

He turned up the burner under the pan of water, rinsed out Tina's demitasse cup, and found a cup, a saucer, and a spoon for himself. There were only three tea bags left in the canister. "I'll have to get more tea tomorrow," he said.

"You sure will."

"Tina, do you know a girl named Lara?"

"I don't know anybody but you."

"You remind me of her. I used to be in love with Lara—that's why I bought you. Lara was the woman in front of the fireplace."

"I don't think you told me about that."

"But I lost her, somehow. I lost her walking through the snow."

"You have to dress really warm for a bluskery day."

He nodded. "I bought the coat, and some other things. I got some money, somehow, and I put it in the bank. That's where most of the thirty-two hundred's from."

"Maybe Lara gave it to you," Tina ventured.

"No," he said. And then, "Yes, maybe she did."

· 27 ·

The Desk

"I'd like to talk to you about it," he said. "That's all."

The ugly woman's voice crackled from the earpiece. "We're talking now."

"I'd rather do it face to face. I could come out to your house any evening that's convenient."

Suspiciously: "Isn't it genuine?"

He inhaled deeply, wanting to lie—and found he could not. "It's perfectly genuine, I'm sure. But it's Indian, even though it was made in the British style. Indian things don't command high prices, as a rule."

"Well, whatever you want to tell me about it, you're going to have to say here and now. Then perhaps we'll meet face to face, if I decide we should."

"Mrs. Foster," (this time he positively gulped for air) "I can offer you a five-hundred-dollar profit."

There was a long pause. "If it's genuine, why should you people want it back?"

"I'm not calling for the store," he told her. "I want to buy it myself."

"You've found out it's worth more than they thought."

"No," he said. "No, not at all." He waited for her to say something; she did not, and he was forced to speak again to fill the silence. "I think that when you bought it I told you I felt it was overpriced. I still do. I study the auction catalogues and follow the results, Mrs. Foster. It's part of my job."

"Go on."

"A piece not much different from your desk went for only a little more than half what you paid, two years ago in New York."

"But you'll give me a five-hundred-dollar profit."

Hope surged. "Yes," he said.

"You'll pay me more than twice what it's worth."

"Yes," he said again.

"Why?"

He tried to speak, but no words came. At last he said lamely, "I don't know if I can explain."

"I'm listening."

"I sell these things . . ."

"You've got a buyer?"

"No, no. I don't mean I'm a dealer myself on the side—I couldn't do that and keep my job. I only meant that I sell the things here, in the store."

"I know that. You sold me this desk. I'm sitting at my desk right now, as it happens. This is where I put the phone."

"I never wanted a piece for myself." He felt that he was talking into a void, pleading with a soulless thing of wire and plastic far less human than Tina. "I'd check out a particular piece, you know—"

"Don't say, 'you know.' It's the one thing I absolutely cannot stand."

"I'm sorry."

"So am I. Go on, Mr. Green."

"I was just trying to say I'd look at a certain piece and think that it was nice—or really not so nice. Or at one like your desk and think that it was a good piece but I wouldn't have priced it quite so high. I've seen hundreds of pieces like that, I suppose, but I never saw anything except your desk that I really wanted for myself."

Again she left him floundering.

"I thought they'd mark it down after Christmas, and then maybe I'd take it." .

She grunted. "You told me you thought it would be lower in January, and you suggested I come back then—when you planned to buy it for yourself. It would have been gone."

Desperately he continued, "I hadn't decided to buy it then. Really I hadn't. Not firmly—I thought I wouldn't. It wasn't until it was gone—"

"That you realized how much you wanted it."

"Yes," he said. "That's right."

"Do you know, Mr. Green, I've felt the same way myself a time or two. May I ask how your wife feels about your spending so much money?"

"I don't have a wife."

"You're divorced?"

"I've never been married, Mrs. Foster."

"Marriage isn't for everyone. Why, I know several men, the nicest, kindest—"

"I'm not gay, Mrs. Foster." He knew that he had lost, and he wanted to hang up. "Once a girl even lived with me for a few days, but I've never married." He made one final effort. "I've got thirty-two hundred dollars. That's every cent I have in the world, and that's why I said I'd give you a five-hundred-dollar profit. I'll make it a thousand if you'll take the second five hundred in installments."

Silence again, stretching on and on; this time he did not speak, and at last she said, "I'm president of the Collectors' Club. Did you know that, Mr. Green?"

"No. No, I didn't, Mrs. Foster. I know about your club, of course."

"We're *serious* collectors, Mr. Green. And I will not sell this desk."

There was a metallic click as she hung up. He hung up too. The desk was gone. He tried tiredly to guess her age: fifty or fifty-five, perhaps. Perhaps there would be an estate sale in twenty years or so. No, she was the kind of woman who hung on forever. He could get her address, as he had her number, from Accounting. He could write her and suggest that she contact him if she ever wanted to sell the desk; but it would do no good.

"Staying late, Green?" It was Mr. Cohen, the Art Gallery supervisor.

"Had to make a phone call, sir. It took a while, I guess. How about you, sir?"

"Getting set for Christmas. You know, firelight, candles, and snow."

The images danced through his mind as he walked to the bus stop: snow—candles—firelight—children and other gifts under the tree. The headline of the paper in the vending machine was SUICIDE RATE CLIMBS.

If I'd made the world, he thought, Christmas would be a good time for everybody.

Quite suddenly he recalled that he had promised Tina a tea set, new clothes, all sorts of things. He left the bus stop and walked down to the arcade, an old-fashioned sort of mall he had sometimes peered into, but never entered.

Old-fashioned or not, the arcade had already gone over to extended hours. More than half of its little shops were bright, and shoppers bundled against the cold stamped up and down the clangorous iron walkways. He passed a travel agency, a beauty salon, and a chiropractor's office, the last dark. A toy store—in both senses of the word, for it was hardly larger than the make-believe stores given to children—provided dresses that he thought might fit Tina and a minute tea set of real china.

"I don't suppose you have any tea?"

The clerk shook her head. "There's a deli. I don't know if they're open, but they might be."

He nodded. "Where?"

"In the annex. Know where that is? Down that way, and the entrance is on your left. Only one level in the annex."

He thanked her and went out. When he reached the entrance, its arch of moldering marble looked dark and somehow ominous, as though all the stores beyond were closed and gates of steel bars might slam down behind anyone who dared to enter.

He went in anyway. A few shops were open even here. As he passed a haberdashery, a small, dark woman darted out and caught him by the sleeve. "There you are! What's the matter with you, you don't want your pants?"

He stared at her. She was sixty or so, graying hair knotted at the nape of her neck. "I think—"

"You think I'm trying to sell you something. Listen, your pants are all paid for. You paid so we'd make the alterations, remember? So how about picking them up? I need the space. Be an angel."

"All right," he said. As he followed her in, he felt that he should remember both the woman and her shop.

"With the pants, I got you a nice varnished hardwood hanger. Last you the rest of your life." She glanced at the yellow tag pinned to its paper dust cover. "Four months now they've been waiting."

"I'm sorry," he said.

"Oh, it's okay." She was studying his waistline. "They might not still fit. Bring them back if they don't, and we'll let them out."

"This is the hotel, isn't it? The Grand Hotel?"

She looked at him quizzically. "We rent from them."

"This is where Fanny worked in the coffee shop. This is where Dr. Applewood has his office."

The woman said, "He's dead now."

He nodded and walked out into the cavernous lower level. Why hadn't he recognized those dusty flags at once, the clawed griffin, the eagle with two heads? And the woman in the toy shop had said the annex had only a single level. There were balconies. Dr. Applewood had leaned over one of those railings to call to him.

He saw the doors to the elevator—the elevator that would take him to the Grand Hotel, the hotel that was so much nearer Lara. He started toward them, slowing as he felt the chill of fear. In the hotel he would have no money and no friends, not even Tina. If he ever found Lara, she would see only a silly middle-aged man. Yes, he was middle-aged now, and it was better to face it. Lara would see a silly man carrying dolls' clothes, a doll's tea set, and slacks that were probably too small for him by a couple of inches.

His finger pressed the buzzer.

The elevator did not come at once, and indeed did not come for a long time. He waited, squaring his shoulders, adjusting the bag from the toy store and the paper-shrouded slacks; and at last the doors slid back.

He stepped in. "Ground floor, please."

Slowly and distinctly, the operator announced, *"This* is the ground floor."

He recalled stepping through a doorway and out into a snow-covered parking lot—the ground floor. "The lobby level, then."

"There's nobody there."

"Take me there anyway," he said.

The elevator rose slowly and smoothly, and it came to him that there was nothing of the Grand Hotel's wire cage about it. When the doors separated, they revealed the deserted lobby of an office building, a lobby a floor above the street. He stepped out and said, "Thanks," then watched the doors close behind him. The world he saw from the windows of the lobby was his own, he felt certain. United and North were not there, and if Lara came it was only briefly and temporarily, to live with some fortunate man or to store her coat.

He should have watched the furrier's; just as the cold had reminded him of this wool overcoat, it would have made Lara (if Lara were here) get her coat out of storage. He had forgotten, and it was too late now.

He went back to the elevator and pushed the buzzer just as he had before. Now the elevator was his only hope; yet he knew the hope was vain.

"I get it," the operator said. "You wanted to use the john. There's some downstairs too—if you'd asked me I could have told you."

He nodded, not speaking, waiting for the doors to open.

"Sometimes kids want to go up, you know? I don't let 'em. I could tell you were okay."

The doors slid apart, and he was in a wide low room without flags. Most of the shops were dark. He went out into the main arcade, drawing up his muffler around his neck and buttoning the topmost button of the overcoat.

The street was dark, empty of everything save the wind. A prowl car went by fast, cops staring threats at vacant doorways. The wind cut his fingers to remind him that he had forgotten to put on his gloves. He set his parcels down on the icy sidewalk and took the gloves from the pockets of the overcoat, pulled each on carefully and fastened its cuff. There was enough tea for tonight at any rate; he could buy more tomorrow if Tina was real. If Tina was really there.

Another bus stop, one stop nearer his apartment, would be nearly as close as his usual one. As he walked toward it, he discovered to his surprise that he was happy. It took him half a block to find the source of his happiness in the knowledge that Lara was real even if Tina was not.

She might laugh at him; she probably would; he laughed at himself, now and then. But he would rather listen to her laugh than to anything that anyone else in either world might say. On television, some woman had mentioned that wild dogs did not bark, that tame ones barked in imitation of human speech. What was the talk of anyone else, of Bridget Boyd or H. Harris Henry, but an animal's imitation of Lara's voice, of the laughter of the goddess? Though she would surely reject him as a lover, would she reject him as a servant? If she did, he would become her slave.

A glance behind him showed a bus coming down the street. Hurrying, he got to the stop just as it pulled up.

It was not until he had risen to get off that he remembered he would have to tell Tina. She would be there, waiting for him in the living room, hiding among the sofa cushions in the place she called her secret fort; she would pop out when she heard his key in the lock. He would have to admit to her then that he had not been able to buy the desk.

Already the taste of failure was bitter in his mouth.

· 28 ·

The Story

" 'm *good* at looking for stuff," Tina said. When his expression betrayed his skepticism, she added, "Yes I am! And I don't like to watch TV."

"Neither do I," he told her mildly. "But at night there's not much else to do."

"There's looking, and you could read me a story while I do it."

"You could listen to the TV," he said. "That would be the same thing." It was not until he had finished speaking that he realized he had conceded Tina's ability as a searcher—probably much too soon.

"It isn't the same thing at all."

He had already turned down the volume; now he switched the television off. "Why not?"

"Reading would help you in school."

"I don't have to go to school any more."

Tina stamped, impatient with his stupidity; the sound was like the tapping of a fingernail. "You'll have to go back next year. It will help you then."

"All right," he said.

"Besides, you would be reading me *stories*. TV's just—just talk to use up the time."

He nodded. It was something that he had felt as well, but never expressed.

"What does it look like?"

He took out his wallet and showed her a dollar bill and a five. "Like these, except for the pictures. They'll be women's pictures instead of men's." He paused. Women and men thought different things important; it was something he had understood half his life, because of his job. Now it seemed to him that it might be important in itself: women would not care as much about cars; women would care far more about children's loneliness, and their education. Women in power might even see to it that there were dolls like Tina.

"Pictures of ladies," she prompted him.

"Really it doesn't matter. Pieces of paper that look like this. Money." He found he associated the money with the smell of roses, though he could not have said why. He was not certain there had been much left—but if he found Lara's world again, even a few dollars might be useful.

"I'll start by looking under things. I'm built for that. When I'm through, I'll need a bath. Then you'll have to pull out the drawers for me, so I can get inside."

He protested that he could look in drawers as well as she could.

"No, you can't," she told her. "I can go inside and poke around. It's not the same at all. Now read me a story while I look under the dresser."

241

He had fewer than a dozen books, all of them inherited from his mother, and little idea what might be in any. At random he pulled a faded red volume from the shelf and flipped through it until he discovered what appeared to be the beginning of a fresh narrative.

"Once upon a time," he read, "there were two brothers who lived by themselves in a little house deep in the Black Forest. Their names were Joseph and Jacob, and Jacob was blind."

Tina emerged from beneath the dresser pushing a dust ball almost as large as herself and coughing histrionically. "You don't dust under here *nearly* enough," she said. "I don't think you do it *at all.*"

"Joseph took good care of his brother, and Jacob did all he could to help, and because they loved each other they were very happy."

"I'll look under the bed now," Tina announced. "Then you'll have to go into the living room so I can look in there."

"But they had little money, and their situation became more precarious every year."

"It's dusty under here, too." Tina's voice sounded faint and hollow.

"Because so much snow falls in the Black Forest during the winter, making it a white forest for whole months at a time, the brothers had to buy enough food in autumn to last until spring. And after several years had gone by, there came an autumn when it could be seen that they could not."

Tina called, "Here's a button. A shiny one!"

He decided she must have spun around with it as a full-sized woman would have thrown a discus; it came flying out like a bullet.

"One day Jacob said, 'Joseph, do you recall how beautifully I used to write?' And when Joseph replied, 'Indeed I do!' Jacob showed him a frame he had made to hold a sheet of paper, a frame with violin strings stretched across it and spaced so that a man might barely have thrust his thumb between them."

"Here's a dime!" The dime shot out like the button and rolled until it struck the wall.

"'With this,' Jacob explained, 'and you, dear brother, to sharpen my pen for me now and then, I can write just as I used to. Perhaps the *Schwarzwald Gazette* will take one of my tales. Then we'll be able to buy more food for the winter.'"

"That's all there is under there," Tina told him, "except for a lot more dust. Don't I look like a chimney sweep?"

In fact she looked like a long-lost toy that had just been found and was about to be thrown away because it would be too much trouble to clean it, but he nodded and smiled, and followed her docilely into the living room.

"So Joseph sharpened a gray goose-quill with Jacob's little knife. He put paper into the frame and made sure there was ink in the inkwell. That done, he went about his work, leaving his brother alone to write."

"Nothing under the couch or the big chair but a lot more dust," Tina reported. "Now take me into the bathroom and run some warm water into the bowl. It would be better if you left it running."

He put his hand down so she could step into the palm and did as she asked. When he was seated on the lid of the commode with the red book open on his lap, he noticed that the light was actually better in the bathroom than it had been in the bedroom and the living room.

No one reads anymore, he thought, but men still shave.

"But when Joseph returned, there were only a few words on Jacob's paper, and Jacob was drumming his fingers on the table. 'I can't write,' he said. 'I used to look out of the window to write.

243

Then I had no difficulty. But now . . .' Jacob lifted his shoulders and let them fall."

Tina pointed to her hair, not wanting to interrupt the story. He poured out a drop of shampoo for her.

"'Perhaps I could look out of the window for you, dear brother,' Joseph suggested.

"Jacob nodded slowly. 'It's worth trying. Look outside and tell me what you see.'

"So Joseph looked, but there were only trees waving their arms in the wind. 'Hmm,' he said.

"Jacob smiled. 'I always felt the same way myself,' he said."

Tina asked, "Felt what way?"

He pulled at his jaw, scratched his ear. "As if there was nothing going on, I guess. And yet, so much going on—so many things that it was hard to choose."

"Uh huh, that must be it. Read some more."

"Joseph saw how silently the blue shadows crept across the hoarfrost beside the trees. 'I see a black wolf,' he said, and Jacob's pen flew faster than the wind. Joseph tiptoed away as quietly as he could."

He paused and glanced at Tina, who was rinsing her hair in the trickle from the tap. "I can hear," she told him. "Don't stop."

"When he came back next time, Jacob was waiting. 'You must look outside again, I fear,' Jacob said.

"So Joseph looked out. A bright bird fluttered above the brambles. 'I see an enchanted princess picking blackberries,' he told Jacob. 'An enchanted princess with wings,' he added after a moment, and Jacob's pen flew faster than the bird."

Tina was drying herself with Kleenex. "Do you think the *Schwarzwald Gazette* will buy Jacob's story?"

He nodded. "I'm sure they will. It's such a good one."

"So am I," Tina said. "Now read some more."

"Soon Jacob's story was finished. He addressed an envelope, and that night Joseph walked to the village to mail it.

"After that, Jacob wrote another story and another, but no answering letter arrived from the *Schwarzwald Gazette*. When the last leaves had fallen, Joseph bought as much food as he could; and when winter came in earnest, and the snow was higher than a man's knees, he made snowshoes. Each day, after he had dressed himself as warmly as he could, he went hunting. He shot several hares in that way, and at Christmas he and Jacob feasted upon a partridge."

Tina stepped into the blue teddy he had bought her in Toys. "All clean," she announced. "We can start on the drawers, but you'll have to open them for me and lift me up."

He carried her into the bedroom and (deciding they might as well be systematic) opened the upper left drawer of his bureau. "You can start in here," he told her. "But I don't think you'll find anything except handkerchiefs."

She hopped from his palm. "I like your hankies. They're so clean. Now go on with the story."

He sat down on the bed and found his place. "And yet there were many days when Joseph shot nothing at all, and he and Jacob supped upon pease porridge and water, for dried peas, water, and firewood were the only supplies that the winter had left them; and on such days, Joseph filled Jacob's bowl to the rim but took only a few spoonsful for himself.

"But on this day, when he saw how few dried peas remained, Joseph resolved that Jacob should have them all and that he himself should have nothing, for he blamed himself bitterly for returning with an empty bag. He set out Jacob's bowl and a spoon, filled two pots with snow, sprinkled all the remaining peas into one, and hung them over their little fire.

"Then Jacob said, 'Brother, I am hard at work on a new tale, but you must look out the window for me.'

"Joseph looked, and to his astonishment saw a fine sleigh drawn by four—"

Tina called, "Look!" She was holding up something thin and brown and shapeless, suspended on a scarlet thread.

"What is it?" he asked.

"Don't you know? I found it in your drawer."

He took it from her and held it up to the light. "It's a root," he said. At once Mr. Sheng's shop rose before his mind's eye, complete with all its queer boxes of incense, paper horses, blue-haloed gas ring, and steaming teapot. "It's a magic charm," he told Tina.

"A real charm?"

"The man who gave it to me said it was."

"Will it make you as little as me?"

"I'm afraid not."

She seated herself on the edge of the drawer, slender legs dangling over what was to her an abyss. "I didn't think so—not really. But we could pretend. Will it make you invisible?"

He shook his head. "It was supposed to bring mail."

"But it doesn't work?"

"I don't know. There was a lot of mail when I got back, but then I'd been gone for a month."

"Will it bring a sleigh with reindeer, like the one in the story?"

"I don't think they were reindeer." He glanced down at the page. "No, chargers."

"I don't know that word."

He groped. "Like ponies," (Tina would surely know *pony*) "but bigger. I don't think it will bring any kind of sleigh."

"Aren't you going to put it on?"

246

"I hadn't planned to," he said.

"It's the first thing I've found. Or anyway the first real thing, because you didn't even pick up the dime and the button. Besides, if you don't put it on how are you going to know if it works?"

"The mail carrier's been here already today," he pointed out.

"Then if you get some more letters or something, you'll know it's a real charm."

He was not often subject to sudden insights, but he had one then; it was that he was arguing with a doll about a magic root. He nodded his surrender and hung the charm around his neck.

"Joseph looked, and to his astonishment saw a fine sleigh drawn by four white ponies. 'What do you see?' Jacob asked him.

"'I see a magnificent sleigh,' Joseph answered. 'It's bright with gilt and dancing golden bells.'

"'Ah! Continue, please,' said Jacob. 'Give me more, dear brother.'

"'A big coachman in a high fur hat and a big brown fur coat cracks his long, black whip above the ponies. Beside him sits a tiny groom in a scarlet jacket, so that they look like a bear and a monkey in the circus. Riding in the sleigh is a woman wrapped in white furs.'

"'Wonderful!' Jacob exclaimed, and his pen danced over the paper so busily that he seemed not to hear the tinkle of sleigh bells as the sleigh stopped before their little house."

"Open this other drawer," Tina instructed him. "And when I jump across, you can shut this one. I think she's the editor of the *Schwarzwald Gazette*."

He pulled out the drawer that held his socks. "Maybe," he said.

"Joseph saw that the woman was a princess, and he bowed to

the ground. 'Are you Jacob?' she inquired. 'The publisher of our little paper has sent all your stories to me, knowing that they are just the sort of thing I like. I forbade him to tell you of it until I had rewarded you.'

" 'No, Highness,' Joseph said honestly, 'it's my brother who writes the stories. If you'll wait a moment, I'll bring him out to pay his respects to you.'

" 'That's certainly not necessary,' said the princess. 'I shall go in to pay *my* respects to *him.*'

"But when Joseph hastened to open the door, he found that Jacob was already in the doorway. 'Your Highness,' Jacob said, 'what my brother has told you is not wholly true. It is indeed he who writes my stories—I, as you see, am blind. I merely write them down.' "

"That was a sad story," Tina said. "Sometimes fairy tales are too much like real life. But I liked it."

He nodded and closed the book. "So did I."

There was a knock at the door.

· 29 ·

Magic!

There was another knock. A voice muffled by the door announced, "UPS."

"All right," he said, and opened it.

The UPS driver was short and dark, and looked angry. "This Seven C?"

He nodded.

"Here it is. You want it out here or in there?" *It* was a big, solid-looking crate on a handcart.

"Is that for me?" he asked.

"This is Seven C? It's for Seven C."

"I wasn't expecting—"

The driver snarled. "Your name Green?"

"Yes, but—"

"Want me to take it off my buggy and leave it in the hall?"

He shook his head. "I guess you'd better bring it inside."

The driver grasped the handles of the handcart and gave a mighty heave, tilting the cart back enough to put the center of gravity of the crate over its axle. "You should have seen me getting this bastard in that elevator. You'd have laughed your head off. Usually a thing like this goes to a loading dock."

He asked, "Who sent it?"

"Hell, I don't know. It says on the side someplace."

He bent to look. "It's just an address."

"If you read it, you know everything I do. Here, I'll move it over so it don't block your TV."

"Leave it in front of the TV," he said. "If you put it over there, I won't be able to get into the dinette." He got a bill from his wallet and extended it to the driver, who accepted it in silence.

Tina called, "You should say thank you." She was standing in the bedroom doorway, apparently having climbed from his sock drawer.

The driver glanced around uneasily. "You say that?"

"No," he said.

"I guess it was something on TV." The driver studied the black screen. "Maybe from the next apartment."

He was looking at the thick, rough boards of the crate and the shiny heads of their four-penny nails. "How am I—?"

His question was cut off by the shutting of the door as the driver went out.

Tina came over to examine the crate. "You should say thank you," she repeated.

"I thought you were talking to the UPS man," he told her.

"I was talking to *you*. I was the one who found the charm and got you to wear it. You should say thank you."

He pulled it from the neck of his shirt; it had not changed color or become larger or smaller. "Maybe we ought to wait till we see what's in the box," he said.

"Something nice," she told him. "It's almost Christmas, and Christmas presents are always nice."

He smiled faintly. "I don't think you'd like it if I got a puppy."

"Or another doll—I'd be jealous. Lift me onto the couch if we're going to talk. I was born on Christmas—have I told you about that?"

He took her tiny waist between his thumb and forefinger and stood her on the cushion beside him. "No, you've never told me much about your past."

"Now *you're* jealous."

"I am not."

"Yes, you are. I can tell. You're a jealous god, like the one they talk about."

"I'm not jealous, and I'm not a god," he told her absently. Another part of his mind was wrestling with the problem of the crate. The custodian would be in the musty basement apartment that came with the job, perhaps. But the custodian did not like being disturbed so late, and might already be asleep.

Tina said, "Not to *you*, you're not. And not to other big people. But to me."

"I see."

"I used to have a goddess."

That got his full attention. "What was her name?"

Tina shook her head. "That's the part I can't remember. I remember a tree—so pretty—and the kitten, because the goddess got a kitten too. I didn't like it, and when you said about the puppy, that made me think of it."

"I'll bet your goddess went to school."

"Uh huh. After Twelfth Night she did."

"Do you remember what grade?" He tried to guess Lara's age; twenty-eight, perhaps. No, she would be older now.

Tina shook her head again. "But she could walk by herself, I remember that, and she used to show me things she made out of paper. Once she made a paper crown, and when she came home she made a little crown for me."

"And then?" he prompted.

"And then something happened. I don't know what— something bad. Then you were holding me and crying."

He nodded. "I remember. Do you know how long you were in the doll hospital?"

"Was I in a hospital? I don't remember that."

"Yes," he said. "I know how it is." He got up and walked around the crate. It seemed to him that there should have been directions of some kind: PULL HERE. There was only his name and address on the UPS label, with a return address in the northern suburbs.

"Is that where you got me? From the hospital?"

"Yes," he said.

The telephone rang. He stared at it. It rang again.

"I'd like to answer—I really would. Only I'm not strong enough to pick up the thing you talk with."

It rang a third time. He said, "Sure, no problem," and picked it up. "Hello?"

"It's *you*. That's wonderful. You've moved."

It was Lara, as he had somehow known from the ring; as he had known all along. "That's right," he said. He wanted to say more, but the words stuck in his throat.

"How are you? Everything all right?"

"I'm fine. Where are you, Lara?"

"It's *Lora*. I'm at home, Mr. Green, and I'm flattered you remember my voice. Naturally you're surprised that I'm calling you from home, but I knew you worked days and didn't want us to phone you at work. Anyway, I looked you up and tried the

252

number before I left the office; but no one answered. Did you tell Dr. Nilson you'd moved?"

"Yes," he said. "Yes, I did."

"I thought you probably had, but she's awful about things like that. I mean, if you dream about a fish that waltzes like your aunt, she writes it down. But addresses and phone numbers are too mundane."

He said, "I still love you."

There was a pause, a silence so long it seemed apt to last forever.

At last Lara said, "I was going to say I went out to dinner when I left the office. With somebody. Somebody took me out to dinner."

"That's okay."

"The thing is, you've got your regular session with Dr. Nilson on Tuesday."

"Yes," he said.

"And she has a chance to pick up a little consulting job. You know she doesn't make much at the Center."

"Yes," he said again.

"Do you feel you could skip this week? Would you want to, and would you be willing to do that as a favor to Dr. Nilson?"

"No," he said.

"The other possibility would be if you were able to come in tomorrow. Pretty often someone cancels, and even if they don't, I could probably squeeze you in."

"You'll be there?" He found he was looking at Tina while thinking of Lara. That was why he had bought Tina, of course—because she reminded him of Lara; but she was not Lara. Lora was Lara.

"I know you must be wondering why I'm back with Dr. Nilson

after being gone for so long. I've been married and divorced. I get alimony and child support now, and I thought of this job. It doesn't pay a lot, but it was the best job I'd ever had, the only one I ever had that I really liked, and I knew if I had to take Missy to the doctor or something, Dr. Nilson would let me off, there wouldn't be any trouble about it."

He hesitated, irresolute among the thousands of things he wanted to say to her, the hundreds of questions he needed to ask. In some weak way he held power for the moment, and it was supremely important he not squander it. Slowly and carefully he said, "If I come tomorrow, I'll be counting on you to get me in to see her. I want to know beyond a doubt that you'll be there, Lara."

"I'll definitely be there. Can you come after lunch? One o'clock?"

He found that he was holding his handkerchief—that he had crushed it into a sodden ball. He said, "The best way for you to make certain I'll be there at one would be to let me take you to lunch. I'd like very much to do that."

Another pause, shorter this time but still long. "Suppose I were to tell you I had to see Missy at the day-care center?"

"I'd like to go with you. I'd like to see Missy, too." He glanced at Tina. "I might even have a present for her."

"I don't, not really." A brief pause. "Not till I get off work tonight."

"You go to lunch at—"

"Noon."

"I'll be there at eleven forty-five," he said.

"Fine. Thank you, Mr. Green. Goodbye."

There was a gentle, final click.

I should have found out where she's living, he thought; and then, She wouldn't have told the truth.

Tina asked, "Are you going to give me to a little girl? Doesn't she have a doll already?"

"I don't know," he told her. "But don't worry. I don't think this little girl really exists. If she has a doll, it probably isn't real either."

He hung up the phone, went to the crate, and took the edge of the middle board in both hands. It felt as though it were cutting his palms, then as though his shirt—no, the muscles of his back were tearing, ripping themselves to shreds of effort and pain. Nails started to give, protesting like mice as they were drawn from their holes, the last surrendering with a jerk that nearly sent him flying backward.

Tina whistled like a tiny teakettle. "I didn't know you were so strong."

"Neither did I," he admitted. He peered through the wider opening he had made. The object within looked rough and nearly black.

"Are you going to pull them all off?"

He shook his head. "I had that one in me. I don't think there are any more."

"Don't lay it down like that," Tina advised him. "You'll step on a nail. Stand it up against the wall."

"You're right," he said.

"Where are you going?"

"To the kitchen. I've got a screwdriver in there."

"I want to show you something first. Will you come over here?"

He sat down on the sofa beside her.

"I'm going to do magic. Put your hand in here." *Here* was the pocket of his overcoat. "What do you feel?"

"Nothing," he said. "It's empty."

She raised one tiny arm dramatically. "Now watch as the

Amazing Tina goes inside for a minute!" She crawled headfirst into the pocket as a full-sized girl might have dived beneath the covers of a bed. A moment after her feet had disappeared, she was climbing out again. *"Now* put your hand in."

He did, and drew out a thin packet of bills. Tina laughed and clapped.

"How did you do that?"

"Well, you couldn't put me in another drawer because you were talking. And I knew after that you'd want to look at the magic mail. Me, too."

"Magic mail?"

"Yes," Tina told him firmly. "Magic mail. But never mind, there wasn't a lot for me to do, and your coat was lying here on the sofa."

As patiently as he could, he asked, "But why was the pocket empty the first time I put my hand in it?"

"Open it and look at it under the light, and you'll see."

He did, sliding to the end of the sofa next to the table lamp, putting the coat on his lap, and turning the three-way bulb to its maximum brightness. A thin panel of fabric, of the same material as the lining of the pocket, divided it into two chambers.

"It's a double pocket," Tina told him delightedly. "Only the middle thing had gotten pushed up underneath the flap. When I got in, I could feel the money on the other side, so I looked to see what it was."

He nodded slowly. "I should have felt it myself."

"You were looking for something at the bottom, probably, not off to one side."

He nodded again. "Thank you, Tina."

"Is that the money?"

"It must be." The packet was secured with a rubber band,

now gone weak. He pulled it off and tossed it toward the waste basket before looking at the bills. There were five hundreds, three fifties, a ten, and two singles, all quite similar to the designs with which he was familiar, but all bearing the faces of women. He had a fifty in his wallet; he got it out and compared it to the ones from the packet. Neither the scrollwork nor the style of the lettering was precisely the same. The fifty with Grant's picture read FEDERAL RESERVE NOTE. The fifties from the packet said GOLD CERTIFICATE REDEEMABLE FOR FACE VALUE.

He laid the money down, struck by a thought. "Tina, you could go inside that crate just like you went into my pocket."

She looked at the crate dubiously. "I guess I could."

"Of course you could. It might have been a little tight before I pulled off that slat, but now there's a big space."

"All right," Tina said, suddenly decisive. "Lift me up."

He returned the Grant fifty to his wallet, put the rest of the bills on the end table, and stood Tina on the board beside the opening. She said, "It's awfully dark in there. Have you got a little flashlight or something I could use?"

"I don't think so, but I can move the lamp so it shines into there."

She nodded. "I think you'd better."

He did, noting as she lowered herself into the opening that her skin was smooth plastic. She's just a mechanical doll, he thought. I've been playing with a programmed doll.

Yet he missed her as soon as she was out of sight.

· 30 ·

Tina's Secret Fort

Tina might tell him what was in the crate; but he would have to open it himself, unless he wanted to wait until tomorrow evening and have the custodian do it. That would be the sensible thing, certainly.

He discovered that he had no wish to do the sensible thing, and it took only a moment of self-analysis for him to find the reason: he would see Lara tomorrow, and he wanted to be able to tell her all about this crate and whatever was in it. He most definitely did *not* want to have to tell her he had been unable to get it open. What would Lara think of a man who could not open a simple wooden crate?

He went into the kitchen and equipped himself with the screwdriver he had mentioned to Tina and a big utility knife that had come with the set from Chef's Shape-Up. Studying its cruel curve, he tried to remember whether he had ever used it before. Probably not; it seemed intended for butchering large hairy animals that were not quite dead. He could hardly start stabbing and slashing at the crate with it until Tina was safely out of the way.

"Tina!" he called. "Are you okay in there?"

There was no answer. He put his ear over the opening and listened, feeling sure that if Tina was moving around inside he would hear her. After a few seconds he could make out the whir of the electric clock and the faint noises of someone preparing for bed in the next apartment, but there was no sound from the opening; it was as silent as a grave.

"Tina, are you playing a joke on me?"

He grabbed another board and tried to pull it off. Whether because it was more tightly secured or because he had exhausted himself on the first, it yielded not the smallest fraction of an inch.

Yet it was slightly cracked. He jammed the big blade into the crack and worked it back and forth. The crack enlarged in a satisfying way and soon reached the edge of the board, depriving one end of the strength of one nail. He drove the blade under that end and pried—he had heard that you were not supposed to pry with the blade of a knife, but he found that he did not give a damn. If the blade broke, he would pry with what was left.

The remaining nail gave instead, shrieking and bending. He threw down the knife, grabbed the board, and tore it off.

The opening was doubled, so that the light from the table lamp he had positioned for Tina shone into it more effectively. The rough dark surface, which he had imagined to be that of the object contained, was revealed to be only some sort of packing material or wrapping. He felt it and pushed against it; the object beneath seemed smooth and unyielding. There was no sign of Tina.

With the knife, he started to work on the third board, then realized he was neglecting a more powerful tool. He slipped the narrow end of the board he had just pulled loose under the third board and threw his weight on the opposite end, using the edge of the crate as a fulcrum. Though its nails complained like the rest, it came up fairly easily. So did the next, and only the board on which the table lamp stood remained.

He tried to grasp the rough packing material and tear it, but it was too tough to tear and too tightly stretched to afford him an effective grip. The big utility knife would cut it, he felt sure. But the knife might also damage whatever the packing sheet was protecting, might even harm Tina. He called to her again, softly, and tried to tell her how worried he was. There was no response.

When he had replaced the lamp on the end table, he tried to pry again with the detached board, but the mechanical advantage it had possessed was gone.

There was no convenient crack into which he could force his knife. He worked it beneath the end of the remaining board and wedged the tip of his screwdriver into the opening he had made; as soon as he tried to pry with the screwdriver, it bent like a coat hanger.

He discovered that he did not want to pry with the utility knife because he was afraid it might break. Earlier he had not cared about it and would have thrown it away any time he needed more space in the utensil drawer. Now it was truly his, like his order book and the silver pen whose writing element he had replaced so many times.

He wedged the blade under the other end of the board and made himself work the handle up and down, gently at first, with increasing force as the nails resisted. When he had enlarged the opening between the board and the top of the crate to about an eighth of an inch, he withdrew the blade and pulled up the end of the board, heaving backward again and again, so that one side of the crate was lifted from the floor.

With the top of the crate gone, he could see inside better than he had when the lamp had stood beside the opening. The rough, gray-brown sheet seemed to have been added when the crate was complete except for its top—draped over the rectangular object inside, its margins shoved down into the crate. Yellow mats of shredded wood had been pushed down around it to give extra protection to the sides. He pulled them out, and when the last was gone lifted off the rough sheet, which was only a kind of heavy cardboard, easily enough.

The rectangular object he had felt was the top of the desk, a single dark panel of tropical hardwood. He knew it at once, knew each scratch and honorable mark of service. The fold-down writing board was folded, the drawers taped shut; but it was the desk, his desk.

Somehow, he felt, the sides of the crate should simply fall away now. They did not; he was forced to pry the boards of one side off one at a time and pile them in a corner. It was only when he had removed the last and paused sweating to search once more through the heap of packing materials for Tina, and admire the desk, that he noticed that the masking tape meant to hold the writing board in place hung free. For a second or two he wondered whether Tina could have done it—whether she possessed the needed strength. She probably could, he decided; her tiny fingers could have loosened a corner easily, and with a corner up, she could peel the tape back. He tugged experimentally at the loose end and found the tape had not adhered well; the desk had been waxed.

Mentally, he traced Tina's path. Finding herself on the thick cardboard sheet, she would have crawled across it just below the remaining boards. The mats of shredded wood would have blocked her at the sides, but she could have—must have —gone down one of the corners. Originally, the cardboard sheet had been flat; it had been bent to fit around the desk fairly tightly, but there had necessarily been a good deal of extra material at the corners. Tina could not have climbed the waxed legs of the desk, but the loose folds of rough cardboard at the corners would have offered her a choice of several easily scaled pipes.

He pulled away the piece of tape. Its makers had provided the desk with a brass lock; but the key had been lost, perhaps for a century or more.

"Here you are, Tina, I've found you," he said as he opened the board.

She was not there. There were eight pigeon holes in the top row behind the board, six larger ones in the bottom row—he had counted them often at the store—and they were empty, all empty except for a single ivory-colored envelope of note-paper size. Thinking that Tina might somehow have secreted herself behind it, he pulled it out. She had not, and as soon as the envelope was out he realized that it would have been impossible. The fourteen empty pigeon holes stared blandly at him; he seemed to hear Tina's delighted laughter.

Sitting in the old brown chair with the cigarette burn in its arm, he tore open the envelope.

Dear Mr. Green:
  Mother gave me an antique doll when I was twelve, and I have been a collector ever since. That's more than fifty years now. Do you know Kipling's poem?

> *There was no worth in the fashion—*
> *there was no wit in the plan—*
> *Hither and thither, aimless,*
> *the ruined footings ran—*
> *Masonry, brute, mishandled,*
> *but carven on every stone:*
> *"After me cometh a Builder.*
> *Tell him, I too have known."*

It was a favorite of my late husband's.

Merry Christmas. You will pardon an old woman her sentimentalities.

Martha Foster

Mail. He read the letter again, as though there were some clue there. In cartoons, people were always climbing mountains and asking the robed and bearded freaks they met to explain the meaning of life. He would never be able to laugh at that again. How could anyone laugh? "There was no worth in the fashion— there was no wit in the plan—hither and thither, aimless, the ruined footings ran—"

He picked up the money Tina had found for him, counted it, and stuffed it back into the pocket.

Tina was hiding, but it was only that she was hiding. She was in the desk or in the heap of packing materials and boards, or—barely possibly—she had slipped unseen out of the crate and was hiding somewhere else in the apartment. If he went to bed now, she would probably . . .

No. Tina might hide briefly as a joke, but not for this long; she would not want to worry him like this. Something had happened to her.

She could not be in one of the drawers because every drawer

was still tightly taped. He tore the strips of tape away just the
same and looked in all of them. He would have pulled them out
of the desk if he could, but they were retained, apparently by
stops attached before the back of the desk had been fastened in
place.

But Tina had not gotten into any of them, anyway. He was
behaving like the man in the joke who looked for his wallet on
the corner because the light was better there. Tina had pulled
loose the tape that had held up the writing board and slipped
behind the board. Was it possible one of the pigeon holes had a
false back? All of them were deep, and all looked equally deep,
but he checked them one by one with a ruler. They were all of
the same depth, and that depth was less than the width of the
top of the desk by a scant three-quarters of an inch. There was
nothing between the bottom of the lower row of pigeon holes
and the work surface of the desk.

Or rather, there was nothing but a smooth panel of nearly
black wood about three inches high. He tried to grasp it and pull
it, but every edge was covered: the top by the bottoms of the
pigeon holes, the ends by the sides of the desk, the lower edge by
the fixed part of the writing surface.

He shifted the table lamp to the desk and studied the blank
wood. How could Tina, under the thick cardboard sheet, have
seen something that he could not see even under a bright light?
Tina could only have felt the panel; in the pitch darkness behind
the writing board, she could not have seen it. Replacing the
lamp, he shut his eyes and traced the panel with his fingers. He
felt nothing.

Tina's fingers were far smaller than his, hardly thicker than
pins. He retrieved the utility knife and slid its point lightly
across the surface of the panel, careful not to scratch it—or
rather, not to scratch it more than it had been scratched already

by two centuries of use, particularly, for some reason, on its left end.

When the tip of the blade reached that end, it slipped into the crack between the panel and the side of the desk. He pushed gently and felt rather than heard the click as the panel swung a quarter of an inch toward him.

· 31 ·

Lunch with Lora

When the waitress had gone, he took out Tina and laid her on the checkered table-cloth.

"A doll?" Lora Masterman stopped fiddling with her chair and took gold-framed glasses from her purse to peer at Tina.

"I bought her because she reminded me of you," he said.

"That was sweet of you."

"She can walk around and talk, and even think about things a little bit, when she's working. But she can't read or crunch numbers. She's not programmed for it, and I doubt if she's got the capacity. If you ask her how much one and one is, she says it's two or three. When you ask her four and four, she says a lot." Hastily he added, "I don't mean that I think you're like that."

Lora was still smiling. "I'm sure Dr. Nilson thinks I am, sometimes."

"I want to tell you about Tina, and about my desk. Is that all right? Do you like antiques?"

"I like them. I don't know much about them."

"I do," he said. "Even the dumbest person knows about some things. Did you ever notice? With me it's antiques and personal computers. I know about those. When we lived together, it was just personal computers, but now I know antiques too. Computers are good, but antiques are better because there's more to know."

Lora said softly, "It was only for a couple of days."

"I know, but I wanted it to last forever. I wasn't smart enough or good-looking enough, and I didn't make enough money. I understand. I'm not blaming you."

"It really wasn't any of those things." Lora took off her glasses and returned them to her purse. "I wasn't good for you. You were one of Dr. Nilson's patients, I was working for her, and I was hurting you. After a few days I couldn't stand that."

The waitress brought icewater, a basket that held butter and a small loaf of warm Italian bread, and their wine.

"How did you hurt me?" he asked.

"You started blocking. You forgot—I mean on the conscious level—that you were a patient, and that was very bad. You even forgot that we'd met in Dr. Nilson's office. You talked about us meeting in the park, because we took that walk during lunch. And now—" Lora's voice had grown fainter as she spoke, until it seemed that she was close to tears, "I'm afraid you're going to start it again. You're constructing a delusional system, with me inside."

"I couldn't," he said. "You're too big. I couldn't wrap my mind around you."

"You did before."

He shook his head. "You were real, just like you're real now.

267

You changed the way you looked, changed it just a little, and you said your name was Lara Morgan. You let me pick you up in the park. But you're telling the truth about one thing: I didn't want to admit I'd been seeing a psychiatrist—not even to myself. Somebody like that wasn't good enough for you—I knew that.

"Just the same, the place I went to when I went through the door, that was real. I met real people there, I ate real food, and I bought this doll. I even met a man there who was from our world, a man who used to work for Nixon."

Lora reached for Tina, but he drew her away. "You think I'm going to break her," Lora said; it was a statement, not a question.

He nodded.

"If you were to walk down this street until you came to a toy store, you could probably buy a doll—"

Smiling, Mama Capini stopped at their table. "You two, you're back together? That's good."

"I'm back together," he told her. "I'm trying to get Lara back with me."

"Girl's got your order?"

He shook his head.

"Take the clams. They're good today."

"All right," he said.

"I'll tell the girl." Mama Capini drifted away.

Lora said, "She remembered me. It's been years."

"You're not that different. Besides, who could forget you? I didn't buy Tina because I thought I was going to forget you. I knew I'd always remember you, that everything that I saw would remind me of you. I got Tina because I wanted to own a little piece of you. If you can't have somebody, you want to have her picture, and you were the model for Tina. You had to be."

She began to object, but he waved it aside. "Okay, Tina just happens to look exactly like you. Let's not fight about that. Anyway, a lady I thought was a bitch sent me the desk, because she knew how much I wanted it. It turns out she's a saint, really, underneath."

"Sometimes it turns out the other way, too," Lora told him.

He nodded again. "You mean I think you're an angel, but you might be a devil—a fallen angel—really. That's all right; I'll follow you back to Hell, if that's where you're going."

He paused to think, but Lora did not speak.

"We've got this Victorian tapestry. It shows a knight and a lady, and behind the knight it's just ordinary. You know, a lot of grass and trees. But behind the lady, everything's very strange. It illustrates a poem, 'La Belle Dame sans Merci,' by John Keats. That was you too, wasn't it? I didn't think of it until just now, because the lady doesn't look much like you. I doubt if Keats had really seen you either—he probably just took some old legend—but maybe he had."

Lora grinned. "This is better than the talking doll. I've always wanted to be in a tapestry."

"Come by the store, and I'll show it to you. Anyway, the desk was packed in a wooden crate. I suppose she had a moving company come in and do it; it looked like a professional job."

Lora nodded.

"I didn't know what was inside it, and I had some trouble getting it open; so when I got the first board off, I sent Tina in to look."

"You really believe all this, don't you?" Lora tossed lustrous brown hair back with an impatient jerk of her head. "You actually think that doll can walk around and talk."

"It's not that far out," he said. "I thought it was myself at

269

first, like magic. The Amazing Tina, that's what she called herself once. But Heathkit will sell you a little robot you put together yourself, and the Air Force has airplanes that will fly and fight and go back to base and land, all with the pilot dead. I couldn't build her, and I don't know anybody who could. But somebody here might be able to, if we put our minds to it."

Tina lay face down on his side of the table, almost beneath his forearms. He had picked up the saltcellar; he toyed with it as he spoke, passing it from one hand to the other.

The waitress brought their clams.

"She didn't come out. I pulled the crate apart and looked everyplace, you know? But I couldn't find her at all. Finally I found out there was a secret compartment in the desk. I don't think the lady who gave it to me even knew about it. I opened it, and Tina was inside. She didn't walk or talk any more—she was just like this." He gestured.

Lora was chewing pasta and clams. She nodded skeptically.

"I should have told you before that Tina was like this when I got her. The clerk told me how to make her work, but I didn't pay much attention." He paused. "I should have known better. I've seen it myself a thousand times when I was selling personal computers and peripherals—I'd tell a customer something, and next day he'd be back in the store asking. Anyway, I wondered what had happened to her, but after a while I figured it out. When you've got a mechanical toy, you don't keep it running all the time; you turn it off when the child's not playing with it. If it's a windup toy, you don't even have to. It runs down. I won't tell you how I started up Tina the first time, but I did it by accident."

Lora patted her mouth with her napkin. "So you couldn't do it again."

270

He shook his head. "That's right. I'm too happy, because I've found you and you're going to take me back."

"I don't know what you mean by that. I may date you again, sometime. I may not."

He nodded. "Tina had told me how she liked her tea, and I made her some; but she only told me that once, and after a while I forgot. When I thought about her lying there, it made sense. She tells the child one time, and as long as the child's really interested he keeps her going. But if he isn't he doesn't do it any more, and she puts herself away so his mother doesn't have to pick her up. Pretty soon she runs down, or maybe she shuts herself off. That way she doesn't get broken, and she doesn't wear out. I wasn't really that interested in Tina any more; I was interested in the crate and you."

He sipped his wine. Lora said, "You expect me to believe all this."

"I know you believe it—you know all about these toys. I think you probably know a lot more than I do. What I expect is for you to admit it, when you see that it's no use to go on the way you are now." He put down his wineglass and picked up the saltcellar again. "Anyway, that's what she'd done. She would always put herself away, more or less, when I wasn't going to be around. She called whatever place she liked that day her secret fort. This time she crawled into that secret compartment."

He unscrewed the top of the saltcellar, poured salt into his icewater, and stirred it with a spoon. When most of the salt had dissolved, he dipped his fingers into the cold salt solution and sprinkled Tina. "When they're already going, they can drink it," he told Lora. "Tea, or plain water with salt in it, I suppose. Once they're off, you've got to do this. It's an electrolyte. Don't bother to act surprised."

A drop struck Tina in the face, and she sat up. "Hello. I'm Tina." Her wide hazel eyes blinked slowly before focusing on Lora.

Lora said, "Hello, Tina," her voice strained.

"I belong to you," Tina announced. "I'm *your* doll, and I can talk."

Lora shook her head. "I'm afraid you don't, Tina. You've got the wrong party. You belong to the man behind you."

He said, "Hello, Tina. Remember me?"

"A little bit."

"We used to play in my apartment. You helped me look for lost things, and I read to you. I got you some pretty dresses, and a little tea set."

Tina nodded. "If you want to have a tea party, I can help you set the table."

"I do," he told her, "when we get back home." To Lora he added, "Sure you don't want her for Missy?"

Lora shook her head. "I know you mean well, and I have to admit you were right about your doll and I was wrong. You were telling the truth, but it's a little bit too much like voodoo or something for me. And for Missy."

"All right, let's forget about Tina for a minute. When you left you wrote me a note, remember? If you're nothing more than you say you are, a divorcée with a little girl, why did you tell me about the doors?"

Lora looked puzzled. "What doors?"

He took the note from his wallet, unfolded it, and smoothed it on the table. A drop of salt water dampened one corner like a tear. As he looked up at Lora, Tina giggled.

Lora asked, "What's so funny, you two?" She had glanced at the note as he opened it; she did not look at it again.

"Your face," he told her. "You've had such great control until now."

She rose, brushing her lips with her napkin. "If you don't like my face—"

"Suppose I call Channel Nine," he said. "Suppose I show them this note, and then I show them Tina. I think the TV news would love Tina. You couldn't come here again for a long, long time."

Tina added, "Don't go away!" A fat diner at the next table glanced toward her and looked quickly aside with the shaken but determined expression of an atheist who has seen a ghost.

"This is crazy," Lora said. "I should have known it would be, so it's my fault. Thanks for lunch."

"I have your picture too," he told her. When she did not reply, he added, "Sit down."

Arms extended, begging to be picked up, Tina piped, "You're so pretty!"

Lora sat. There was no fussing with her chair this time, and her shoulders were squared. "I never allowed you to take my picture."

"I didn't." He paused, trying to frame what he had to say. "Things sort themselves out, don't they? The things from your world and the things from mine each get together with their own kind. When I was a little boy, my mother used to give me Corn Flakes for breakfast, and I could never figure out why a flake that I put in the middle of the bowl always floated over to one side. I still don't know, but I don't think it's magic, and I don't think this is, either. It's probably some sort of law of nature, like gravity. What happens when something belongs to both places?" He waited for her answer.

"Let's call my world the sea," Lara said. Her voice was

suddenly new; the alteration was minute yet vastly significant —she had given up a hopeless game that no longer entertained her. "And yours the land."

There were freckles beneath her makeup, and her eyes blazed green.

· 32 ·

Lunch with Lara

He sighed, releasing breath he had not been aware of holding. "All right."

"Heavy things belong to the sea. You may be able to draw them out—" Lara glanced down at Tina, "but if ever they come near the sea again, they will eventually fall in. And when they fall in, they will sink."

He nodded to show that he understood.

"Lighter things belong to the land. If they happen to fall into the sea, they float. Eventually they are washed to some shore. You wanted to know about things that belong in part to both."

"Yes," he said.

"Think of a broken timber from a wreck. It is wood, which floats; but in it are several large nails. The nails are iron, which sinks. If the timber floats at all, it will float nearly submerged. If its wood becomes waterlogged, even a little, the timber will sink;

but for a long time it will not lie heavily upon the floor of the sea. The sand will not bury it for years, because for years it will move with the tide enough to shake the sand off. When a storm comes, currents will scour the bottom; then it is possible the timber will be washed ashore."

There was a sudden silence. At last Tina asked, "Are there really storms like that?"

Lara nodded. "I am the storm." To him she said, "Now show me my picture, please, and tell me how you got it."

"All right." He took a locket of tarnished gold from his left jacket pocket and snapped it open. Lara leaned forward to look; but he did not let her see it for a moment, studying it himself instead. In colors time had softened rather than faded, the old miniature showed him her face in profile, half smiling, a delicate choker of Flemish lace circling her neck, grass-green jade ornaments at her ears.

"If I say I love you," Lara asked him, "will you give that to me?"

"I love you," he told her. "Won't you let me keep it?"

With warm, slender fingers, she turned his hand until she could see the miniature, then nodded.

"Your name's inside the lid—or one of your names, anyway. Leucothea Fitzhugh Hurst."

Lara nodded again. "Where did you get it?"

"It was in the secret compartment with Tina. The old sea captain must have had that compartment built so he could hide his valuables in it, and this locket was what he kept in there. I suppose it was in there when he died, and nobody else knew about it."

"And you want to keep it because you believe it's a picture of me."

"I know it's a picture of you."

"And Tina." Lara glanced down at her, a goddess regarding a toy. "Tina's me as well."

Tina exclaimed, "I am not!"

He said, "So is Marcella, the movie star. You practically told me so, over the phone when I was in the hospital. You like having names that begin with *L*, but you don't always use them."

"Lara's a fairly new one," she admitted.

"I didn't know then that it's the one you store your coat under when you come here—Lara Morgan. I found that out later, after I got back."

She smiled. "That was clever of you."

"Thanks. I tried to get a job there, but they didn't want me."

"You wouldn't have been happy if I had been Lora Masterman, because Lora Masterman was your psychiatrist's receptionist; so I was Lara Morgan for you."

"Uh huh. Maybe you can tell me about something I've been wondering about."

"What my real name is? No."

He shook his head. "What was wrong with me when I went to Dr. Nilson to start with? Now it's you, but what was it then?"

Tina asked, "Don't you feel good?"

"Yes, I do, Tina," he said. "I feel wonderful."

"Depression, mostly. There's a certain kind of lonely man who rejects love, because he believes that anyone who offers it wouldn't be a lover worth having. You were one of those lonely men, whether you would admit it to Dr. Nilson or not."

"'I wouldn't belong to any club that would accept me as a member.' Groucho Marx said that. I watch reruns a lot." He shrugged apologetically.

"He put it well. You were an only child, and your parents separated while you were still very young. Your mother was your

GENE WOLFE

best friend—in fact, your only friend. After your mother died, you managed to cope for a year or so. But you wouldn't talk to customers, sometimes, and you were drinking too much. The store you work for sent you to Dr. Nilson."

"You felt sorry for me."

"I felt sorry for all of you," she said. "I still do. You were—you seemed like the best choice."

"But you didn't love me."

"Yes, I did." She paused so that her next words would sink in. "I loved Captain Hurst, too."

He had forgotten the locket; he saw it now, lying between their soiled plates, as though he had never seen it before. "Do you really want it?"

"No. I wanted it to remember him by, but that was silly of me and selfish. I couldn't remember Billy by keeping a picture of myself, not for long; and I think you need it much, much more than I do."

"His name was Billy?" He was astonished.

She smiled. "It was William, actually. Everyone called him Billy, of course not to his face: Blaze-Away Billy Hurst." Her hands had been in the purse in her lap; they appeared above the edge of the table clasping a black-bordered handkerchief. "I wish I could cry for him," she said. "He deserved it. He was brave, and gentle even when he wasn't sober. But I can't, not really. I hadn't thought about Billy for years."

He snapped the locket shut and dropped it back into his pocket.

Her fingers touched his, then fled. "Would you do me a great favor? Please?"

"Anything," he said.

"You have Billy's old desk now? You own it?"

He nodded. "I suppose it must have been his."

"Then you'll keep things in it—your papers and so forth. I want you to keep that locket where he kept it. Will you do that for me?"

He nodded again. "If you'll tell me how he got you to marry him."

"There isn't much to tell. We met on shipboard; he was the captain, I was a passenger. If we had merely done what you and I did, it would have been the gossip of the fo'c'sle in an hour. Billy would have done it—he was mad about me—but things would have been very difficult for both of us afterward. There was a parson aboard, so we got him to marry us—a big social wedding, as shipboard weddings go, with the first mate as Billy's best man and more than half the women as my attendants. It was our celebration of rounding the Cape, too."

"I see," he said. "Did one of the passengers paint the picture in this locket?"

Lara shook her head. "It was done in Bombay by the British governor's wife, after we docked. She was an amateur but really very good."

"How long did you stay with him?"

"Until he sailed. By that time I had fallen ill and had to be left behind."

"And I don't imagine you were still there when he returned. Tina, you'd better go back. Too many people are admiring you." He picked her up and replaced her in the breast pocket of his jacket.

"No," Lara said. "What is it you want of me? That I love you? I do already, as much as I'm capable of love; if I hadn't loved you, I would have stayed with you far longer. That I stay with you for the rest of your life? I can't do that."

He told her, "I've been thinking about why you picked us—the captain and me; it was because we wouldn't be believed.

If we went through a door and came back to tell about it, nobody would pay any attention to us. Nobody believes sailor's yarns, and Hurst was a drinker and a hell-raiser from what you've said about him. I'm a mental patient, and that's why you took your job, and why you went back. What is it you want from us?"

"Your love. I want to be loved by a man who doesn't die because he made love to me. Is that so terrible?"

He shook his head. After a moment he said, "I think you like *Billy*—like the name. Anyway another Billy told me once that you had a lover called Attis. After I got back, I saw a thing on TV about people down at the library who'd look things up for you. I talked to a woman there, and after she told me about Attis, I asked about books on antiques. I've read all of them now, and a few of them three or four times. So I owe you something."

Lara waved the debt aside.

"Anyway, Attis cut—cut himself for you, because that was what you wanted."

"No," she said.

"All right, because he thought that was what you wanted."

"I wanted him not to die!"

"All right," he said softly.

"But what is it you want from me? I've told you what you can't have, and I've told you that you have my love already. I love you as much as I can—as much as I can afford. As much as the old woman at the next table loves some little dog, possibly. What more?"

He knew that she was trying to insult him, but he was not insulted; instead he was happier than he had ever been before. "I want what that dog wants," he said. "I want to follow you, when I can, I want to help you, whenever I can be of any help, and I want to hear your voice."

Her fingers drummed the table.

He waited in patient silence; and at last she said, "We'll have a test, as such things were tested long ago." She picked up her wineglass and offered it to him, grasping it between her thumb and forefinger at the rim. "Hold the stem with your left hand."

He did so.

"Now tear off a crumb of that bread. Not a tiny crumb—a piece as big as a crouton. Don't squeeze it."

He pulled a small piece from the soft loaf in the basket by the ashtray.

"Now drop it into the wine. If it sinks, you're free to follow me as long as you wish. But if it floats—"

"If it floats," he told her, "I will die."

She nodded. "You will anyway."

For a moment it seemed the bit of bread scarcely lay upon the wine. Lara murmured something—a prayer, perhaps, or a curse, that he did not understand. Red as blood, wine raced up the snowy sides of the bread, and it sank like a stone.

"So be it," Lara hissed. She released the glass, and he nearly let it fall.

He did not understand, and would never understand, how she got her coat without going near the hook where it had hung. He snatched down his own and ran after her, ignoring an angry shout from one of Mama's sons.

· 33 ·

To the Fights

At first it seemed that she had vanished in the throng of office workers; then he glimpsed her sleek head, its hair returned to the copper he remembered by the level light of the setting sun. He hurried after her, lost sight of her, found her and lost her once more, yet hurried forward still. Streetlights were coming on, section by section, all over the city.

The streetlights—and yet it had been lunch, surely lunch, that he had shared with Lara. He passed a church where services were in progress; he could hear the throb of the organ and the singing of many voices. Lights within made the stained-glass windows glow like gems. One showed Lara, with a spear in one hand, a mirror in the other. He stopped for a moment to stare, then hurried on.

Someone caught him by the shoulder. "Just where the hell have you been?"

He turned and saw North; as he did, North's fist slammed into his right kidney. He gasped with pain and doubled over, but the crowd on the sidewalk was so thick, shouting and shoving as it fought to reach three ticket windows, that no one seemed to notice, though perhaps it was only that those who saw them ignored them.

"That's for leaving me," North said. North grasped his tie as if it were a leash and led him out of the crowd and into a narrow alley. There he jerked the tie away and swung wildly at North's face. North stepped inside the blow, there was a red flash of pain, and he was sitting on the filthy bricks clasping his belly and retching.

"That's twice," North said. "Get up!"

Tina's voice, tiny and muffled by his jacket, asked, "Are you sick?"

He smiled and said, "Yes," suddenly glad that both blows had been too low to harm her.

"What the hell are you grinning for?"

"I'm still alive." He stumbled to his feet. "Isn't that enough?"

"For you," North told him. A door opened, throwing a beam of strong yellow light into the dark alley. "Come on." North led the way down a steep flight of concrete steps.

"Where are we going?" he asked. It was an effort to speak, but a distraction from the pain.

"To put on a show." North chuckled. "Like we did before."

The steps ended in a wide concrete corridor that stank of sweat. A middle-aged man in a torn T-shirt and khaki trousers hurried past them carrying a stack of clean towels and a bucket of water.

North said, "We've got lots of time. They haven't started the preliminaries. He'll have one of the big rooms close to the elevators."

The corridor turned and turned again, growing still wider and still more brilliantly lit. Tight-lipped young women with notebooks and lounging men with cameras clustered at one end. North shouldered them out of the way, seemingly oblivious to their protests and threats. "Come on!" North snapped. "Follow me!"

He followed as closely as he could. They stopped before a wide metal door painted dark green. A big cardboard sign neatly lettered in India ink had been taped to the door at eye level: JOE JOSEPH.

North knocked so loudly it seemed likely that the knocking alone would open the green door, smashing its latch and hinges. A bald man opened it instead and swore. North strode inside, leaving the bald man to push back the men with cameras and the intense young women with notebooks. A flash filled the whole bare room like a bolt of silent lightning before the bald man closed the door.

It was not until he was nearly in the center of the room that he realized that the bald man at the door had been Eddie Walsh. Eddie's prizefighter, Joe, sat on a masseur's folding table, wearing blue-and-white boxing shorts, a blue satin robe, and gym shoes, and looking as big as the store.

W.F. glanced up from taping one of Joe's enormous hands and grinned at him. He tried to grin in return, then bit his lips as he sought to recall the name of the serious-looking blonde in the crimson dress. That would be Jennifer, of course, whom he had never met. Joe's wife, Jennifer.

North was speaking to Joe in a low, crisp voice that seemed to imply that they were the only significant people in the room, the only people who mattered an iota. "Meet your new handler," he said. "I'll be in your corner with Walsh tonight, and believe me, my being there is bound to bring you good luck—the greatest fight of your entire career. You know who I am?"

Joe did not reply or change his expression even slightly. The big hand he held out to W.F. neither moved nor trembled; the blank, blue eyes stared sightlessly at something far away. If the fighter was thinking about anything at all, it appeared to be utterly unconnected with the events taking place in the room. A saint contemplating God or a gourmand contemplating Dinner might have worn the same open, empty face.

"We've got a couple of dozen men up there," North told him. "Not because we need that many, but because I want them to see you in person. They'll be watching you before you get into the ring, and they'll watch you fight, and they'll still be watching you when you come out, memorizing the way you look and the way you move. Four men in two cars are watching your car, just in case you're dumb enough to try to use that. You *may* get home okay, if you're God-damned lucky. Maybe. But either you play along, or you'll be dead by this time tomorrow night. Her too." North jerked his head to indicate Jennifer. "Maybe these two nobodies from noplace you've been carrying, if they happen to get in our way. But you for sure. You and your wife, and you can take that to the bank."

Joe's voice was as slow and big as he remembered. "You want me to throw the fight."

"Hell, no," North said. "You can fight as good as you want to. I don't care whether you win or lose. But I'm going to be one of your handlers."

"Bullshit," Walsh told him.

There was a knock at the door, a nearly inaudible tap. Walsh hurried over to open it, and Lara came in.

· 34 ·

Prelims

Walsh cleared his throat, looking slightly embarrassed. "Laura, this is North, the guy I told ya about. My lawyer, Miss Nomos. This other guy—"

Lara nodded frigidly. "Mr. Green and I have already met."

North nodded too. "This isn't a matter for attorneys. I didn't know you were a fight fan, Miss Nomos."

"There are a great many things you don't know, Mr. North."

North whirled on him. "So—you know her. Are you working for her?"

He nodded. "I'd do anything in the world for her."

North's hand drew back, then inched forward. It seemed to him that the entire world had gone to slow motion. He clenched his fist, knowing he could hit North—a dozen times if necessary—before the blow landed.

Lara's eyes stopped him. They were brilliantly blue-green, matched aquamarines set in her lovely face, brighter far than the stained-glass eyes of the church window. They told him that this was not the moment to resist.

North's open palm smacked his cheek, jerking his head to the right. He felt a flash of pain, but it was no more than pain—millions endured far worse every day. Backhanded, North's knuckles raked his mouth, splitting his upper lip.

Walsh stepped between them. "'At's enough!"

He got out his handkerchief and dyed it at his lip. Above their heads, muted by two feet of concrete and steel, the crowd growled low.

Lara said, "Exactly what is it you want, Mr. North?"

North was glaring at the bald man. "Walsh told you."

"I prefer to hear it from you."

North turned to face her. "Simple. Tonight I want to be out front where everybody can see me. I want to be associated with a popular male figure—a truly masculine man. I want the best seat in the house for the title fight."

"And that is?"

"Joe's allowed two handlers in his corner. I'm going to be one of those handlers."

Lara shook her head. "That would be extremely irregular. The Boxing Commission—"

"God damn the Boxing Commission! I told you what I want. You know what's going to happen if I don't get it."

Unexpectedly Jennifer asked, "If you do, are you going to hurt Joe anyway?"

North shook his head. "Not if I get what I want."

Lara said, "Then tell me what you'll do if you *don't* get what you want, Mr. North. Again, I prefer to hear it from you."

"To start with, I'll tell the police about Walsh. He's an

escaped mental patient. You know that—so do I. He hasn't been picked up because you're his lawyer and Secretary of Security Klamm's supposed to be your stepfather." One corner of North's mouth went up. "You think anybody really believes that?"

Lara said, "He and I do. It happens to be true."

"Then you wouldn't want to see him hurt. Or the President, and anything that hurts Klamm is going to hurt her politically. The papers haven't connected the little bald guy who broke out of United with Joe's manager; but they'll sure as hell connect Walsh with you, and you with Klamm. With a little help, they might even connect Walsh with Green here, and he's as crazy as a blue crab."

He shook his head, thinking how tired Lara must be getting of being threatened with the media. First him, now North.

She said, "Eddie, you were correct to ask me to come. I'm supposed to protect you, and he's using me to get at you."

"'At's not it. I was hoping you could see a way out."

Lara turned back to North. "All you want is to be one of Joe's handlers?"

North nodded.

"But we have no assurance you won't use the same threat again and again."

"I'm going to give it to you now," North told her. He took a folded paper from his pocket. "This is a confession of murder, to be signed by me."

It had seemed that nothing could surprise Lara, but that did; for an instant her eyes opened wide. "May I ask who you murdered?"

North nodded. "A doctor named Applewood. The police were about to get him, and he would have talked. He was a low-level

288

man, but because he was a doctor he knew more than a low-level man should have." North had taken a pen from his pocket. "That was about four months ago. Maybe you read about it."

To him, Lara said, "You knew him—Dr. Applewood."

He nodded. "Years ago."

Walsh was staring at North. "Ya really going to sign that thing?"

"And give it to you," North said, "or rather to Miss Nomos to hold in trust for you, when you agree to let me act as one of Joe's handlers. You're going to be the other, and do the actual handling."

Slowly Walsh shook his head.

Lara said, "In other words, you trust us."

W.F. had finished with Joe's hands. He said, "But *we* don't trust *him*. No way!"

North shrugged. "Naturally not. That's why I wrote this. You have to promise me, on your honor, that you won't use it or talk about it unless I threaten Walsh again. I know you won't break that promise. But if you do, I'm free to tell the papers what I've told you I'd tell them. I might add that some of my friends will see to Joe and Jennifer for me."

The noise of the crowd above them had become so constant that he had ceased to notice it. Now those thousands of throats fell suddenly silent, so that when Lara spoke her voice seemed unnaturally loud. "I think we should do it," she said.

Walsh glanced at her incredulously. "Let this guy handle Joe?"

North said, "I'll do whatever you tell me. You have my solemn word."

Walsh shook his head. "It won't be me telling ya. It'll be W.F."

W.F. yelped, "Wait up!"

Walsh said, "W.F., ya not losing ya chance t' second the champ 'cause of me."

"Hold on—Joe need you. You got strategy for him, all that stuff."

The big fighter, who had been listening (as it seemed) with no more interest than an ox, nodded emphatically.

Lara asked, "Would you like a ringside seat, Eddie? Close to Joe's corner? I can get you one if you wish."

"Yeah," Walsh told her gratefully. "Yeah, I sure would." Sweat beading the small man's head vanished before a yellow handkerchief.

"Perhaps when Mr. North has been seen sufficiently, you and he might change places."

North nodded. "Perhaps. But the decision must be mine, not Walsh's." There was triumph in North's voice.

"That's understood. Sign that paper, then, and it's all arranged." Lara turned to him. "You look doubtful."

He asked, "Aren't you going to read it?"

"What would be the good—"

Someone pounded on the door. A voice called, "Time, Joe! You ready?"

Like a lion, Joe slid from the masseur's table and drifted toward the door. W.F. followed, carrying a red-and-white kit as big as a small suitcase. "You a handler now?" W.F. asked North. "Okay, you fetch the waterbucket and all them towels."

"Sure thing." North signed the paper and gave it to Lara.

She unfolded it and glanced at it. "Jennifer? A seat for you? It'll be no trouble."

The blonde shook her head. "I never watch. I'll wait right here."

Lara nodded to him. "Then come along."

He wanted to say that it had not been "come along" when she had left Mama Capini's. W.F. opened the door for Joe; there was a thunderclap of questions from the reporters and an incessant lightning from the flashguns of the photographers. Walsh was walking on tiptoe and talking rapidly to Joe, lips as close to Joe's ear as possible. Joe pounded glove against glove.

He was going with them, but Lara held him back. "They'll ride up in the same elevator," she said. "Eddie, Joe, and W.F. That's their privilege. North too, I'm afraid, but that can't be helped. When they reach the ring, Eddie will have to leave them. That will be hard enough." After a few seconds, they stepped out into a corridor that was now empty, and she pulled the green door shut behind them.

"Where are we going?" he asked.

"To join my stepfather. Two of his guards will have to surrender their seats to you and Eddie. They won't be happy about that, but they can stand in the aisle."

"May I ask a few questions?"

"Certainly." Lara sounded preoccupied, and he was as much astonished as delighted when he felt her hand slip into his.

"It was lunch time—almost one—when we left Capini's."

"Lunch for us," she said. "Some other people were having dinner. You didn't notice."

"My watch," he glanced at it, "says it's a little past two. What time is it here?"

"After ten. Why should you expect it to be the same time in different places? If you'd called London after lunch, would you have expected them to tell you they'd just sat down to tea?"

"It's been years for me." He tried to count them, but he could not. "How long for Eddie and Joe and W.F.?"

"What does that matter?" They had reached the elevators. Lara pushed the button with the hand that held her purse.

"How long?" he insisted.

"About four months, or so North said."

"You're a goddess." It took an effort for him to force the words to his lips; he made the effort, and they came. "You live forever?"

As they entered the elevator, Lara turned to look at him. For once there was no hint of mockery in her eyes. "There are many forevers," she said. The elevator rose.

He took her in his arms, not suddenly or violently, but enfolding her as a flower would enfold a bee, if the bee were indeed its lover and no mere go-between. Her kiss stung his lips, smooth and sunwarmed.

Tightly pressed between their bodies, Tina yelled, *"Hey!"* They ignored her.

The elevator doors slid back. "I am Laura Nomos," Lara told him. "I am an attorney, and the stepdaughter of a cabinet officer. You are an acquaintance." In a lower tone she added, "You needn't wipe your mouth—women paint theirs to look like me."

The whisper was no more necessary than the wiping of his lips; Sailor Sawyer had grabbed the ropes and vaulted into the ring, and half the audience was on its feet, cheering wildly.

"They applaud him now," Lara murmured. "But in a few years he will be dead, and so will they. Let them all engage with Death, an opponent worthy of any strength."

"I thought you liked Joe," he said as they made their way down the aisle.

"I do. He's like a big, solemn child, so eager to please and to do what is right. And Eddie, because he'll reshape the world to fit his dream or die. And W.F., because he loves them both."

Klamm had already taken a seat in the first row when they arrived; there was an empty seat to his right. Lara gestured to the man on the other side of it, who rose and went to the aisle. She sat down beside Klamm and patted the now-empty seat next to hers.

He sat. She said, "Stepfather, this is my friend Adam K. Green. Adam, Adalwolf Wilhelm Klamm."

The old man leaned across her to shake hands, eyes stupid as though with sleep. "A great pleasure, Herr Kay." The words were thickly accented.

He said, "It's a very great honor, sir."

"So," Klamm remarked to Lara, gesturing toward Sawyer. "You t'ink still your Joe will beat him?"

With mock firmness Lara announced, "I *know* it."

"Then I bet you. Theater tickets, any play you wish. Or any play I wish, which is how it shall be."

Lara said, "Never give a sucker an even break," and they shook hands solemnly.

Tattoos covered every visible inch of Sawyer's skin from the neck down, pictures and bannered inscriptions that writhed and flowed with the muscles beneath them.

Tina said, "That dragon's alive!"

He looked down and saw that she had clambered far enough out of his pocket to peep past the lapel of his coat. "It's just a picture somebody drew on his skin," he told her.

"I'm a doll, but I'm not *just* a doll."

Joe's robe was off. Eddie Walsh, who had replaced the other guard, had it in trust. As the referee reached for the microphone lowered to her from the rafters of the arena, W.F. opened the red-and-white kit on the canvas just beyond the ropes. North stood to one side, incongruous in a three-piece suit.

Lara whispered, "Do you want to read this?" and handed him North's confession.

This is to state that I, the undersigned Wm. T. North, did upon the morning of January 21 shoot and kill Dr. Cecil L. Applewood in his office in the concourse of the Grand Hotel. I acted in self-defense only in that I feared disclosures Applewood might make to the police. I had been observing a confederate and saw he was being followed by an officer. My confederate visited Applewood, whom he knew to be one of us, and the officer overheard their conversation. When they had gone, I entered Applewood's office and shot him twice in the chest, knowing that he was not the man to withstand a sustained interrogation. I then entered the hotel room occupied by my confederate, intending to kill him when he returned, but he did not return.

William T. North

"I was the confederate," he whispered to Lara.

She nodded. "I thought you were."

The bell rang. Joe and Sawyer left their corners, circled, and jabbed. An indescribable sound filled the arena, the whine of a huge animal about to be fed.

. 35 .

Main Event

At the end of the first round, he felt Joe had gotten the worst of it, despite a few good punches. Joe had fought defensively, covering up, edging away, keeping Sawyer at a distance. Vaguely he recalled a night in Walsh's room. Joe had said his opponent had been an expert boxer but, "I had the reach." Something like that. Joe had the reach again now, by an inch or two; or so he thought. Was that really so important here? An inch or two?

As the death of a parent or a summer job awakens a boy to manhood, as the accidental lifting of a theater curtain shows us the hurrying stagehands and the sweating actor behind Lear or Willy Loman, so these dim musings gradually permitted him to see Joe and Sawyer. He had always supposed boxing a mere matter of someone strong and brave clubbing someone else who was less so. Thus had his schoolyard defeats been, or thus he had judged them.

It was not true. Joe and Sawyer played a game as complex as chess, and played it with the unequal pieces awarded each by birth and time.

The bell rang, and the fighters rose at once. For half a minute, both appeared to feint and circle as before. Quickly the dragon closed, wrapping Joe in golden scales. They were so near he could hear the *smack-smack* of their punches through the roar of the audience; yet he could not see . . . did not see what had happened. They separated, circling as before; there were fiery splotches on Joe's chest; Sawyer's head was shaking as if the champion sought to clear it.

Lara freed her breath in a deep sigh. "I thought that was it," she said. He asked what she meant, but she only shook her head like Sawyer.

The fighters closed again toe-to-toe, and this time he had a better view. Sawyer's head was bent over fists pounding like pistons. Joe's head and shoulders held Sawyer away while Joe's muscled forearms absorbed the blows. As they separated, one of those arms flew out, driving a brown-gloved fist where Sawyer's chin met the collar bone.

Now it was the champion who was backing off and jabbing, while Joe advanced with little bobbing steps, swaying to right and left as Sawyer tried to circle.

"Look 'at 'im weave," Walsh shouted to Lara. "God, ain't he beautiful!"

The bell rang, Joe rejoined W.F. in the corner, and three things happened at once. Walsh sprang from his seat and rushed to Joe's corner. W.F. yelled, "Water!" to North. And North flourished both hands, somewhat like a stage magician, somewhat like a small girl fastidiously wiping her soiled fingers on her pinafore; this last caused a blue-black automatic to appear in each hand.

For a moment North posed with these pistols, an actor in the spotlight. During that moment, Klamm dove to the floor and Lara screamed. It occurred to him that neither had much reason to be afraid; North's guns had already swung toward him. They went off together, deafeningly loud. He grabbed the ropes as he had seen Sawyer do a few minutes earlier, vaulted clumsily, and used his momentum to drive his foot into North's groin.

North stumbled backward, one gun firing into the rafters. Joe and Sawyer were on their feet. The referee was ringing her bell, ringing for the fighters to fight again, he thought, and they were going to do it across North.

No, North was up, scuttling toward the ropes, still holding one gun. Klamm's men were firing from the aisle. North's gun barked at him, spitting flame and leaping like a big, angry dog; but W.F. had thrown the red-and-white kit, and it struck North's arm.

Then he held the gun, too. He twisted it up and back. It fired—its flash half-blinded him, and the sound of the shot was deafening. North's jaw was a red horror, yet North struck him again and again. He heard his own nose break, a terrible sound; something had invaded his head and was working destruction there. He gasped for breath, drew in blood and spat it out. More blood was streaming down his face.

Joe's padded glove slammed North's ear. After that, North no longer wrestled him for the gun. It was in his hand, but he did not know what to do with it—and then it was gone. North's corpse sprawled on the canvas near the center of the ring, in a widening scarlet stain.

"Set down now," W.F. told him. "We got to get a ice-pack on your nose. Stop that bleedin'."

He discovered there was a stool behind him. He sat, wanting to say something about bananas or tomatoes, to joke with W.F.; but he could not speak, could not ensnare the fleet thoughts in syllable and phrase. He had lost teeth, and his tongue explored the places.

Klamm was in the ring, waving to the audience, muttering to the fighters, a hand upon the shoulder of each. Each was a head taller than Klamm.

Joe squatted in front of him. "You okay?"

The ice-pack was on his face, but he managed to nod.

"That was a brave thing you done." The words were muffled, slurred by Joe's mouthpiece.

The bell rang once, sharply. Klamm had struck it with the case of an old-fashioned pocket watch.

"Gotta go," Joe mumbled. "But you're a real champ."

"Hol' still," W.F. told him.

Klamm said, "This fight. It is to take their minds off it. You will make this a long round, *ja?* Because perhaps at the end they are nervous once more." Klamm was talking to the referee, not to him.

A hard-faced man he recognized as one of Klamm's body-guards asked, "Where's his other gun?"

Walsh handed it over sheepishly, butt first. "I only got one shot at 'im," Walsh confessed. "Somebody was always in the way."

"Good thing you didn't try for two."

Walsh nodded. "Ya never can tell."

"We take him to a hospital," Klamm was explaining to W.F. "To a doctor. You must see to your man, *ja?*"

W.F. took away the ice-pack and changed the cotton in his

nostrils. Klamm's bodyguard helped him through the ropes. He looked around for Lara, but she was gone.

"She is not here, Herr Kay," Klamm told him.

It was as though he had spoken aloud—but it was too hard to speak. Klamm had known; Klamm had read his thought, or at least had read his expression and noticed the direction of his eyes. For the first time it struck him that one did not become a cabinet officer by chance, that the sleepy old man with the dyed mustache probably possessed extraordinary abilities.

The bodyguard asked if he could walk. "He walks," Klamm declared. "He is a tough one, a *Raufbold, ja?*"

The pain of his broken nose was like fire on his face. He wondered vaguely whether he had been hurt anywhere else. Those teeth, of course; that was drowned in the other pain.

Outside several hundred men were milling around the arena. "North is dead." *"North's dead."* "In there—they just killed Bill North." He caught the words everywhere; he could not tell who had spoken them because everyone was speaking them. A man of about his own age wept without shame, sallow cheeks flooded with tears. Klamm's guards had their guns out—in one case a strange-looking gun with a long curved magazine. He decided it was probably a machine pistol.

Three black cars—one an enormous limousine—stood at the curb. "He rides with me," Klamm told somebody. "You need not come."

A uniformed driver with a gun opened the rear door. Klamm got in first, sliding across the wide leather seat to make room for him. The door clicked softly behind him.

"We speak in private, Rudy," Klamm said, and a thick sheet of glass slid from the back of the front seat to the roof. A moment later, the limousine pulled smoothly away from the

GENE WOLFE

curb. One of the sedans was ahead of it, and he suspected the other was behind it, but he did not bother to turn his head to see.

"You haff saved my life," Klamm said. "I shall reward you, if I can. I haff some money, and I am not without authority in this place."

"No," he said. He managed to shake his head a little.

From his pocket Tina announced, "He needs your help, Papa."

"Then he shall haff it. Whatever I can give."

He said, "I want to find Laura."

The old man sighed. "So do we all, Herr Kay."

"She's your daughter—your stepdaughter."

"She is a grown woman, my stepdaughter. She goes where she wants. Sometimes she tells me because she loves me, such is her way. More often not. I will help if I can, but I cannot say to you her apartment is here, she is in that hotel."

"No," he said. "That's not right."

"What is it you mean, Herr Kay?" Klamm leaned back in the corner, eyes sleepier than ever.

"Laura says she's your stepdaughter, and you say she's your stepdaughter. But she can't be, not really, so you know. She's the goddess."

Klamm opened one eye wide. "She told you that?"

He tried to think back. "I figured it out. She admitted it. She knows I know."

"Yes, Herr Kay, she is the goddess."

He understood then, and could not understand why he had not understood before. "Then you're her lover—or one of her lovers. Or you were."

"Yes, Herr Kay." Klamm's eye had shut again. Now both eyes

300

opened. "Long ago, when I was younger than you. But she is still fond of me, *nicht wahr?* I hold her hand. She holds mine. Perhaps we kiss when nobody sees. That is all. Do you envy an old man so much, Herr Kay?"

"No," he said.

"I assist her when I can. For her I perform certain little services. She does not require them, but she knows it makes me happy to do these things. At times she assists me, as she saved me tonight. She brought you, Herr Kay, and without you I should lie dead at this moment."

He waved that aside. "I want to ask you about her, but I don't know what to ask."

"She is very beautiful, always. She believes she can hide her beauty when she chooses, but she is wrong in that. It is only that sometimes it is open, this beauty—the beauty of one who knows herself to be beautiful, *ja?* Other times, the closed beauty of one who does not know, and then we must look. If we begin by saying, 'Why is that woman not beautiful?' we never see it. But if we search—you know, I think."

"Yes, Lora Masterman. Mr. Klamm, once while I was in the hospital I tried to call my apartment, and you answered."

Klamm nodded sleepily. "I answered, and you hung up your telephone. You wish to know how such a thing could happen?"

"Yes, sir."

"It is so simple. She thought you might call. Sometimes one can, from here to there or the other way. So we arranged that such calls should ring at my desk. A special instrument, you understand. She told me of you, and that I was to assist you, should you ask my assistance. You did not."

"And another time I got another man."

"One of my agents," Klamm explained. "I am very much at

my desk, but not always. When I am gone, another must answer my calls. Sometimes we must act at once; then he acts for me, in my name."

"He wanted to know where I was. Lara knew where I was. She sent flowers."

"But we did not, nor did we know that Laura knew. She does not know everything, you see, though she knows so much. Nor does she tell me a tenth what she knows. Perhaps she only sends your flowers as an experiment; if the florist had said, 'There is no one there with such a name,' she would have known that you were elsewhere. We too often make such experiments. That United was a good guess she made, *ja?* Visitors are often brought there."

It was the word Fanny had used. He asked, "Am I a dangerous Visitor or a harmless one, Mr. Klamm?"

Klamm chuckled softly. "Harmless, very much so, exactly like me. But Herr North, he is a dangerous Visitor, you see? And so we must question all Visitors somewhat. You become the responsibility of one of my subordinates. She will keep you from harm, and it might be someday Laura comes for you."

"One more thing, sir. I told you about the other man, who answered the phone in my apartment."

"Ja."

"I saw him on TV one time. I just switched on the TV, and there he was, answering the phone in my apartment."

Klamm nodded. "No one else was looking? Perhaps another would have seen what you saw, Herr Kay. But perhaps not. More often, not. She was near you then, and she brings such dreams; I cannot explain why."

That was the end of their conversation for a time, and it seemed to him that the limousine should have pulled up in front of a hospital when Klamm said, *I cannot explain why.* In point of fact, it did not, but followed the black sedan for another mile at least while he considered what had been said and Klamm slumped in the corner apparently asleep. Even when they reached the hospital—St. Anchises's, according to a sign illuminated by the headlights—the limousine did not stop in front but circled to the emergency entrance in the rear.

"Good-bye, Herr Kay," Klamm said, once again extending his hand. "No, at such a time you haff a right to the correct name. Good-bye, Herr Green, my friend. May good fortune go with you! I only call you Herr Kay because I remember an old friend, that was myself also."

He shook Klamm's hand. "Good-bye, Mr. Klamm. You can call me anything you want."

One of the bodyguards opened the door.

"You know how to reach me at my desk, *ja?* Or another who will act for me."

The dome light had come on when the door was opened, and he saw with astonishment that there were tears in Klamm's eyes. He said, "Yes, I do, sir."

"Take care of him, Ernest. See he has a good doctor."

The bodyguard replied, "I will, Mr. Secretary," and he got out; as soon as the door closed, the limousine glided away.

Tina said, "What a nice old man."

The bodyguard glanced down at her and grinned. "You got one of those? I used to have one myself."

Tina told him, "You should get another one."

He followed the bodyguard into a brightly lit room, where an Oriental who had been sipping from a battered china mug rose to attend to him. "Good to see you again," the Oriental told him. "But not here. Have a seat."

He sat down. "It's good to see you again, too, Dr. Pille." After a moment he added, "I thought you were at that other place."

"I am, when they need me. It's only a block away. You had a concussion that time, remember?"

"Sure," he said. *"Ow!"*

"Your nose is broken," Dr. Pille told him. "We'll have to set it. I'll give you an anesthetic, but it will still hurt a bit. You get in a fight?"

A nurse answered for him. "With an assassin, Doctor. It was all over TV."

Still examining his nose, Dr. Pille nodded. "Really?"

The bodyguard asked, "Can you keep him overnight, Doc? Somebody will come by to get him in the morning."

"Certainly." Dr. Pille straightened up and began filling a hypodermic.

· 36 ·

Decision

A nurse woke him to ask what he wanted for breakfast. "You lost a couple of teeth," she told him. "So no toast or anything like that. Do you think you could manage a coddled egg?"

He nodded and sat up in bed. "I'm hungry. Guess I missed dinner last night."

She grinned. "That would explain it."

When she was gone, he looked around the room; it was bigger than the one he had occupied at United, much smaller than the open ward in which he had slept with nine other patients in the psychiatric wing of some hospital whose name he could not quite remember. Like his room at United, it held a locker, but this locker was unlocked. His jacket, his trousers, and his overcoat hung inside. His shoes were on the bottom. He recalled that he had not had his overcoat when he had been in the limousine with Klamm. Someone had brought it.

He peeked into the breast pocket of his jacket, and Tina said, "Hello—good morning," and stretched.

"Good morning." He held out his hand, and she climbed into it. "Back in the hospital," he said.

"Were you in the hospital before?"

"Yes, but you were asleep. I've been in hospitals a lot."

The nurse came in with his tray. "Those are against our regulations," she said.

"I'm sorry," he told her. "I didn't know."

"I really should take it and lock it up. But you're going to be discharged today anyhow, so it's really not worth all the trouble. Just don't let anybody else see it."

"I'll hide," Tina promised.

"What would you like to drink? We've got coffee, tea, and milk."

He asked whether he could have both tea and milk, and she nodded and brought them in, managing to get a cup, a little hot-water pot, and the glass of milk all on his tray.

"The tea's for you," he told Tina when the nurse had gone. He put the teabag into the pot and sprinkled salt from an old-fashioned glass saltcellar into the cup.

"Goody!"

He held the cup for her while she drank. "You don't need any food? Just this?"

"This is all," Tina said. "And this was plenty. Eat your egg so you'll grow up strong."

With a napkin to protect his fingers, he unscrewed the top of the white porcelain dish.

"Don't you have to go to school today?"

"I don't think so," he said. There was a soft roll on his tray as well. He tore it in small pieces and mixed the pieces with the egg, adding pepper and the pat of butter. "Somebody's coming for me, but I don't think it's to take me to school."

"Where *are* they going to take you?"

"I don't know," he said. After a moment he added, "I'm not sure I'll even go."

About an hour after the nurse took his tray, she returned with a wheelchair. "I'm afraid you've got to ride in this," she said. "Regulations."

He looked around for Tina.

"It's under the sheet. You'll be back in an hour or so."

He hesitated, then said, "All right. Where are we going?"

"To see the dentist."

He stared curiously as she wheeled him to the elevator; the hospital seemed merely a hospital like any other, a little less modern than the ones he recalled seeing on TV. Perhaps they all were.

The dentist was a large woman who gave the impression of disliking him and the nurse equally. "Open wide," she told him, and when he complied leaned so close it seemed she was trying to thrust her head into his mouth. "One came out clean, and one left a piece of root." She turned to the nurse. "This will be a local. You can go if you want."

The nurse shook her head.

The dentist shot something into his gum, after which he and the nurse spent a quarter of an hour in the outer office waiting for it to take effect. "If I'd gone," the nurse said, "she'd have had you out like a candle." He nodded, wishing she had; he had never liked having his teeth worked on and saw nothing wrong with being out like a light.

There was a stack of magazines. As he leafed through one, it struck him that he had read almost nothing here. Tina would rebuke him if she knew; thinking of it made him feel guilty, and he studied the magazine with more care. It seemed very similar to those of his own world up until page forty, which showed Lara sitting with a pink drink in a tropical garden. Lara's hair was gold, her skin bronze. "Marcella Masters relaxes at home before beginning work on *Atlantis*," read the caption.

He tore the page out, folded it, and put it in the pocket of his pajama shirt. The nurse seemed scandalized but did not protest. After that he flipped through magazines energetically until the dentist summoned him back to her chair, but he found nothing more.

Fanny was waiting for them when they returned to his room. She showed the nurse her badge and a letter, at which the nurse appeared impressed. "He's all yours, Sergeant, if you want him."

Fanny grinned at him. "I do."

The nurse opened his locker and glanced inside. "I'll have to get his laundry. It shouldn't take long."

"Okay," Fanny told her. To him she said, "You look pretty damned awful with all that tape on your face."

He told her he felt all right.

The nurse said, "He's lost a couple of teeth too, Sergeant. In a week or so he should see a dentist about getting a bridge. In two or three days a doctor should check his nose. You can take him to Dr. Pille's office or bring him here. Dr. Pille set his nose last night."

Fanny said, "Okay."

When the nurse had gone, Fanny said, "You went back to wherever it is you come from, didn't you? That time in the restaurant."

He nodded. "I didn't mean to, but I did, and I couldn't get back. Well, once I did, but it only lasted a few minutes. Then I found Lara again and followed her—I think she let me—and here I am."

"I hope you stay here," Fanny told him. "I'm responsible for you now, and I'll catch hell if I lose you. Do you have to sit in that thing?"

"No," he said. He stood to show her, then sat beside her on the bed. That reminded him of Tina; he reached beneath the sheet and pulled her out.

She said, "Hey! They're not supposed to see me here."

He told her, "It doesn't matter. We're leaving."

Fanny sighed. "You'll throw that thing away when you've been with me for a week or two."

He wanted to shake his head, but he did not.

"You don't die, do you?" Fanny whispered. "They don't die where you come from. We can do it over and over, as often as we want to."

Her dark eyes made him uncomfortable, so that this time he did shake his head, thinking of Lara.

The nurse returned with a bundle wrapped in brown paper and tied with string. She handed it to him, and she and Fanny left his room, shutting the door behind them. He broke the string, unwrapped the bundle, and unfolded his shirt on the bed. The laundry had bleached out the bloodstains, leaving the shirt as white as it had been when it was new. He took Lara's picture from the pocket of his pajamas and put it into the pocket of the shirt.

Tina asked, "Are we going with that lady?"

"For a while," he told her.

"I don't like her," Tina said.

309

"I do," he told her. "But not enough." He pulled off the pajama top and tossed it onto the bed. "Now turn around and shut your eyes."

She did, and he untied the cord of his pajama bottoms and let them drop to the floor. When he had buttoned the clean shirt, he permitted her to look again.

"You should have waited till you had your pants on," Tina lectured him. "Are you going to let those ladies come back in now?"

"I'm wearing jockey shorts," he explained. "Besides, the shirttail covers me." He carried his trousers to the window, where the light was better; they were dotted with dried blood, rusty and stiff. "I wish they'd sent these to the cleaner," he said.

His wallet was in the hip pocket, still holding money that would be useless here. Bills that could buy things were in the double pocket of the overcoat, though his gloves seemed to have fallen out; the map was in the other pocket. He put the scarlet thread that held Mr. Sheng's charm about his neck and thrust the charm inside his undershirt, then knotted his blood-smeared tie as neatly as if he were going to work at the store. When he was fully dressed and Tina had been stowed in his jacket pocket and cautioned to keep quiet, he opened the door.

"I'm afraid you have to ride in my chair again," the nurse told him. "We can't let you walk until a doctor says you can walk."

He sat down obediently, and she pushed him as before, this time with Fanny walking beside them. Fanny signed him out at the main desk. "You won't need your coat," she told him. "It's beautiful outside." He folded the coat over his arm.

She was right. A spring breeze stroked his cheek as soon as they had left the hospital smells behind them. Jonquils in stone tubs waved to them from both sides of the walk leading to the street.

"You're not too steady on your pins, are you?"

He was holding on to the rail as he went down the steps. "I'm fine," he said.

"We can take a cab. They gave me expense money."

"I can walk." He was looking up and down the street; it was hauntingly familiar. "And I think we'll have to. Do you see any cabs?"

Fanny shook her head.

"You didn't bring your car?"

"No," she said. They had started down the street. "You're thinking of that time I was at the Grand, but that wasn't really my car."

"How did you get to the hospital?"

"On the trolley," Fanny said.

"Then we can ride the trolley back. Is there a stop around here?"

"A stop?"

"Where the trolley stops and you get on."

Fanny shook her head again, making her tight black curls bounce in the sunshine. "Is that how you do it where you come from? Here we just flag them down. What are you staring at?"

It was a shop window, the window of a narrow little store that sold sheet music. The song displayed there, open upon a gilded music stand, was "Find Your True Love." It had been in the window so long that its dusty paper had turned yellow.

"There's a cab," Fanny said, and called, *"Taxi!"*

He looked down the street for the doll hospital. Its sign hung there, displaying a picture of a doll dressed like a nurse.

"The cab's stopping." Fanny tugged his sleeve. "Come on."

He nodded and turned to follow, feeling more lost than he ever had since he had run down Mr. Sheng's alley. Fanny opened the door for him, and he said, "Thank you," and got in.

"Where to, sir?" The driver was a man, a bit younger than he was and surprisingly clean. Fanny was walking around the rear of the cab. He considered the matter.

"Where are you and the lady going, sir?"

Casually, he reached across the seat and depressed the lock button. "To the railway station," he said, rolling up the window. "But she's not coming."

"Like that, huh?" The driver grinned as he put the cab in gear.

"Yes," he said. "Like that." He turned to look at Fanny, left standing in the street. He felt that she should have drawn her gun or at least shaken her fist at them. She did neither, and there was something achingly forlorn about her small, dark figure.

"We're out of that hospital, aren't we?" It was Tina, thrusting her head past the lapel of his jacket.

"Yes," he told her.

"Where are we going?"

"To Manea." He spoke softly, so that the driver would not overhear him; the driver might be questioned by the police.

"Lovely country, they tell me," the driver remarked. "Close to Overwood."

"I didn't think that you heard me," he said. "Yes, I know it must be."

They passed a fountain, and its splashing recalled Klamm— the tears in Klamm's eyes. Klamm had followed the letter of the law; but suddenly he knew that no one would question the driver or pursue them. Fanny might be reprimanded; but there would be no investigation, no all-points bulletin.

Not far away the whistle of a steam locomotive blew, echoing and re-echoing among the surrounding buildings. He smiled. It blew again, singing of lovers' meetings in distant places.

Tina looked out from her vantage point beside his necktie. *"Whooee!"* Tina said. "A-whooee, *a-whooee!"*

THE TOR DOUBLES

Two complete short science fiction novels in one volume!